By the same author and illustrator

Jessica Haggerthwaite: Witch Dispatcher
Jessica Haggerthwaite: Media Star

Sam and the Griswalds

Emma Barnes

illustrated by

Tim Archbold

BLOOMSBURY

First published in Great Britain in 2004 by Bloomsbury Publishing Plc
38 Soho Square, London, W1D 3HB

Text copyright © Emma Barnes 2004
Illustrations copyright © Tim Archbold 2004
The moral rights of the author and illustrator have been asserted

A CIP catalogue record of this book is available from the British Library

ISBN 0 7475 5906 6

Typeset by Dorchester Typesetting Group Limited
Printed in Great Britain by Clays Ltd, St Ives plc

All papers used by Bloomsbury Publishing are natural, recyclable products
made from wood grown in well-managed forests. The manufacturing
processes conform to the environmental regulations of the
country of origin.

10 9 8 7 6 5 4 3 2 1

For Steve and Abby – EB

To Rosie and John and friends at
Ednam Primary School – TA

Chapter One
Sam in the Rain

Sam Harris first met the Griswalds when Elfrida Griswald set fire to his hair.

The Griswalds had been living in Bellstone for almost a week when the meeting took place, and they were already famous in the town. The reason for this was, quite simply, that they were *different* from the other kids in Bellstone. Some people thought they were different in an entertaining kind of way; and some people thought they were different in a downright criminal kind of way. But they were different – there was no doubt about that.

Sam Harris was one of the few people in Bellstone who had not heard of the Griswalds. He had been suffering from a slight cold that week, and even though he was meant to be starting a new school, Mrs Harris, who was inclined to fuss, had kept him home. He had spent the whole week in bed, being fed ever more poisonous-tasting vitamin pills, and being told to 'wrap up warm and toasty' and 'keep out of the draughts, dear, and sit still and don't run around'.

On Saturday afternoon the rain cleared and Mrs Harris finally agreed that Sam could take a walk round the garden. After taking off the thick jumper and scarf she had made him wear, he went to sit in the old swing under the beech tree which held his old tree house. As he swung gently, he wondered what his chances were of being allowed to go to school the following week, or whether he would be forced to stay home instead.

Not that Sam was looking forward to school *at all*. But if he had to go, then it would have been better to start with everybody else. Now he was going to be the only new boy – and the longer his mother kept him home, the more difficult that would be. It would be impossible to be invisible, starting so much later than everybody else. And being invisible was what Sam chiefly asked of school.

Or mostly he did. But he had been at home so long, and was so bored out of his mind, that he could at least pretend to himself that he had other ambitions. And one of them was so secret he had never admitted it out loud, until now. 'I'll never get on the team if Mum won't let me go back,' he said suddenly to the squirrel that was foraging amongst the tree roots. 'Not that I would have anyway. And there's nothing else worth doing. Bellstone,' he told the squirrel, 'is probably the most boring place in the Universe.'

There was a cold hard lump in his stomach, like a block of ice, only it wasn't ice, it was misery. At that moment he would have given anything to have someone to talk to: a brother, a sister, a friend or even a pet. Even the squirrel had abandoned him and disappeared into the undergrowth. As if to add to his unhappiness, a light rain began to fall. But Sam could not be bothered to get up and go inside. He was fed up with being inside. And he felt as if nothing exciting would happen, probably for the rest of his life.

And then something did happen.

'Yowwwwww!' Sam felt an excruciating pain somewhere above his left eyebrow. He leapt up, clutching his head. Pain shot through his hand. There was a horrible burning smell. And then, almost immediately, the pain stopped – or at least lessened.

This was good. What was not so good was that what felt like a gallon of cold water had just been tipped all over Sam, and most of it was streaming down his neck.

'Quick thinking, Spider,' said a voice from somewhere above Sam's head. There was a pause, then it added, 'Pity about the ginger ale, though.'

For a horrible moment, Sam thought it might be Brandon Bullock, who lived next door. But he would have recognised Brandon's voice anywhere, and this voice simply was not spiteful enough. He could not look to see who it actually belonged to because some of the liquid (it did indeed taste of ginger) had ended up in his mouth and he was too busy choking and spluttering. Then, when he was about to demand exactly what was going on, something else happened. For the third time in as many minutes, something landed on his head. Worst of all, this time the something was *alive*.

Sam knew it was alive because it bit his ear.

Sam said a very rude word and grabbed. He felt fur, and at first he thought the creature was a cat or a squirrel, these being the kinds of animals that usually jump out of trees. But then he caught sight of it and immediately realised it was a rat. A big, war-torn old rat, with sharp teeth and an evil expression; one of its ears was missing, and it had lost its tail too – probably in a fight with another rat.

The rat slid through his fingers and down to the ground.

'Catch him! Quick!' called a new voice – this time a girl's. Sam grabbed, but he was too late. The rat went scurrying through the grass towards the garden fence.

'Stop him!' howled the voice again. Sam flung himself full length – and landed in the compost heap. Still, it was a wonderful dive – the sort of thing he always dreamed of, but never actually managed to pull off, when playing in goal at school.

Somebody else was thinking along the same lines. 'Great save!'

'Did you get him?' demanded the girl's voice anxiously.

Sam lay still, all the breath knocked out of him. He had, after all, been burnt, soaked and bitten in quick succession, and as if that was not enough, had ended up covered in bits of old grass cuttings and potato peel. Now it seemed there were a load of dangerous maniacs loose in his garden, and they had with them a rat which bit. It was not turning out to be a great Saturday.

'He'd better not have hurt him –' the girl continued.

'Hurt *him*? I don't think a Rottweiler with rabies could hurt him –'

As he listened to them arguing, Sam felt more and more indignant. Usually, he was shy with strangers. But these strangers had sneaked into his tree house without his permission, and attacked him with fire, flood and a savage animal. He rubbed at his hair and a charred bit came away in his hand. This tipped his mood from indignation to anger.

'Who do you think you are?' he demanded, scrambling to his feet. 'And what do you think you're doing in my garden?'

There were three kids, he now saw, two boys and a girl, sitting in a row on the platform of his tree house. They stared at him and for a moment nobody said anything.

Then the smaller boy said, as if it was something Sam should have known all along, 'We're the Griswalds. I'm Jake and that's Spider and Elfrida. We live next door.'

The Griswalds all had dark hair, and they all had the same alert, interested expression – like a family of weasels staring at a rabbit.

Jake looked about Sam's age (which was eleven) although he was a good bit taller than Sam. He had untidy, spiky hair and heavy brows. His nose was slightly squint, as if it had been broken in a fight (as, indeed, it had). Spider was a few years older; tall, skinny and extremely pale, with immensely long arms and legs, and strangely shifting grey eyes. His hair was covered by a black woolly hat and unidentified clanking objects hung from his belt. He was holding an empty plastic bottle. Elfrida had lots of tangled brown hair and a fierce expression. Although she did not look much older than eight or nine, she was holding a lighted cigar. The smoke from it was drifting up into the branches.

What the Griswalds saw was a sturdy, jeans-clad boy with chestnut hair, now rather singed around the edges. He was clutching a rodent to his chest and breathing heavily, as if he was not used to taking much exercise. He was also glaring angrily. The Griswalds were not too concerned by this. They were used to people glaring angrily at them.

'What's your name?' asked Elfrida.

Sam hesitated, not knowing whether to reply, or to tell these strangers who were so calmly sitting in *his* tree house that they could mind their own business. Before he could make up his mind, Jake said, 'Hey, why don't you come up here, out of the rain?' And the next moment, rather to Sam's surprise, the Griswalds had all jumped down onto the grass, and Spider and Jake were helping Sam brush off the potato peelings and ginger ale, while Elfrida took possession of the rat and checked that he was all right. Then Spider gave them all a leg-up back into the tree house.

'What is your name, anyway?' asked Jake, when they were settled again.

'Sam Harris. And now,' said Sam, taking a deep breath, 'tell me what you're doing here.'

'Why shouldn't we be here?' asked Elfrida.

'Because it's not your garden. You can't just go and sit in other people's gardens!'

'Why not? We often do.'

Sam gaped at her, aghast.

Jake said, 'Yeah, it seemed peaceful. And we felt like a bit of peace and quiet.'

Spider nodded and Elfrida said, 'Yeah, that's right.'

Sam stared at them suspiciously. Even on such short acquaintance, the Griswalds did not strike him as lovers of peace and quiet. 'What's wrong with your *own* garden? It's peaceful, isn't it?' Sam looked towards the part of next-door's garden which was visible over the fence: while resembling the Amazon Jungle in terms of undergrowth, it certainly looked peaceful enough.

'It's not the garden,' said Jake. 'It's more – the people who might be in it, if you know what I mean.' The Griswalds exchanged meaningful glances with each other, but did not elaborate further.

Sam felt more and more confused.

'All right,' he said, trying to seize on something concrete. 'So what were you doing with that cigar?'

'Oh that.' Jake looked relieved by the change of subject. 'Well, the thing is, we thought if we were going to come and sit in your garden, then this would be the perfect moment.'

'The perfect moment for what?'

'For Elfrida to smoke her first cigar. You see, we've had the cigar for ages. Spider nicked it off Dad, but there's never been a good time to smoke it. We don't want to smoke it where Dad might see us – he was given it for his birthday and he's been saving it for a special occasion.'

'But why don't you want him to have it?' asked Sam. He was beginning to feel that the longer this conversation continued, the less sense it was making.

'Yeah, well, the thing is – smoking is bad for you. Didn't you know?'

The Griswalds looked pitying. Sam felt wrong-footed – as if suddenly *he* had to justify himself to *them*. 'Well, of course I know that,' he said hastily (as indeed he did – Mrs Harris went on about it all the time).

Jake continued, 'Also, Spider likes to keep in practice.'

'At what? Smoking?'

'No. Nicking things. It's sort of a hobby of his, you see.'

Sam screwed up his eyes, to cut out all the Griswald eyes intent upon him, while he tried to come up with a satisfactory answer to this. There were lots of things he wanted to say. But in the end all he could manage, in a half-strangled voice, was: 'I see. But then why – I mean why did you give the cigar to Elfrida?'

'Ah – that was an idea Spider and I had. If she smokes a cigar now, then most likely it will put her off smoking for life. Think of all the money she'll save – and she won't get lung cancer either. Anyway,' he added, 'Spider and I don't like the taste.'

'Me neither,' said Elfrida with feeling. 'It tastes horrible.'

'I'm sorry she dropped her ash on your head, though,' said Jake magnanimously.

Sam opened his eyes. The Griswalds were all grinning, looking highly pleased with themselves, as if everything they had just said and done made perfect sense.

'You're really weird, you know that?' said Sam.

The Griswalds looked surprised. But before they could reply there was the sound of the back door opening and a voice called, 'Sam! Where are you? Are you coming in now?'

Instinctively, Sam signalled to the Griswalds to be quiet. Somehow he just knew his mother and the Griswalds were not going to get on. He could just imagine what his mum would say about kids who encouraged their little sisters to smoke cigars, especially in other people's gardens. There was also the matter of how Sam was going to explain his burnt-off hair.

Luckily, the Griswalds were well practised in not being heard or seen. Jake drew back into the darkness, Elfrida crouched low upon her branch, and Spider, with one easy movement, went slithering silently up the side of the tree house and on to its roof, where the leaves hid him.

'It's OK, Mum – I'm up here.' Sam leaned down from the platform and waved. He was glad the rain had stopped. Otherwise his mother would never let him stay out.

'Oh dear!' Mrs Harris started off on her high-heeled shoes towards him. 'I do wish you wouldn't play up there.

It's so high up. And what if you fell on a rusty nail and got tetanus?'

This did not sound very likely to Sam, but then a lot of Mrs Harris's worries sounded unlikely. 'Mum!' said Sam, rather desperately. 'I'm OK. I've been indoors all week. Please let me stay out a bit longer.'

Mrs Harris, whose heels were slowly sinking into the mud, slowed down. She realised she was wearing new shoes, and that it was even muddier under the tree. 'Well, remember you're not well,' she said. 'Don't stay out too long.' Then her voice sharpened. 'What's that in the bushes?'

There was a rustling noise in the blackberry bushes, and Sam caught a glimpse of a waving brown and white tail. With annoyance he realised the Griswalds had brought a dog into his garden, as well as a rat.

'I saw a hedgehog there last week,' he said quickly.

'Oh!' Mrs Harris regarded the bushes nervously. 'Well, don't go near it, they carry fleas. And I'm sure I've heard that hedgehogs bite.'

Sam felt like saying it was too late to worry about that – he had already been bitten by a rat. But thankfully, Mrs Harris was disappearing back inside.

The Griswalds emerged from their various hiding places. Sam thought the time had come to hint that they think about going home, but before he could do so, Jake said, 'I think it's safe to go back to ours now. Come on, Sam. We've rigged up a pulley between our pine trees.'

'Err – well –' Sam began, wondering how to explain that he had promised his mother not to leave the garden. But Spider and Jake had not waited for an answer; they had swung themselves down from the tree house and were already halfway to the fence. Sam followed more cautiously. Elfrida waited for him to reach solid ground, then said, 'Will you take Morris for me?'

'I suppose so,' said Sam, eyeing the rat without favour, 'if he doesn't bite me this time.'

'Of course he won't bite you!' Elfrida handed him down carefully into Sam's cupped hands. Sam had just taken him when, out of nowhere –

Pow! Something hit him right in the chest.

It was the brown and white dog. It was trying to get at the rat, of course. Sam lost his footing and fell backwards onto the compost heap, and Morris streaked through his hands. The dog snapped at Morris and caught Sam's hand

instead. Then the dog went bounding straight over Sam and after the rat, barking merrily. Morris gave a squeak, and disappeared through a hole in the fence. The dog collided with the fence, bounced back and lay next to Sam, stunned.

As if from a great distance, he could hear Jake and Elfrida making a great hue and cry.

'He's gone! He's escaped!'

'I didn't know Morris could run that fast!'

'How could he have let him go?'

'It was the dog that did it. Wow, he bowled him over like a canine cannonball!'

Sam managed to sit up. 'Shut up! Or you'll have Mum out here again.'

Jake shut up and, for the second time that afternoon, came to help Sam remove the mud and potato peelings. Spider chased the dog (which had recovered and was chewing at Sam's jumper) into the blackberry bushes. Elfrida, however, was too worried about her pet to be quiet. She ran to the fence where he had disappeared, which was on the opposite side to the Griswalds' garden. But the fence was too high to see over.

'We have to get him back this minute! He'll be scared and wanting to go home. And,' she added, eyeing Sam, 'you should help. It's mainly your fault that he's gone.'

'It was not my fault! And I don't care about your rat.'

'What do you mean, rat? He's my hamster!'

'That's a *hamster*? What's his name? Basil?'

Jake and Spider both laughed, but Elfrida was not amused. 'He's called Morris. Morris Algernon the Third.'

'Well, whatever he's called, you can just forget about him! Do you know who lives on the other side of that fence? The Bullocks, that's who. And if you go into their garden for any reason whatever, then you're mad. They're a dreadful family. Brandon's the biggest scumbag you'll ever meet, and Christabel is *worse*. And Mrs Bullock – she's the scariest person I know. She'll probably kill you.'

Jake turned and looked at his siblings. 'I don't think we've met Mrs Bullock, have we?'

'I think she's one of the ones who've been round to complain about us,' Elfrida said. 'The one that looked like a rhinoceros.'

Spider nodded.

'Oh yeah – Old Big Nose.' Jake turned back to Sam. 'What's the matter? Are you scared of her or something?'

'Of course I'm scared of her,' said Sam defensively. 'So'd you be, if you had any sense. Why don't you just see if – err – Morris comes back by himself?'

Personally, Sam thought it would be no great loss if Morris didn't. But it was clear from their expressions that the Griswalds thought this suggestion incredibly tame.

'No way!' said Jake.

'Of course we're fetching him!' Elfrida declared.

Spider didn't say anything, but just nodded his head in agreement. Only then did Sam realise he had not heard Spider speak a single word all the time he had been there.

Occasionally, he nodded or shook his head, or raised an eyebrow, but that was all.

'So are you coming or not?' demanded Jake in a threatening kind of way.

Sam hesitated. As far as he was concerned the whole idea was madness. It was not as if he really cared about Morris. And he hated and detested the Bullocks, and had no wish to risk meeting any of them while trespassing in their garden.

Yet, he did not say so. For one thing, he knew if he did he would not see much more of the Griswalds. Their expressions told him so. And while he was not sure he even wanted to see more of them – and he certainly did not want to climb into the Bullocks' garden with them – somehow he did not want to end the chance of a friendship before it had even begun.

The truth was that for ages Sam had been hoping some decent kids would move in nearby. He had no brothers or sisters, and since his parents had divorced he seemed to have spent most of his time alone. His mum was a worrier, and the thing that worried her most was what might happen to Sam. In her mind, the world beyond their own house and garden was a dangerous place full of speeding cars, out-of-control buses, forest fires, charging bulls, dangerous youths, axe murderers and other such hazards. As a consequence, she did her very best to stop Sam going anywhere much beyond Thistle Lane, where they lived, or taking the bus alone, or being out after dark. As Mrs Harris didn't have a car any more, since his dad had left, it was very difficult for Sam to see his friends. And the less he saw of them, the less they really *were* his friends.

Consequently, some decent kids moving in nearby would make a big difference in Sam's life. Admittedly, Brandon and Christabel Bullock already lived next door, and they both went to Bellstone High, and Brandon was even in the same year as Sam. But they were not even halfway decent kids: in fact, they were absolutely repellent kids. When he wasn't wishing some new kids would move in, Sam spent quite a lot of his time wishing Brandon and Christabel would move out.

And now some new kids *had* moved in. They seemed a bit unusual – if not downright crazy – but at least they did not seem to be mean and spiteful, the way Brandon and Christabel were mean and spiteful.

But in the end it was none of this that made up his mind. It was the way the Griswalds were staring at him, with a mixture of contempt and 'dare you' in their eyes. He just couldn't say no.

'Sure. If that's what you want to do, let's do it.'

The Griswalds whooped. The next moment they were swarming up the fence like so many ninja assassins. Sam followed reluctantly. He could not help wondering just what he had let himself in for.

Chapter Two
Morris Meets his Match

Sam had expected the Bullock fence to slow the Griswalds down and, with luck, even defeat them altogether. It was extremely high, difficult to grip, and worst of all it had big spikes on the top. But Spider Griswald did not hesitate for a moment: he reached out a hand, extended a foot, and the next minute was moving smoothly up the surface of the fence.

He reached the top and wedged himself between the spikes. He took a metal hook from his belt and attached it to the top of the fence, then uncoiled a length of rope. While Sam was still wondering if the Griswalds always carried mountaineering equipment with them, Spider made a few magical knots and loops and suddenly there was a rope ladder of sorts extending to the ground.

Five minutes later everybody, even, to his own amazement, Sam, was perched rather uncomfortably on top of the fence.

'I can't see Morris anywhere,' said Elfrida with disappointment.

They all gazed into the Bullocks' garden. It was a big garden, and it would have been almost impossible to detect an animal the size of a hamster in it, except that it was immaculately tidy. In fact, it was unbelievably tidy. Sam could remember there had once been trees in the Bullocks' garden, a rolling lawn, steep banks and a rock garden. Now, all that was gone. Mrs Bullock had hired bulldozers to level it all, and had put in a cement patio, and a huge lawn as flat and dull as a bowling green. There was an ornamental lily pond in the middle of it, but it was not the kind of pond that fish or water lilies would ever want to live in, consisting as it did of metallic-coloured water in a blue, plastic shell. There was only one tree left, and even this was the tidiest tree imaginable: a poplar, with its branches slanting upwards and taking up the least possible space. Apart from that there were a few hideously ugly, but expensive, garden ornaments (one of them, Sam had been told, had cost a thousand pounds), a pink-plastic bird table and a garden shed with a padlock on it.

Sam thought it terribly depressing, but not surprising. Mrs Bullock was a great believer in tidiness. In fact, she was famous for it. She had been leading Bellstone's campaign to be chosen 'Tidiest Town in England' for the last five years, and after Bellstone had narrowly missed winning last year (due, some said, to graffiti on the bus shelters) she had sulked for months.

Sam saw Morris first. He was sitting on the bird table. There was no bird seed or crusts there, of course (Mrs Bullock would have thought this terribly untidy), but Morris was scratching around as if he thought he might find some. And almost immediately Sam saw something else, watching Morris. It was Delilah, the Bullocks' cat.

Sam could see now that Morris was a hamster, not a rat. But he was the biggest, most scarred and battered hamster Sam had ever seen. He had a malevolent expression and very pointed teeth. But Delilah's expression, as she watched him from the top of the Bullocks' shed, was every bit as malevolent. She was a huge cat: black and white, with yellow teeth. She often watched this bird table, but rarely had much luck. No sensible bird ever went near the Bullocks' bird table.

Sam nudged Elfrida who was sitting next to him. 'Look there,' he muttered.

As it turned out, this was the worst thing he could have done. They were all very precariously situated on the narrow fence. The nudge unbalanced Elfrida, who clutched at Jake, and for a moment there was a lot of jostling and struggling, made worse by the fact that nobody wanted to get impaled on one of the spikes. The next moment, Jake and Elfrida had both fallen from the fence back into Sam's garden. Sam and Spider remained on the fence: Sam because, if truth be told, he was somewhat plumper than either Jake or Elfrida, and so was wedged that bit more tightly between the spikes; Spider because, although extremely skinny, he had the balance of a cat – or a spider.

'You glumphing graeth idjot!' shouted Elfrida. Her voice was muffled, as if she had fallen into something soft and smothering; which she had – the Harris's compost heap.

Jake just said, 'Ow!' He was stuck in the Harris's blackberry bushes.

Spider pointed. Sam looked and saw that Delilah was about to pounce. 'No!' he yelled. Morris must have heard, for he looked up just as Delilah sprung. Sam would never have thought a hamster – however large – could take on a strong and powerful cat. But Morris uttered an evil squeak, drew back a paw and cuffed Delilah round the nose. Then he sunk his teeth into her leg. She was so surprised she fell with a yelp off the bird table, grasped the edge and hung there by her front claws. Then her powerful back legs levered up behind her, and she made to spring.

Spider took his closed Swiss Army knife from its loop on his belt and sent it hurtling through the air. It hit Delilah full on the nose, and with a squeak she fell back off the bird table. Morris jumped down, and fled for his life down the path.

Sam did not even have time for a sigh of relief before he saw something truly terrible. Coming down the path, like an armoured tank charging into battle, was Mrs Bullock herself. She was singing loudly and trampling heavily on unsuspecting slugs and snails as she passed.

Spider and Sam froze. All their attention was riveted on Morris, who was hurtling straight towards her. With a couple of feet to go and just beneath Sam and Spider, Morris spotted Mrs Bullock – and Mrs Bullock spotted Morris. Morris stopped short with a terrible squeak. Mrs Bullock stopped likewise, and stood with her feet planted, hands on hips, and with a terrifying scowl on her face. As for Delilah, she was delighted. She could see Morris was trapped. With a yeowl, she sprang to catch the unfortunate hamster.

Spider Griswald launched himself off the fence and landed right on top of the unsuspecting cat.

Sam watched horrified as Spider scrambled to his feet, holding the struggling Delilah. Mrs Bullock was glaring at him as if she wanted to blast him into smithereens. Morris, very sensibly, was hiding behind a piece of rock that marked the border of the path.

'Who are you,' demanded Mrs Bullock, 'and what are you doing in my garden?'

Spider said nothing.

'Do you know you are trespassing on my property?' continued Mrs Bullock.

Spider said nothing.

'Wait a minute!' Mrs Bullock leaned closer. 'I know who you are! You are one of those Griswald hooligans. Let me tell you this, you are in deep trouble! Wait until I speak to your parents. You are going to wish you had never come to this town!' Mrs Bullock was red in the face, her expression resembling that of a boa constrictor gathering itself up to strike.

Still Spider said nothing.

Sam could feel his hands shaking. From the scuffling sounds behind him, it was clear that Jake and Elfrida were both caught fast in the blackberry bushes. Sam wished he was too. He swallowed nervously, crossed his fingers for luck and before he could think better of it – jumped.

He was not as practised at hurling himself off tall objects as Spider, and instead of leaping clear onto the path, he merely slithered uncomfortably down the fence. At the bottom, he staggered straight into Spider and Delilah. Spider, taken by surprise, let go of Delilah. Sam grabbed at her and, for the third time that day, got bitten (this time on the arm). She struggled and scratched at him but he did not let go.

Sam looked up to find Mrs Bullock scowling horribly at him. Her eyebrows were looking particularly bushy and she was baring her teeth in a very unpleasant manner.

'Good afternoon Mrs Bullock,' said Sam, hoping his voice wasn't shaking too much.

Mrs Bullock did not bother with any social pleasantries. 'What are you doing in my garden, Sam Harris?' she snarled. 'And what are you doing with my cat?'

Sam felt like a rabbit caught in headlights just before it is mowed down. His mind was completely blank. Then inspiration struck. 'We were bringing Delilah back to you,' he improvised. 'We found her in my garden, and she was hurt. So I thought I'd better bring her straight round. But then she escaped and we've been chasing her round your garden.'

Mrs Bullock glared at him. 'A likely story! Give me that cat! I'm warning you, Harris! If I find you've been lying to me – well!'

She reached out and grabbed Delilah. Then she caught sight of the cat's leg where Morris had bitten her. It was still bleeding. 'Hmm,' she conceded reluctantly. 'She does seem to have been hurt. I will have to make sure the vet sees her. Now get out of my garden, and don't come back.' With a glance at Spider she added, 'And I wouldn't associate with those Griswald children if I were you, Sam Harris. I don't like them. I shall be telling your mother the same thing. Now get out, both of you!'

Inwardly seething, Sam turned to go, forgetting that he would be unable to get up the fence without Spider's help. He was thinking, strangely enough, about a teacher in primary school who had told Sam's class that she was convinced there was good buried within everybody. Sam thought that any good within Mrs Bullock would need to be extracted with a pickaxe. 'And she might have said *thank you*,' he added to himself. He had forgotten all about Morris, who was still cowering next to the path.

Unfortunately, Mrs Bullock had not.

From behind him came the words, 'Good Kitty! Now kill the horrible rat!'

Sam stood transfixed as Mrs Bullock flung Delilah at Morris. There was a horrible hamster squeal as Delilah's paw pinned Morris to the path. Then a kind of crunching noise.

A terrible silence followed. Then Delilah began to purr.

* * *

Sam and Spider returned to Sam's garden by way of the street. They were both in shock, and too weak to climb the fence even if they'd wanted to. Jake and Elfrida had finally fought free of the brambles and were both covered in scratches, not to mention bits of straw and potato peelings. Elfrida was crying.

'He was just a sweet, innocent hamster,' she sobbed.

'I'm sorry, Elfrida,' said Sam miserably. He meant it too. He thought Morris's end was the most rotten thing he had ever seen. Then he caught sight of Jake, and took a step backwards. Jake's eyes were so furious he looked positively dangerous.

'We shall go next door right now and – and –' Jake struggled to think of a sufficient revenge.

'Kill her!' Elfrida supplied. She looked as if she could have done it single-handed.

To Sam's alarm, neither Jake nor Spider dismissed this idea outright. In fact, they looked as if they were seriously considering it.

'We can't kill her!' Sam said hastily. 'I don't even think we should go round there. If we do, she'll lock us up in her shed, and report us to the police or something.'

'Then let's go round there,' said Jake, 'and lock *her* up in her shed, and report *her* to the police.'

Immediately the Griswalds surged forward. Sam ran after them protesting, so horrified that he could hardly manage a coherent sentence. 'Can't – crazy – dangerous – disaster – terrible trouble!' he bleated, but the Griswalds took no notice. 'There has to be –' he began again.

The Griswalds stopped short – but not because of Sam. Thistle Lane was usually a peaceful place on a Saturday afternoon. But now there were the sounds of footsteps – gates and doors slamming – then the wail of a police car's siren.

Suddenly they heard voices.

'What on earth is going on?'

'What's happened?'

'Is there a fire? Is there an accident?'

Sam recognised the voices of various neighbours. Then he heard a voice that boomed out above the rest like a football stadium loudspeaker.

'It's a disgrace – that's what it is! And I know who's to

blame. It's those children – that's who! Letting down the neighbourhood – no-good hooligans – little brutes – well, *they're not going to get away with this*!'

It was Mrs Bullock, of course. And somehow Sam had no doubt at all that she was referring to the Griswalds. Judging by the looks on their faces, the Griswalds agreed with him. They turned round and made for Sam's back garden.

Elfrida began, 'Do you think they've found out about –'

'Yes,' said Jake.

'And d'you think it's our house the police –'

'Yes,' said Jake again.

'Mum's going to be absolutely –'

'Yes,' said Jake, and for a fleeting second he looked almost worried. Sam, who hadn't thought any of the Griswalds capable of such a feeling, wondered if he had imagined it – especially as the next moment Jake was looking his usual confident self.

'Sam,' said Jake, 'there's a lot of sense in what you say.'

'Huh?' Sam gaped at him.

'Yes. Sometimes it's not a good idea to be hasty. I thought you were just scared, but I was wrong. I should have listened to you. You were really quick-witted, making up that stuff about the cat. We need to think of a more – umm – subtle revenge to take on Old Big Nose –'

'Right,' said Sam, greatly relieved.

'We need time to come up with a truly cunning plan –'

'Exactly,' said Sam, who thought any plan would be an

improvement on trying to lock up Mrs Bullock in her own garden shed.

'And I think we ought to be going now.'

'Good,' said Sam. 'I mean – that's a shame – but perhaps you'd better –'

'You see,' said Jake, 'we don't like to leave Mum to talk to the police by herself. It's not fair really, is it?'

'What!' yelled Sam before he could help himself. Then he continued hastily, 'I mean – no – err – I suppose not. I mean, I know how it is.'

Actually he did not know – it was not an issue he had ever had to consider before. And he was not sure, either, whether to be relieved that the Griswalds did have some better feelings after all or horrified that they were involved with the police. He still hadn't decided when they reached the fence and Elfrida turned and took his hand in a tight grip.

'You did your best to save Morris, and I'll never forget it,' she declared passionately. 'We Griswalds don't forget our friends, and you're our friend, now, the best friend we have in the whole of Bellstone!' Her sincerity was obvious, and the effect only slightly spoiled when she added, 'Anyway, the rest of Bellstone are pigs!'

Sam went red. He watched as the Griswalds disappeared over the fence, then he went back to the house. Strangely, despite the tragic events of the afternoon, there was a warm glow inside him. It was good to think he had some allies at last in his eternal battle with the Bullocks. And from what he had seen, allies who were not only capable of taking on the Bullocks – but perhaps even of winning.

* * *

Luckily for Sam, Mrs Harris had rushed out onto the street with everybody else, and so he had a bit of time to disguise his injuries and clean up before she saw him. Even so, enough evidence of bite and burn remained to make some explanation necessary, and in the end he told her he had got that way playing with Brandon and Christabel Bullock. Mrs Harris never believed him when he tried to tell her how vile the Bullocks really were, and was always saying he should become more friendly with them, so Sam reckoned it would do no harm if she thought his injuries were their fault. He counted on Mrs Harris being too scared of Mrs Bullock to actually go round and complain.

He was right. Mrs Harris muttered something about how she *would* go round and see Mrs Bullock, only Mrs Bullock was so busy 'what with that fire, and everything' that she did not want to bother her. Sam immediately pricked up his ears.

'What fire?' he asked.

Mrs Harris looked cagey. 'Oh – nothing. I wasn't going to mention it. Well, all right,' she went on as Sam glared at her. 'It seems there has been a slight – err – accident to the bus shelter. You know, the one on the corner. It seems it's – well, it's burnt down.' She immediately turned away and became very busy putting a pizza in the oven.

Sam gaped. 'How could it burn down?' he demanded.

But the moment he said it, he knew how. The Griswalds had done it.

Mrs Harris came to sit down at the table. She was fidgeting, the way she always did when there was something she would prefer not to tell him. As she preferred not to tell him anything she found at all worrying, or strange, or upsetting, or even just out of the ordinary, he was well used to the signs.

'Mrs Bullock is saying that the new children next door are to blame,' she said, reluctantly, at last. 'But I don't think that's likely. I don't see how they could possibly burn down a whole bus shelter . . .' Mrs Harris's voice faltered. She reached forward and opened her box of cigarettes. Then she shut it again. She tried hard never to smoke in front of Sam, as she knew the smoke was not good for him, and she did not want to set him a bad example. 'You know, Sam,' she said suddenly, 'it might be as well if you didn't get friendly with those children. The Griswalds, I think they're called. It sounds like they might be – well – a bit strange. In fact, the truth is, I didn't mention them to you until now because I'd rather you didn't get to know them.'

'Mum!' Sam was so fed up he forgot about everything else. 'That's just typical of you. You can't just not tell me things, and hope I won't find out! Do you think I wouldn't have noticed that new people had moved in next door?'

'I'm only thinking of what's best for you, Sam!'

'What were you going to do – force me to stay home for the rest of my life, so I wouldn't meet them?'

Mrs Harris's willpower failed her, and she reached for a cigarette. 'Now, Sam, I just don't want you mixed up in anything. These children sound a bit wild to me. I have to look out for you. After all, now that your father isn't here, I'm the only one to do it. I have to do the job of two parents and it's not easy –'

Usually when Mrs Harris talked this way, Sam just sat and listened, while that cold lump of misery inside him grew bigger and bigger. But today – perhaps because of everything that had already happened – something snapped. 'That's not fair!' Sam leapt up, knocking over his chair. 'You always say that! You always drag Dad into it and it's not fair!'

He ran out of the room. As he went through the hall he thought he could hear strange noises coming from the garden. 'It's probably nothing,' he muttered to himself, 'but I suppose I'd better check it out, before she hears and decides it's murderers or terrorists or something.'

He flung open the back door. The brown and white dog was sitting there, looking up at him and making whimpering noises.

Huh! thought Sam, not very impressed. He had forgotten all about the Griswalds' dog, but that did not mean the Griswalds should have. People who owned dogs had responsibilities. And he thought people who had just had one pet murdered under their very noses might try not to lose the other in the same afternoon.

He knelt down and rubbed the dog's chest, and it wagged its tail and whined at him.

'What are you doing, Sam?' called Mrs Harris from the kitchen.

'Nothing!' he yelled. Then he grabbed the dog and ran it upstairs to his bedroom. He could not tell her it belonged to the Griswalds, for he had not admitted to meeting them, and if he pretended it was a stray, she would not let it in the house. Stray dogs, especially stray dogs that bit people, were well up her list of worries. He could almost hear her now: *rabies, fleas, diseases* . . .

'I expect the Griswalds are wondering where you are,' Sam told the dog, emptying a cardboard box for it to sleep in. 'I expect they're really worried about you. Well, they deserve to worry. In fact,' Sam added, heartlessly, 'I hope they're really suffering.'

* * *

Had Sam been able to view what was happening next door, he would have been disappointed. It was true that the atmosphere around the kitchen table was not a happy one. Mr Griswald and the older Griswald brother, Luke, were not there, but Mrs Griswald was, and in such a bad mood that you could almost see it crackling out of her like static electricity. But the only actual suffering taking place was in the gastronomic line.

'Oh Mum, not dumplings again,' complained Elfrida, as her mother slammed down a platter of these objects on the table. Mrs Griswald had been taught by her Czech grandmother how to make more than twenty different kinds of dumpling. Her offspring loathed all of them.

'After the events of today,' observed Mrs Griswald darkly, 'you don't deserve even bread and water.'

'I'd prefer bread and water,' muttered Elfrida, but her mother didn't hear her.

'Don't you think you're overreacting, Mum,' suggested Jake. 'After all, it was an accident.'

'An accident!' Mrs Griswald speared a dumpling on the prongs of her fork, like an Eskimo spearing a seal. 'Is that what you call it? I call it the most *irresponsible*, *reckless* . . .'

Her children helped themselves to dumplings and, in Jake and Spider's case, chicken and boiled cabbage. When their mother seemed to be running out of insults to throw at them, Elfrida, who had never been noted for her tact, intervened.

'Well, it *was* an accident. And in a way it was *your* fault. If *you* hadn't suggested –'

'*My* fault?' Mrs Griswald looked so dangerous that Elfrida fell silent. '*My* fault? Of course it was *my fault*. I should have realised that you weren't to be trusted for a moment –'

Elfrida looked at her brothers and shrugged, then chewed on her dumplings. They weren't very nice. They tasted like wallpaper paste might if it was rolled up into balls and allowed to go dry. Elfrida thought Luke was lucky to be out with some of the other students from his new Sixth Form College. She looked hungrily at her brothers' plates, and at the full plate that was still waiting for her father. Mr Griswald was often a bit vague about mealtimes. In fact, he was a bit vague about most things.

'Hey, you keep off!' Jake had noticed her looking at his food. 'You're a veggie, remember? There's hardly enough chicken for us.'

Elfrida scowled. She had been a vegetarian for the last month, and was determined not to give up. But there were times – like now as she stared at the horrible, grey, doughy balls sitting all alone on her plate – when she felt extremely tempted. It was true she could have eaten some cabbage. But Elfrida hated cabbage. In fact she hated most vegetables – an unfortunate thing for a vegetarian.

'Eat up – don't let them go cold!' Mrs Griswald snapped. Everybody obeyed. Not because they were obedient by nature – they were not – but because Mrs Griswald's dumplings had much in common with quick drying cement. Eating them cold was like chipping at rock.

Her food eaten, Mrs Griswald laid down her knife and fork. 'Now, I want a word with you. And this is important.'

'Mum!' Jake protested. 'Not again! It *was* an accident –'

Mrs Griswald shook her head. 'It's not about that. It's about that neighbour of ours – Mrs Bullock. She's been round to see me three times this week already! And as well as telling me our house is a disgrace to the neighbourhood, and that I should chop down the apple trees and concrete over the lawn' (Mrs Griswald sniffed loudly to show just what she thought of this advice), 'she's been complaining about you lot. Footballs through car sun roofs –' (she glared at Jake) ' – and cats howling through the night –' (she scowled at Elfrida) '– and people lobbing water-bombs off the roof –' (she turned to look at Spider). 'Well, I'm sick of it. So, I don't want any of you doing a single thing – do you understand me, *not one single thing* – that will give her an excuse to come round here again.'

Mrs Griswald scowled round at her children. They gazed back at her, a picture of hurt innocence. None of them looked as if just two hours before they had been planning to lock the same Mrs Bullock into her garden shed. Their mother continued, 'Now it seems that Mrs Bullock has this campaign she runs, to make Bellstone the Tidiest Town in England. She gets very, very worked up about it. She doesn't want anything to go wrong.' Mrs Griswald paused significantly. 'So, it had better *not* go wrong, do you hear me? You lot are going to be *tidy*, for once in your life. And if that's impossible,' added Mrs Griswald more realistically, 'at least you are not to do anything majorly untidy. And that includes any more accidents with bus shelters. Do you understand me?'

'Yes,' said her children, meaning that they understood her perfectly. It did not mean, however, that they planned to do what she told them. Mrs Griswald would have been wise to clarify this point.

'Just keep away from her!' Mrs Griswald declared.

She then departed with the plate of food for her husband, who had obviously forgotten all about the meal, leaving her children with strict instructions to do the washing-up. This they did, although perhaps not in quite the way she had intended. Elfrida stood on a stool by the sink, sending tidal waves of water overflowing across the kitchen; Jake juggled the plates as he dried them, then lobbed them across the room to Spider, who caught them one-handed and put them away – but in his own fashion, which meant that he leapt lightly from counter to counter across the large kitchen, and never once let a foot touch the floor.

'What d'you think of Sam?' asked Jake. He flicked his wrist, and the dumpling platter went hurtling towards Spider, who was sitting on top of the fridge.

'I like Sam,' said Elfrida. 'He tried to save Morris.' She plunged a saucepan into the water, sending spray everywhere. Spider, who was now clambering up the shelves of the dresser, nodded his agreement.

'I think he has possibilities,' said Jake. 'He did good work today. He just needs livening up. A bit like Bellstone really. After all, he *said* he wished Bellstone was more exciting.'

He grinned.

Sam, if he had been listening, would have been horrified.

Chapter Three
Next Door

Sunday morning dawned bright and peaceful in Bellstone. Old ladies on their way to church waited to take the bus from where the bus shelter had been before the Griswalds turned it into a heap of smouldering ash. Mr Bullock trimmed the Bullocks' lawn, undisturbed by Mrs Bullock, who was prowling around Bellstone looking for things that needed tidying, and people to bully into tidying them. Mrs Harris drank tea and smoked a secret cigarette before Sam could come down and catch her. Even the Griswalds were being peaceful – or at least they were not doing anybody any harm. In fact, most of them were asleep. Only Spider had woken early and was currently sitting on top of the chimney pot.

Sam was not feeling peaceful. He had spent a terrible night with the dog. It seemed to be a typical Griswald in that it combined large amounts of energy with no respect for authority. It wanted to play; it wanted to bark; it wanted to chase imaginary hamsters and to climb the curtains in Sam's bedroom. Stopping it from doing these things, and most of all from waking Mrs Harris, exhausted Sam. He got little sleep, and when he did drop off, he slept late. He woke up feeling out-of-sorts, with his scalp stinging where the Griswalds had burnt it, and his arm and ear throbbing where the Griswalds' dog and hamster had bitten *them*. He no longer felt a warm glow when he thought about the Griswalds. On the contrary, now that he knew they were dangerous arsonists who neglected their dog, he was no longer sure he wanted to have anything more to do with them.

The dog was lying on Sam's feet, snoring. Sam finally managed to shift it and trailed downstairs. His mother quickly stubbed out her cigarette. 'Really, Sam,' she said. 'If you look this tired and sleep this late, you can't be well. I wonder if I should keep you home another week?'

This did nothing to improve Sam's mood. As soon as he possibly could, he smuggled the dog out of the house, and went next door.

He was in such a hurry, he forgot to check the lane as carefully as usual before stepping out of his own gate.

'Hey, look, it's Sam. What have you got there, Fatso? A new dog?'

'A dog?' added a high, shrill voice. 'More like a mutant toad. Hey Sam – where are you off to?'

Brandon and Christabel Bullock were smirking at him from further up the lane. Brandon was big and stupid-looking, and Christabel was small and spiteful-looking. Sam had never been able to make up his mind which of them he liked least. While Brandon's feet and fists left the bigger bruises, Christabel's needle-sharp comments could hurt for months afterwards.

Sam set off down the lane, the dog loping along beside him, but Brandon and Christabel were coming right after him – and gaining. Sam pulled up at the Griswalds' front gate.

'Hey, you're not going to see those Griswalds, are you?' asked Brandon.

'Yes, they're real *weirdos*,' said Christabel. 'Nobody will talk to you at school if you hang out with them. Not that they would anyway.' Christabel Bullock was quite pretty. But her dainty heart-shaped face, surrounded by gold-red curls, was able to screw itself up into the most amazingly ugly expression. Brandon stepped forward menacingly as Sam backed into the gate.

Then an amazing thing happened. Just as Brandon was about to attack, the dog stepped forward, snarling, and with its hackles rising. The Bullocks took one look, turned and fled up Thistle Lane. Sam gave the dog a pat. He was still feeling rather shaky as he reached the Griswalds' front door and rang the bell.

Mrs Griswald answered the door. There was something brisk and fierce-looking about her, which made Sam sure she must be the Griswalds' mother. Her face looked as if it was chiselled out of solid rock. Her hands were covered in soil.

'Just when I was in the middle of killing off that bindweed!' she exclaimed. 'Can nobody else in this good-for-nothing family open the door?'

Sam was a bit taken aback by this. He did not like meeting strangers in any case, and found he was stammering slightly as he said, 'Hello. Umm, I'm from next door and I w-was w-wondering –'

'I hope you're not one of those Bullocks,' Mrs Griswald interrupted.

'No! I'm Sam Harris and –'

'Good! Because I can tell you I'm in no mood for any more Bullocks coming round here. Do you know that woman told me to cut down my apple trees! I mean, why do you think we bought this house?'

Sam blinked. He had never heard of anyone buying a house for its apple trees, especially apple trees as gnarled and twisted as the ones in the Griswalds' garden. Then again, there were not many good reasons for buying the Griswalds' house. It was very old and one side of it looked as if it was falling down. Sam's mother had once said that whoever bought it would have a real job on their hands making sure this did not happen. They would also have a job containing Mrs Bullock, who had been trying for ages to have the place condemned so that a nice, new, and above all *tidy*, modern bungalow might be built there instead.

'And no bonfires – forbidden, she says! Who does she think she is?' Mrs Griswald sounded as if she could continue all day.

'Err, Mrs Griswald –'

'I suppose you're friends with the children,' said Mrs Griswald, eyeing Sam as if this were no recommendation. 'You can come in if you like. Actually you look quite harmless.'

Sam could feel the anger welling up inside him. After all, nobody likes to be described as *harmless*. 'Actually,' he said furiously, 'I came to return your dog. Look, you haven't even noticed he's here! And if you want to know, I think your kids are disgusting to have a dog and then forget about it, and not even to have a collar with its address on –'

'*Our* dog, you say?' Mrs Griswald was staring at the dog with a thunderous expression on her face. The dog was wagging its tail in a friendly way, but Mrs Griswald looked as if she was about to hit somebody. Sam took a quick step backwards. Then Mrs Griswald turned and bellowed, 'ELFRIDA!!!!'

During the silence that followed, Sam did not dare say a word. Then Elfrida appeared.

'Oh hello, Sam,' she said. Then she spotted the dog and her face lit up. 'Hello doggy –'

'Elfrida,' interrupted her mother in a terrible voice.

'What have I told you? What have I said to you again and again? NO MORE PETS! And now I find you have gone behind my back and –'

'But Mum,' said Elfrida, 'this isn't my dog. He's yours, isn't he Sam?'

Sam glared at her. This was too much. Yesterday he had thought he might be friends with the Griswalds, but now he was altogether sick of them.

'No, he is not,' he snapped. 'You know perfectly well you left him in my garden.'

'I never did! You liar, Sam Harris!'

'You're calling *me* a liar! That's rich, that is!'

A ferocious argument began. Attracted by the noise, Jake and Spider appeared, followed by their brother Luke (even taller than Spider and with an earring in one ear). Then one of Elfrida's cats, Pomfret, came searching for her. Pomfret and the dog exchanged one look, then with a yowl and a hiss they went for each other.

Everybody stopped shouting and tried to pull the animals apart. Eventually, Elfrida and Jake pinned Pomfret down on the sofa, Spider and Sam sat on the dog, and something like peace was restored.

And then finally, the truth emerged. Nobody knew who the dog belonged to. While Sam had assumed it belonged to the Griswalds, they had assumed it belonged to Sam.

'It was in your garden, after all!' Elfrida yelled.

'Yes, but *you* were in my garden too!'

Elfrida turned to her mother. 'I told you it wasn't mine!

You never believe me!'

'And can you blame me? After that stray cat you smuggled into the cellar – not to mention that rat you bought without telling me.' Nevertheless, Mrs Griswald did look a bit shamefaced. She added defensively, 'And those animals of yours are eating us out of house and home.'

'That's all you care about!' Elfrida howled. 'Food! Even though you're eating other living things!'

'Don't worry, Elfrida,' said Jake. 'I'm almost sure that chicken last night was dead.'

Luke Griswald chuckled, and disappeared upstairs.

Elfrida changed tack. 'Please Mum, let me keep the dog! Please! I'll be good for ever, I promise – and I won't burn down any more bus shelters –'

'No! You have ten pets already. Ten is enough.'

'But I don't have ten any more,' Elfrida howled. 'Morris died! A cat killed him!' And at the terrible memory, she began to cry.

This revelation shook even Mrs Griswald. She turned to Sam and in a subdued voice asked if he was planning to keep the dog, but Sam explained that his mother would never allow it.

'Please, Mum,' said Elfrida.

'I don't think – I mean – humph!' declared Mrs Griswald. And with that she went sweeping out of the room.

Elfrida immediately perked up. She gave the dog a huge hug.

'But what are we going to do with him?' Sam asked worriedly.

'What do you mean? He's staying with us, of course.'

'But your mum – she said –'

Jake shook his head at him. 'She didn't say no, did she? And that's good enough.'

Sam blinked. He had never looked at things that way before – and he was pretty sure Mrs Harris would have something to say if he did. Still, he did not argue. The dog needed a home. Besides, he felt rather awkward for having misjudged the Griswalds so badly. Luckily the Griswalds did not seem to resent his accusations; they were very pleased with their new pet, and immediately went off to find something to use for a collar and lead.

Sam followed them, staring curiously around the house as he went. It was as different from Sam's home as he could have imagined. In his house, everything was polished and gleaming, and Mrs Harris had flowers and pictures and tasteful ornaments. The Griswalds, however, would have no more thought of polishing the furniture than of baking a cake for Mrs Bullock, and any tasteful ornament would have been broken before the day was out. They had plenty of other stuff, though: boxes of flea powder, a surfboard, mud-caked football boots, old padlocks, a stuffed ferret in a case, boxes of birthday cards, cat-worming pills, mountain bikes, a saxophone, several crates of ginger ale (the Griswalds obviously liked ginger ale), fishing rods and books with intriguing titles such as *One Hundred and One*

Things to Do with Dumplings and *The SAS Survival Guide*.

Sam could see that the Griswalds were never going to get on with Mrs Bullock. They could never win a prize for tidiness. Or even be runners-up.

When they arrived in Spider's room in the attic, Sam stared more than ever. It was a huge, bare space; ropes hung from the rafters, and spikes had been hammered here and there into the walls and the enormously high ceiling. In some places, hand-holds had been gouged out of the plaster. In a flash, Spider went clambering up to the beams, where he untied some rope, then swung down. Soon, he had fashioned the dog a halter and lead of sorts.

'From that window,' Jake told Sam, 'he has three different routes onto the roof. Don't you Spider? One of them's dead easy – Elf and I could do it. We're going to try it some time, when Mum's after us.'

To Sam's relief, he did not suggest they tried it now. Instead, they went to Elfrida's room, so the dog could meet some of her other pets. Elfrida's room was covered with posters of animals, with slogans such as 'Eating Meat is Murder' and 'Ban Blood Sports!' There was also an enormous dolls' house, which seemed to be occupied by gerbils and, Sam noticed with amazement, a nun's habit thrown over one chair. Unfortunately Elfrida's pets (two gerbils, a green budgie, two mice, a goldfish and a house rabbit) did not take to the dog at all. The dog, on the other hand, seemed keen to meet them. In fact, it was obvious to everybody that he thought a gerbil or budgie would make a tasty snack.

'I'm going to call him Biter,' announced Elfrida, after they had dragged the dog out onto the landing. 'After all,' she added, as she ruefully inspected a finger that had come between Biter and her favourite gerbil, 'that seems to be what he likes doing best.'

'Whose room is that?' asked Sam as they filed out onto the landing. Through an open door, he could see what looked like an easel.

'Oh that's Dad's studio,' said Jake quickly, 'but he doesn't like to be disturbed.' He quickly ushered Sam in the opposite direction. 'Come and see my room.'

Before he turned, Sam thought he caught sight of a small man with grizzled hair bent over the easel. And he had the brief impression of lots of pink, fluffy bunny rabbits. But Sam felt he must be mistaken: it was just too difficult to imagine that the man who had married Mrs Griswald, and fathered the young Griswalds, should spend his time painting fluffy, pink bunny rabbits.

Sam forgot about Mr Griswald as he peered into Jake's room, which looked more like a mechanic's workshop than a bedroom. At first glance, he saw what might be the insides of twenty different toasters heaped up on the floor. 'What's all that?'

'All what? Oh, you mean my motorbike. I'm rebuilding it to make it run off electricity.'

Sam stepped back hastily. He had a healthy respect for electricity, ever since the time Brandon Bullock had tried to electrocute him, accidentally-on-purpose, during a science experiment at school.

'It used to be Mum's,' said Elfrida sniffily. 'She only let Jake have it because it doesn't work.'

'But you're not old enough to ride it,' Sam could not help pointing out.

'Yeah, well – to be honest, by the time I get her to go I probably will be,' Jake admitted. 'What I've found is: taking her to bits is easy, but putting her back together isn't quite so simple. But isn't she a beauty? I reckon she looks a bit like a Harley –'

Sam was not really listening. His eyes took in the

trophies (for football and karate), the skateboard lying in one corner, the poster of Jackie Chan, and the banners for Tottenham Hotspur and the Brazil football team.

'I like football, too,' said Sam suddenly.

'Yeah? What position do you play?'

'Well – usually they make me play defence. At school they did. But really,' he confided, 'I'd like to play up front.'

'Great, we can join the school team together. Then there will be two of us to take on that prat Brandon.'

Sam's heart fell. 'Oh, is Brandon Bullock on the team?' he asked casually – although secretly he had always known he would be.

'Yeah – but think,' said Jake encouragingly, 'if we're on the team too, how many chances we'll get to kick him.'

He continued talking about the team as they drifted outside, with occasional contributions from Elfrida. ('Football's boring – why d'you have to talk about it all the time?') Sam was silent. He felt a bit alarmed that Jake seemed to be taking it for granted that they would both join – or at least try out for – the team. Personally, Sam was not sure he wanted to belong to any team which included Brandon Bullock – and it wasn't much of a consolation knowing he was unlikely to be picked for it anyway.

Once outside, they tied Biter to a large pine tree to keep him away from Elfrida's two cats: a tortoiseshell named Arthur, and the greyish tabby Pomfret. Then Sam followed the Griswalds into the branches of the tree. (The Griswalds, thought Sam, clutching hard to his branch, seemed to have a natural affinity with heights.) From there, Sam had a good view of the Griswalds' garden. In one corner, Mrs Griswald was hacking at the undergrowth with what looked like a machete. In another, the Griswalds' beaten-up old caravan stood surrounded by a sea of bindweed, thistles and wild garlic. In between was a wilderness of rippling grasses, gnarled apple trees, a half dried-up fish pond, a muddy stream and a collapsing shed.

'Right,' said Jake. 'Now let's think of a plan to get back at Mrs Bullock. What we need is a strategy.'

'Wait a minute,' said Sam. 'First of all – what *did* happen to the bus shelter?'

'Oh, that,' said Jake casually. 'We burned it down.'

Sam almost fell off his branch. Not because they had actually done it, but because they were so brazen about it. 'But you can't just burn things down!' he yelled. 'I mean – people don't do things like that. Not in Bellstone, anyway.'

'I know,' said Jake calmly. 'We reckon Bellstone needs livening up.'

Sam just goggled – and while he was goggling, Jake and Elfrida explained.

It was, they said, Mrs Griswald's fault really. She had wanted them out of the house because she was still unpacking after the move, and after they had dropped the second box of plates she had decided they were getting underfoot.

'She said we should go out and have a picnic,' Elfrida said bitterly. 'She said that was the kind of thing people did in places like this. We said *not when it's raining*, but of course she wouldn't listen.'

Jake took up the tale. 'We didn't fancy it. I mean – who wants to get wet? But then we thought – why not have a picnic in the bus shelter?'

'The bus shelter?'

'Yeah – good idea, wasn't it? Nobody was using it. But it was cold, so then *I* said, let's light a fire to keep warm.'

'Spider'n'Jake are good with fires,' put in Elfrida.

'I bet they are,' said Sam grimly.

'So then,' Jake went on, 'we thought if we were having a fire, we might as well cook something on it. So Spider went home and filched some potatoes and sausages, but they didn't cook fast enough because the fire was too small.' He paused, and looked meaningfully at his sister.

Elfrida said: 'I had a good idea. Well, it seemed a good idea at the time. I remembered I'd seen an old can of petrol, in the garage . . . and I'd heard that petrol was good for fires . . . '

Sam stared at her, aghast. 'You don't mean –'

'Yeah.' Jake's eyes gleamed. 'She chucked the whole lot on! We didn't have time to stop her!'

'It was meant to be a lovely surprise,' said Elfrida defensively.

'Surprise? It was an inferno!'

Sam swallowed and didn't hear what Jake said next. He was overtaken by a vision of enormous flames, orange and yellow, licking up around the side of the bus shelter, which was slowly turning black and melting; and the Griswalds all around, screaming and yelling.

'You could have been killed,' he croaked.

'Well, we weren't,' said Elfrida crossly. 'You sound just like Mum. After all, it was the sort of accident that could happen to anyone.'

Sam doubted this. Most people managed to go on picnics without setting fire to their surroundings. And into his mind there came two thoughts: one, the Griswalds were off their heads; and two, if Mrs Harris ever found out the full story she would never let Sam see them again. Then something else struck him. 'So d'you mean you just legged it and hid in my tree house?'

'We called the fire brigade first,' said Jake, 'from the phone box on the corner. And we gave our names and addresses and everything.'

'But we thought there was no need to stick around,' Elfrida said confidingly. 'You see, we didn't want to get in the way of the firemen –'

'I bet you didn't,' muttered Sam.

'– and as it was still raining and your tree house seemed nice and sheltered and . . . out of the way, we thought we'd go and sit in there for a bit.'

'Only then we heard the police arrive,' Jake concluded. 'So we had to face the music.'

'What did your parents say?'

For the first time, the Griswalds looked glum.

'Dad didn't say much – he never does –'

'He just sort of looks at you –'

'But Mum was furious –'

'Never seen her so angry –'

'Says we've disgraced her already –'

'Of course, it was only a matter of time –'

Jake and Elfrida fell silent. Spider remained inscrutable, several branches above them. Sam did not know what to say.

'By the way,' said Jake at last. 'I'm sorry you had to deal with Old Big Nose yesterday. We never meant to abandon you like that. But Elfrida and I were stuck, and Spider's not very good at talking, are you Spider?'

Spider shrugged apologetically.

'That's all right,' said Sam. 'It wouldn't have helped.' And in fact he was completely sure the Griswalds would have backed him up if they could. It gave him a kind of warm feeling inside, and at that moment he discovered to his own amazement that he really *did* want to be friends with the Griswalds. Despite the fact that they were dangerous arsonists, he liked them.

'Anyhow, you did great,' said Jake. 'We're glad you're on our side. Old Big Nose had better watch out!'

'Yes,' said Elfrida. 'And now we must swear a solemn oath to avenge Morris's blood!'

Some of Sam's warm feeling ebbed away. He had the unpleasant feeling that the Griswalds had misunderstood the kind of person he was: they thought he would be a brave and reckless ally in their campaign of vengeance against the Bullocks, whereas Sam really spent most of his time trying to avoid the Bullocks altogether. Still, he did not mind swearing the oath. Elfrida wanted them all to shed blood for the occasion, which she claimed would 'affirm their fellowship', but as Spider's Swiss Army knife was still lying in the Bullocks' garden, and Jake's penknife was rusty and extremely blunt, they decided to abandon this idea. But there was spitting, and slapping of hands, and stamping of feet, and linking of little fingers, while Elfrida avowed that none by the name of Griswald (or Harris, added Sam, getting swept up into the spirit of the thing) would rest until the evil and wretched Bullocks had been made to pay for their despicable crimes. (Sam had suggested that *all* the Bullocks should be included, as Brandon and Christabel were every bit as revolting as their mother, if not more so.)

'Aye, aye,' chorused Sam and Jake (Spider nodded vigorously). And so it was agreed.

With that, Sam realised he had been gone for ages, and his mother was probably already summoning the police. The Griswalds escorted him to their side of the fence and showed him the footholds they had made.

'I'll tell you what,' said Jake, about to give Sam a leg-up. 'We'll come by and fetch you for school tomorrow.'

'No thanks,' said Sam quickly. 'I mean – I might be late – I don't want to keep you waiting.'

'Don't worry about that. I don't expect you could be later than us if you tried.'

'Actually, I just remembered – I might need to be in school early –' He petered out. He could not think of any reason why he should need to be at school early.

The Griswalds looked at him. Their faces were not as friendly as they had been. 'I expect Sam has his own friends,' said Elfrida stiffly. 'I expect he wants to go with them.'

Sam felt himself go red. 'I don't,' he said in a low voice. 'It's not that at all.' He swallowed hard. 'I'll tell you what. I'll stop by tomorrow and collect *you*.'

The Griswalds agreed to this, and Sam heaved a sigh of relief. Now that he had decided he *did* want to be friends with the Griswalds after all, he certainly did not want *them* deciding not to be friends with *him*. The only problem was how to keep his word. Suddenly he found he was dreading school more than ever. Even supposing that Mrs Harris let him go in the first place.

Chapter Four
School

Sunlight filtered through the trees and onto the pitch. Sam sat on the substitutes' bench and watched Brandon Bullock lurk, as he always did, near the open goal. Just because he was tall, he thought he could spend all his time there, waiting for somebody else to boot the ball to him.

At that moment the midfielder did just that. The ball hurtled towards the goal, and Brandon went straight for it.

But so did the other team's central defender. There was a horrible crunching noise, and Brandon let out a yelp; the next moment, he was hobbling towards Sam with a face like thunder. Sam was getting up to take his place.

And now here was the ball coming towards him: Sam stopped it with his left foot; he was sliding it in towards the goal; the goalkeeper was leaping but it was too late; everybody was cheering; Sam felt as if his heart would explode –

'Sam!' shouted Mrs Harris. 'Time to get up!'

Sam opened his eyes and groaned.

* * *

In the kitchen, the sun was pouring in with relentless brightness. Sam crept into the room, somehow smaller and less significant than he had been the day before. He was already practising to become invisible.

Mrs Harris was busy preparing Sam a packed lunch. Sam thought about mentioning that there was a cafeteria at school, then decided it wasn't worth it.

'Now Sam, if you feel in the slightest bit unwell I want you to call me at work straightaway, and I'll come and fetch you –'

'Yes Mum,' muttered Sam, who had no intention of doing any such thing.

'I've made you sandwiches, and some home-made cake; they're in this little box here –'

'Yes Mum.'

'And you will be careful, won't you, not to get into any rough games at break?'

'Yes Mum.' (He could not help feeling extremely grateful that the Griswalds were not here to listen to all this.) He slid into his seat in front of the cornflakes Mrs Harris had set out for him. He did not feel like breakfast. He did not feel like anything, much. Then he remembered he was supposed to be meeting the Griswalds and began shovelling in the cornflakes.

'Don't bolt your food – it's important to chew properly if you don't want to get indigestion.' Mrs Harris came to sit down opposite him, and Sam was forced to eat more slowly. 'I expect you're looking forward to starting your new school, aren't you?' said Mrs Harris brightly.

Sam stared at her. Did she not realise how awful it was to start a new school a whole week after everybody else? He just grunted and bent his head over his cornflakes.

'The thing is to have a positive attitude. Now if only you had some interests, that would help you to make friends. How about bird-watching, or fossils?'

'I do have interests,' said Sam in a low voice. 'I like football.'

'Oh, yes.' Mrs Harris did not sound enthusiastic. 'That's just watching television, though, isn't it?'

'I want to get on the team at school,' said Sam. He had not admitted this to his mother before, but he thought it was better than being forced to join the bird-watching club. 'Although I expect I won't be able to. They probably chose the team last week. And I expect I wouldn't have been picked anyway.'

'Oh, well.' Mrs Harris, to Sam's annoyance, sounded relieved. 'It's a rough game, isn't it? And I've never thought of you as sporty. Now, how about archaeology? That would be interesting, wouldn't it?' Mrs Harris had been trying to get Sam interested in archaeology ever since they had watched a TV programme together about the pyramids.

'What – you mean going on digs in Egypt or Africa?' said Sam hopefully.

'Err – no, I was thinking more about those Roman sewers they're digging up in Lower Titmarsh,' Mrs Harris admitted.

Sam stirred his cornflakes around gloomily. He didn't think he cared *what* he did, even if it was digging up a field in Lower Titmarsh. But with Mrs Harris's next idea he realised that he did. 'Or there's that Tidiness Campaign that Mrs Bullock runs – now that would be fun, wouldn't it? And I expect plenty of people at school belong to her group.'

'Mum! I'd rather die!'

'Well, there must be *something* you're interested in, besides football,' said Mrs Harris in a petulant voice.

'There is. I'd like to have a dog.' As soon as he said it, Sam thought about Biter, and to his surprise, a pang of loss went through him. He remembered Biter snarling at Brandon. 'If I had a dog then the other kids –' He stopped short.

Mrs Harris was not listening. 'You're allergic to dogs.'

'Mum! That's an absolute lie!'

'Well, I'm sure you were breathing strangely that time we stayed with Aunt Fiona and her Yorkshire terriers,' said Mrs Harris defensively. 'Anyway, we've discussed this before and you know there are plenty of good reasons why we can't have a dog. Now, I'll just fetch my coat. We don't want to miss the bus, do we?' She got up.

'Look, Mum,' began Sam, rather desperately. 'I'm eleven years old and I really can go to school by myself. All the other kids will laugh, if you come too.'

'Don't be silly, Sam.' Mrs Harris laughed in a tinkling kind of way. 'If you agreed to ride in the Bullocks' car that would be one thing, but you refuse to go with them and I won't have you travelling by yourself. Now, where did I put my handbag?'

Sam was prevented from further argument by the front-door bell. He opened it, and to his dismay found Spider, Jake and Elfrida Griswald standing on the door-mat, grinning at him.

'Mum threw us out of the house so we thought we might as well collect you,' Jake explained.

Mrs Harris appeared, already wearing her coat. 'Oh, hello children,' she said, looking at the Griswalds without enthusiasm.

'Mum,' said Sam, with all the firmness he could muster, 'these are the kids from next door. We're going to catch the bus together. I'll be fine. I'll see you later. All right?'

And he crossed his fingers and hoped his mother would not humiliate him in front of everyone.

Mrs Harris hesitated. Her eyes roved over the Griswalds, and seemed not to like what they saw. But at last she said, very reluctantly, 'Well – as there are four of you – I suppose you can't come to much harm. But cross the road at the crossing, Sam. And don't speak to strangers, and remember your sandwiches –'

Her voice followed them down the garden path.

Elfrida said, 'Our mother never says stuff like that.'

Sam flinched, but then he realised that Elfrida was not being mean. In fact, she sounded envious.

'What does she say?' he asked.

Elfrida thought about it. 'Today, she said, "Put a foot wrong at that school and I'll kill you."'

There was a brief pause. Then Sam said in a low voice, 'My mum fusses because my dad's left us.' He turned red and waited for the Griswalds to ask all about it.

'Well, our dad might as well have left us,' Jake remarked. 'I don't think he's spoken to us since last Wednesday. Can you remember if he's spoken to us since Wednesday, Elf?'

The Griswalds immediately began a lively argument about this (Spider shaking his head or nodding as required) and were only distracted from it when Sam spotted the bus for school, pulling in where the bus shelter used to be. 'We've got to run,' he yelled, taking off. But the Griswalds did not follow. Sam stopped short, feeling stupid.

'We don't take the bus. We've been banned from the

bus,' Jake explained.

'Why? What did you do? I mean, you've only been here a week.'

'We didn't do anything – much. Elfrida took Morris on the bus and he escaped and bit someone –'

'Well, *you* were riding your skateboard in the aisle,' Elfrida pointed out.

'– but I think what really did it was Spider climbing out the window and riding on the roof.'

Sam gasped. Kids had got into trouble on the bus before: for smoking at the back, or chucking litter, and three of the older boys had once bared their bottoms at the window as the coach went by that was taking the Bellstone's Over Sixties on their Day Out. But nobody had ever tried riding on the roof before, not that Sam had heard. He was so astounded he forgot all about the bus, and by the time he remembered, it was pulling away. He had no choice but to walk with the Griswalds. 'Come on,' he said. 'We'd better hurry if we're going to get there any time today.'

As it turned out, they were not as late as Sam had feared. This was partly because the Griswalds were all good walkers – the result, no doubt, of years of being banned from buses. But it also had something to do with the route they took. The Griswalds believed in taking the direct approach, and if that meant they had to cut across people's gardens, squeeze through hedges, crawl under locked gates or scale six-foot fences, then so be it. Sam was soon panting, as he tried to keep up with them. But the result was that while they arrived at school looking a good deal more scratched and muddy than when they set out, they *did* manage to get there before the bell rang. In fact, there were still some children getting out of cars at the school gates.

'Really, have all these people lost the use of their legs?' Elfrida said scornfully, surveying the clean, well-scrubbed children (who were looking at the dishevelled Griswalds in some surprise). 'Don't they know that petrol fumes cause pollution?'

Jake pointed at the vehicle pulling up in front of them. It was not a car, but an enormous four-wheel-drive Jeep. It would have been just the thing for driving on dirt roads or through swamps and jungles, had there been any of these around Bellstone – which there were not.

'Isn't that the Bullocks?' asked Jake.

Sure enough, Christabel and Brandon Bullock climbed out, both dressed in immaculate school uniform. They stopped and stared at the Griswalds, and the Griswalds stopped and stared at them. It felt very much like Pomfret and Biter meeting for the first time. The air crackled with hostility.

'Where's your car?' demanded Brandon in a lofty tone.

'We walked. We don't need *Mummy* to take us everywhere,' responded Elfrida scathingly, as Mrs Bullock drove off in a cloud of exhaust fumes.

'Sammy does,' Brandon sneered. 'Sammy's mother goes

with him on the bus, and holds his hand. Doesn't she, Sammy-baby?'

Sam blushed furiously. Jake said, 'Don't be stupid. He's with us.'

'More fool him!' said Christabel. 'You lot are a disgrace, my mum says. Look at you! You're not even wearing school uniform!'

'Why should we?' demanded Elfrida fiercely. '*We* are the Griswalds. We don't want to look like everyone else.'

As it happened, there was little danger of this. Even before they had crawled through mud and climbed through hedges, the Griswalds had looked odd, wearing a strange assortment of clothes, none of which matched. Spider, long and lean, was dressed all in black except for his fluorescent green trainers, which were not ordinary trainers but climbing shoes, and he had so much climbing gear attached to his belt that he clanked when he walked. Jake wore a Tottenham scarf, and a hooded sweatshirt with a picture of Jackie Chan doing a kung-fu kick at some unlucky person's head. Elfrida was wearing a purple skirt, green top, pink cardigan, red tights and blue shoes. It was difficult to look at her for more than a few

seconds without getting a headache. She also wore a badge which read 'Stop Animal Cruelty Now!'

'You spoil the look of the school!' squeaked Christabel. 'And I can't believe your parents make you walk. What will you do if it rains?'

'What will you do if you have to get on your fat little legs and go anywhere?' countered Jake.

Christabel scowled. 'I am *not* fat! Sam's much fatter, anyway!'

Once again, Sam's face burned. But he did not have to say anything, for the Griswalds were immediately hot to his defence. They jeered and yelled at the Bullocks, and the Bullocks jeered and yelled at them; and it seemed that things might escalate in a dangerous and even violent manner when, fortunately, the bell rang. Jake grabbed Elfrida, who had been about to throw herself at Christabel, by the scruff of her neck and shoved her in the direction of her primary school next door. Then, with a few last taunts and insults, everyone made for his or her own classroom.

* * *

After this beginning, Sam hardly had time to dread school. Nevertheless, as they hurried to class, and he hunched himself further and further into his jacket in an attempt to ignore the staring eyes around him, he could not help thinking that if he wanted to make himself invisible, then hanging out with the Griswalds was not the best way to go about it. They were just not inconspicuous people.

Still, nobody said anything to Sam until mid morning

70

when he was about to follow Jake out of chemistry. Then somebody grabbed his arm and said, 'Oy, Sammy.'

Sam turned round and with a sinking heart recognised Martin Silcoe, who had been at Sam's primary school, and never once let him play on his team in the lunch-time football game.

'Is it true you're mates with those Griswalds?' demanded Martin.

Sam hesitated. He heard a horrible voice in his head (it sounded suspiciously like his mother's) saying: *Say you've nothing to do with them, that's the sensible thing*. But then he remembered the Griswalds sticking up for him that morning against the Bullocks. He stood up straighter. 'Yeah, I am actually.'

'Oh yeah?' Several others were staring at them now. Then Martin said, a note of yearning in his voice, 'And did they really travel on top of the bus?' And suddenly there was a whole crowd around him, eager to hear of the Griswalds' exploits.

All in all, the day turned out better than he had expected. True, Brandon Bullock was in his class, and already seemed to have made friends with the biggest, toughest-looking boys, including the Biggerstaffe twins. But, as Sam had discovered, there were advantages to being friends with the Griswalds. Paths opened through the teeming hordes of kids whenever Jake or Spider wished to go somewhere; even the teachers treated them with respect. And a lot of the meaner, tougher kids, whom

Brandon had primed to taunt Sam with 'Mummy's boy' or 'Fatty', suddenly thought better of it when they saw he was friends with Jake and Spider. Burning down bus shelters, riding on the roof of the bus, not to mention climbing the tower over the chemistry lab (as Spider had done the first day) or being an expert at kung-fu (as Jake Griswald was rumoured to be) were all reasons for taking the Griswalds very seriously indeed.

But aside from the Griswalds' fearsome reputation, it was just nice, Sam thought, to have a friend. With Jake in his class, he had somebody to exchange grimaces with during religious studies, somebody to partner up with during lab work, and despite being new, he did not get lost once.

By lunch time, Sam had gathered enough confidence to abandon Jake for a secret errand of his own. But once he was standing outside Mr Sturgeon's classroom door, his courage suddenly failed him. He hunched his shoulders and had turned to creep away, feeling miserable, when the door opened and Mr Sturgeon, the coach of the under-twelves football team, shot out.

'What do you want?' he demanded. 'Who are you, anyway? Speak up!'

'I'm Sam Harris but –'

'Sam Harris? Oh, yes – you're trying out for the team this afternoon.'

'Am I?' gasped Sam.

'You'd better be,' said Mr Sturgeon grimly. 'Trying to

change the time, were you? Well, it's inconvenient enough as it is – you should have tried out last week. I'll see you there.' And he strode off down the corridor.

Sam was still feeling stunned when he finally found Jake in a crowd of kids near the school gates. Most of the kids were watching Spider doing handstands on the top of the gate. Jake was standing on one leg and reading a book called *Kung-Fu of the Mind*.

'What's up?' Jake asked. 'You look like someone slapped you in the face with one of Elfrida's goldfish.'

'The thing is, someone told Mr Sturgeon I'm trying out for the team this afternoon.'

'Oh yeah, that was me.'

'What!'

'Yeah, I wanted to try out and knew you did too.'

Sam opened his mouth to say he didn't want to try out after all, but what he heard himself actually say was: 'Thanks.' And as the afternoon wore on, through seemingly endless stretches of maths and geography, he was able to convince himself that it really would be OK, that Brandon would trip over a clump of grass or score an own-goal, and Sam would play out of his skin, make every goal, and be given pride of place as centre forward.

But as he walked across the playing fields later that afternoon, his mood changed. He could see the rest of the team already doing fitness drills, and they all looked faster and stronger than him. Then he spotted Brandon Bullock, looking a *lot* faster, and a *lot* stronger. As the ground grew muddier, Sam's footsteps became slower and slower.

It did not help that Jake had been delayed by the maths teacher, who was convinced he had cheated in last week's test.

'What are you doing here, fat boy?' yelled Brandon. He turned and stared hard at the rest of the team, who chortled obediently. 'Come to try out as the replacement ball, have you? I think you're a bit too soft for us. You need blowing up.'

There was a chorus of laughter. Then somebody kicked the ball. It took Sam by surprise, thudding into his stomach and winding him. He stood rooted to the spot, gasping. Then he chucked the ball back and turned to walk away.

'Sam wants to be a professional footballer, you know,' he heard Brandon telling his giggling friends. 'He wrote an essay on it last year: *What I Want to do When I Grow Up* –'

Sam's face burned. Not for the first time, he wished he had never written that essay; and even more that Mrs Peterson had not chosen to read it aloud to the rest of the class. It had been one of the most humiliating experiences of his life.

He was so wrapped up in the memory that he did not see Jake running up.

'Hey, what's up?'

'I'm off.' Sam took a deep breath. 'See, the thing is, I didn't tell you – I'm rubbish at football.'

'Huh?' Jake stared at him.

'See, in my head I can do it just fine. It's my feet – they let me down.'

Jake did not laugh. Instead, he said, quite seriously, 'In your head is the most important place. It's like this book I'm reading about kung-fu – you need to know it in your head first, then you can teach the rest of you. Give it a chance. Besides,' he added, 'when else will you get such a good opportunity to give Brandon a kick?'

Sam grinned unwillingly.

'And another thing,' Jake went on, 'I saw the way you grabbed Morris. You'd be great in goal, if nothing else.'

Sam said, surprising himself, 'I don't want to play in goal. I want to play up front.'

Jake nodded. 'I prefer the midfield myself.'

Then Mr Sturgeon came up and Sam had no chance to get away. Mr Sturgeon asked why they had not tried out the week before.

'I was detained,' said Jake.

'Not by the police, I hope,' said Mr Sturgeon in a nasty way that showed he had heard all about the bus shelter.

'No, detention.'

'I don't like troublemakers.' Mr Sturgeon looked at Sam. 'And I don't like sickly kids either. They just can't be relied on and Brandon tells me that you're that kind of kid. Well, I'll see what each of you can do. But I warn you, I'm not likely to be impressed.' He blew his whistle.

For the next ten minutes they did sprints and squats; then they did drills; and Sam panted, and flushed, and struggled to keep up. He was constantly aware of Brandon Bullock smirking at him. At one point, when he was supposed to be practising shooting, he actually managed to trip over the ball and fall flat on his face. At least he had Jake to be his partner whenever they were doing a drill in pairs. But Sam could not help noticing that Jake was a lot better than he was: faster, stronger and much more skilful with the ball.

Then they were split into two teams for a game of six-a-side. Jake and Sam were on Brandon's team, and they soon realised that nobody on their side was going to pass the ball to them. Fortunately, Jake was perfectly capable of getting hold of the ball for himself, by a combination of skill and brute force. Soon, just the sight of Jake loping towards them was enough to make whoever had the ball abandon it.

But Sam did not find it so easy. He could see the spaces all right; but even when he managed to run into them he never seemed to get the ball.

'Don't think you're playing with us, Fatty,' declared Brandon, loping up behind Sam, who was making a run down the wing. He gave him a quick shove, and Sam went flying into the mud just as Jake was about to pass the ball to him. Sam got slowly to his feet, a great lump of misery set like a brick in his stomach. He looked up just in time to see Brandon try to do the same thing to Jake. But this was Brandon's mistake. Jake staggered and lost the ball, but he soon regained his balance and saw Brandon running with

the ball ahead of him. Jake flew through the air in a tremendous kung-fu leap, and Brandon went over like a ninepin. Jake took the ball, ran a few steps, flipped it neatly in the air, and volleyed it into the net.

It was one of the worst tackles Sam had ever seen but one of the best goals. Even Brandon's friends cheered – at least while he was still lying in the mud and could not see them. Sam yelled until he was hoarse.

'Stop!' Mr Sturgeon, who had been gossiping with another teacher on the sidelines, had turned back just in time to witness Jake's tackle. He strode up, eyes blazing, and grabbed Jake by the shoulder. 'What were you trying to do? Break Brandon's leg?'

'Of course not,' said Jake, and added, 'If I'd wanted to break it, I could have snapped it like a twig.'

'What!' Mr Sturgeon looked as if he was going to

explode. 'Who taught you to kick like that, I'd like to know? They ought to be locked up.'

'My mum.'

Sam thought the teacher was about to kill Jake. 'Right, that's it. There's no way you're playing on this team! I've heard about you Griswalds – I should never have let you try out. And you –' he pointed at Sam '– are just useless! Get out of my sight!'

* * *

Sam and Jake began the long trudge back to the changing rooms, both horribly aware of Brandon's triumphant grin.

Jake was unrepentant. 'Of course, you're only supposed to use martial arts for self-defence or to further world peace,' he told Sam. 'But when I meet creeps like Brandon I always forget.'

'You shouldn't have told Sturgeon your mum taught you,' said Sam. 'I thought he was going to blow up.'

'But Mum *did* teach me. That particular kick, anyway. She learnt it in the army. Anyway, I don't care. I don't want to play on a team with Brandon Bullock. And that Sturgeon's only interested in chatting up Miss Lambert who coaches the cross-country team.'

Sam said nothing. Even though he had not expected to get on the team, he still felt dismayed to have failed. Furthermore, he could not help thinking that it is one thing to be booted off the team after a tremendous kung-fu kick; quite another to be dismissed for being useless.

As if to rub salt into their wounds, they immediately ran

into Christabel Bullock. She was with a group of girls, all of whom were wearing a bright red T-shirt with 'A Tidier Bellstone is a Better Bellstone' emblazoned across the front. They were carrying a big bin-liner, full of old crisp packets and chocolate wrappers, plus all the chewing-gum they had confiscated from the smaller kids that day.

'Thrown off the football team were you?' Christabel demanded, tossing her red curls and smirking when she saw she had guessed right. 'Well, you needn't think you can join us. My mum says she needs everyone possible if we're going to be Tidiest Town in England, but she says she wouldn't let you Griswalds join, even if you begged her!'

'Yeah – well, you can tell your mother from us –' Jake began, but at that moment there was a ringing noise, and Christabel fetched a mobile phone out of her pocket. 'Yes, Mum,' she said into it. 'We're on our way.'

'Would you look at that,' said Jake disgustedly. 'A mobile phone!'

'Some of us are up-to-date. We plan a place in the modern world,' Christabel informed him.

'Yeah – as litter collectors.'

Unable to think of an answer to that Christabel flounced off, and Jake and Sam made their way home.

Chapter Five
Biter Needs a Home

Sam and Jake soon forgot their frustration about the team, for when they arrived back at Thistle Lane they found Elfrida and Spider waiting for them outside Sam's house. They were looking extremely glum, unlike Biter who was sitting at their feet looking very contented with life despite having a bandage wrapped around one paw. When he saw Sam he jumped up and greeted him like an old friend.

'Oh, there you are, Sam,' said Elfrida. 'We've been looking for you everywhere. I need to ask you an enormous favour.'

Before she could reveal what it was, the front door opened and Mrs Harris appeared. This made Sam rather uneasy. He was sure that any 'enormous favour' a Griswald wanted was best revealed out of earshot of Mrs Harris; and besides, the less the Griswalds and his mum had to do with each other the better.

Mrs Harris ignored the Griswalds. 'Ah, Sam,' she said reproachfully. 'I was just about to go looking for you. Come in out of the cold and have a hot drink.'

Sam considered pointing out that it was not cold but a beautiful sunny afternoon, and that the last thing he needed after football practice was a hot drink; but all he said was, 'OK.'

Elfrida said, 'Please, Mrs Harris, can we come in for a hot drink too?'

Mrs Harris was forced to stop ignoring the Griswalds. With a distinct lack of enthusiasm, she agreed that they, too, could come in for refreshments. The Griswalds trooped shamelessly into the kitchen after her, and sat down opposite Sam at the table.

'Now, Sam,' said Mrs Harris. 'I want to hear all about your first day at the new school.'

'Never mind that,' interrupted Elfrida, not very politely. She turned to Sam. 'It's Biter. The thing is, we can't keep him after all.'

'Biter?' asked Mrs Harris from the sink, where she was filling the kettle.

'Biscuits,' said Sam quickly. 'She means their dog, Biscuits.' He stared hard at Jake and Elfrida, who took the point and started agreeing with him, although so noisily that anybody would have been suspicious. 'Biscuits.' – 'Yes, Biscuits.' – 'Like ginger biscuits.' – ''Cos he likes eating them, you see.'

'Has your mum changed her mind?' Sam asked, cutting through this.

'She certainly has,' said Elfrida gloomily. 'Says she never wants him to set foot in our house again.'

'But what's he done?' As soon as the words were out of his mouth, Sam regretted it. But it was too late.

'Just about everything. Fighting with the cats and howling in the night –'

'Trapping the postman in the garage,' Jake added.

'– and this afternoon he ran off with a whole chicken. Mum was given it at work. She's got a job, you know, at RightPrice supermarket. Anyway, she ran after him with her gardening shears but by the time she caught him the chicken was all chewed up.'

The Griswalds sat in sorrowful silence: in Elfrida's case, for the loss of Biter; in Jake and Spider's, more for the loss of roast chicken.

'Still, that was probably a one-off,' said Sam, with a sideways look at his mother.

Elfrida said, 'Mum says he's *uncontrollably awful* and *diabolically badly-behaved*.' She paused to relish these phrases: Mrs Griswald had often used them of her children, but Elfrida seldom had an excuse to use them herself. Before she could go on, Sam kicked her under the table. Elfrida caught sight of Mrs Harris's horror-struck

face and backtracked
hastily. 'Oh; but he's not,
he's the most wonderful,
sweet-natured dog in the
whole world, truly he is,
and terribly smart and
intelligent. It's just he
doesn't get on with the
cats. Or the gerbils. Or my
budgie –'

'Of course, we don't
have any pets,' said Sam
quickly. He looked at the dog, which was grinning at him,
tongue lolling. 'Mum, can't he live here?'

Biter came and leant heavily against Sam's legs, with his
head resting on Sam's knees. Mrs Harris looked at all the
beseeching eyes fixed on her, and wavered.

'You know I don't like dogs, Sam. Never mind a dog like
this, which comes from goodness knows where. You told
me yourself he was a stray –'

Before she could continue, Jake and Elfrida burst into
speech.

'Go on, Mrs Harris –'

'Please, Mrs Harris –'

'He's a good dog really –'

'You can't throw him out –'

'It would destroy his faith in human beings –'

'Not that he had much to begin with –' concluded Jake,

forgetting for a moment the object of the exercise. Spider nudged him, and he shut up.

'I just don't know,' said Mrs Harris.

Sam felt Biter lick his hand. 'Please, Mum,' he said.

Mrs Harris put a hand to her forehead. 'I feel one of my bad, sick headaches coming on,' she announced plaintively. 'Well, you can keep him for the moment.' But even as Elfrida whooped with joy, she went on, 'But not for ever. You must phone the police, and the Dogs' Home, to see if anybody wants him, and put up notices, and go round the neighbours, and do everything you can to find his real owners.'

'And if we can't find them?' asked Sam, his spirits sinking.

'Then he goes to the Dogs' Home.' Mrs Harris stood up quickly and went to the door, as if she suspected she had been rather mean and wanted to get away before anybody could point this out.

The Griswalds, surprisingly, did not.

'Thanks, Mrs Harris –'

'You won't regret it –'

'We'll put up posters,' Jake told Mrs Harris. 'We'll make big ones with pictures of Biter – I mean Biscuits – and your phone number and everything. That will find his owner, if anything does. You leave it to us.'

Mrs Harris looked pleased. 'That's an excellent idea,' she said, almost warmly. Then she left the room, quickly, before she could be talked into anything else.

'You didn't have to say that about posters,' said Sam, when the door had shut. 'I mean, I don't want to find his owner.'

Jake winked. 'Don't worry.' He tapped the side of his nose and added in a lowered voice, 'Salami strategy.'

'*Salami strategy?*'

'Yep. It's a well-known tactic in international politics. You take a slice at a time, but you end up with the whole sausage.'

'I call it pizza strategy,' Elfrida added. 'You take a slice at a time, but you end up with the whole pizza. The whole *vegetarian* pizza.'

Sam could not see what salami or pizza had to do with anything. And he was not comforted to hear that the Griswalds took an interest in international politics. It was bad enough what they got up to when confined to Bellstone. But Jake said, 'Don't you see? You need Biter to get his foot in the door. That's the first slice. Now, let's get started on the posters. Maybe Luke will do the photos.'

Luke Griswald was practising the bass guitar for a band he had just joined called the Horny-Nailed Toads, and was not pleased to be interrupted for a photo-shoot with Biter, but they eventually persuaded him. Biter was not keen either. He kept baring his teeth at the camera.

'There's no way anybody is going to take that mutt off your hands once they've seen these photos,' Luke predicted, before disappearing into the house.

Suddenly Sam understood. 'I get it. This way we keep Mum happy –'

'And scare off the punters at the same time,' Jake concluded.

Sam had to go back home then, but after he had escaped from Mrs Harris and her hundreds of questions ('And did you find out where the nurse's room is, Sam? And I hope people walked at safe speeds in the corridors –') he went next door and joined Jake in the branches of the pine tree. They sat and watched Spider, who was trying to reach the roof of the Griswalds' house by a wholly new route, and had an enjoyable pine-cone fight with Elfrida, who was sitting with Pomfret two branches below. Jake kept mulling over plans for vengeance on the Bullocks, but as each plan sounded more far-fetched than the last, Sam was not too worried. He was more concerned when Jake said suddenly, 'I'm going to find another team. I bet there's one round here we could join.'

'Oh right,' was all Sam said. He had almost forgotten the humiliation of the afternoon, but now a small, cold slug of misery oozed its way into his mind. And he knew that *nothing* would persuade him to go through that again. He had never felt such a fool in his life.

* * *

Still, he thought, as he lay in bed that night with the comforting weight of Biter on his feet, most likely it would all come to nothing. There was no point in worrying about it now. After all, he realised with some surprise, last night he had been lying awake worrying about how terrible school was going to be. And, apart from the tryout, it had not turned out like that at all.

Sam rolled over and fell into a deep, contented sleep.

* * *

Next day, the photos were ready. They were every bit as bad as Luke had predicted. In one of them, Biter was lunging at the camera, apparently trying to bite it. They used this one for their poster, and Jake and Spider photocopied it in the school office when the secretary wasn't looking. After school they divided into pairs and set off to stick them up.

Jake and Spider headed towards the town centre, leaving Sam and Elfrida to do the area round Thistle Lane. Sam would have preferred to go with Jake or Spider, but he knew his mother would go mad if she found out he had

gone so far into town. Soon, Biter was snarling down from every tree and every lamppost.

'But,' Sam could not help saying to Elfrida, 'what if somebody does recognise him and wants him back? I would.'

Before Elfrida could reply, Mrs Harris came into sight. She was very pleased about the posters (luckily she did not inspect them too closely) but she did not leave things there. 'Now Sam,' she said fussily, 'have you been round and asked the neighbours if anybody has lost him? And the Dogs' Home – have you called the Dogs' Home, Sam –'

'Aww, Mum –' Sam began, but Elfrida pinched him, hard.

'We're just going round to all the neighbours now,' she said.

Sam nodded reluctantly, and Mrs Harris went on her way.

'What'd you have to say that for?' said Sam, rubbing his arm. 'We don't want to go round to all the neighbours.'

'I know that, stupid. But it's better than calling the Dogs' Home, isn't it? And we can just visit the people you know don't have dogs.'

Sam had not thought of this. The Griswalds were just full of natural cunning, he decided, as they set off on a tour of the neighbourhood, with Biter snuffling along behind. At first, Sam hated knocking on people's doors, but it turned out quite well on the whole: Elfrida did all the talking, and some people even invited them in for cake or biscuits. Then they found themselves outside the Bullocks' house – and Elfrida insisted that they call there too.

'It's a chance to check out enemy territory!' she hissed, grabbing his arm. Reluctantly, Sam followed her up the garden path. He knew there was no risk that the Bullocks would lay claim to Biter, but still he didn't want to visit them *at all*.

Elfrida rang the door bell. It was one of those bells that play a tune and, much to their surprise, it played *If You're Happy and You Know it Clap Your Hands*. The next minute Mrs Bullock was standing there, not looking happy at all.

'You know perfectly well, Sam, that I do not own a dog,' she thundered, when she had understood their errand. 'My darling Delilah would never stand for it. And if I did, it would not be a runtish-looking creature like that. Besides, dogs are untidy, unruly creatures, causing all kinds of mess – even when their owners clear up after them, which is by no means always the case. That is why I have placed a proposal before the Bellstone Council Parks and Recreation Committee that dogs should be banned from all the public parks in Bellstone.'

Sam was so furious at hearing Biter described as 'runtish' that he was momentarily speechless, but Elfrida replied.

'That's not very nice of you,' she said. 'Where are people going to take their dogs for walks?'

'People should think about that before they get dogs,' returned Mrs Bullock.

'Why shouldn't *you* think about it, before you put forward your proposal?'

Before this discussion could go any further (and Sam, for one, would have been interested to hear Mrs Bullock's reply) Delilah appeared, sliding around Mrs Bullock's ankles. She caught sight of Biter and he caught sight of her. Elfrida and Sam made haste down the path, dragging a snarling Biter with them, while Mrs Bullock disappeared inside, bearing the struggling Delilah. 'Savages!' she shouted over her shoulder. 'Barbarians!' It was plain enough that Elfrida and Sam would not be welcome at the Bullock residence in the near future.

On top of everything else, as they came out of the gate they walked slap-bang into Brandon Bullock, coming back from football practice.

'Got a girlfriend, have you, Sammy?' he sneered. 'And a nice doggy – even if he does look like a mutant toad?'

'He does not!' began Sam hotly, but nobody heard him, for Elfrida was already in full flow.

'You're just jealous,' she bawled at Brandon, 'because you don't have any friends, and even the friends you think you have hate you really! Even that horrible cat of yours hates you, because you're mean and a bully, and nobody will ever talk to you or be friends with you, and you'll live by yourself until you die and then the rats will eat you! And even they won't like the taste!'

Brandon goggled at her. Sam almost felt sorry for him. It seemed that for the first time in recorded history,

Brandon Bullock did not know what to say.

But Brandon did not need to speak. He stepped forward, a very menacing expression on his face. But at that moment, a football swooped down apparently from nowhere and hit him on the head.

Brandon grunted, and sat down in the gutter. Elfrida and Sam started laughing. And Jake and Spider came running up. 'Sorry about that, Brandon,' said Jake, insincerely. He retrieved the ball and started playing keepie-up.

'You've ruined my new jeans!' Brandon yelled, inspecting the damage. 'And they're *designer*!'

'Have to practise your headers, then, won't you?' Jake said. He dummied the ball to Sam, then flipped it up neatly and volleyed it at Brandon. Brandon ducked, then ran off, yelling abuse over his shoulder. The ball went skimming along the lane, bounced off a lamppost and into the dilapidated structure that was the Griswalds' garage. Jake went to fetch it, and came out looking thoughtful.

'It's not fair for that snot-nose to be in the team and not us,' said Sam.

'Hah!' Jake sent the ball flying upwards in a triumphant lob. 'He can keep his team. I've found us another one.'

'What?'

'Yeah, they play on Bellstone Meadows. I saw them practising when we were putting up posters there. So I went and talked to their coach, and he says they're looking for new players.'

'Oh right,' said Sam weakly. His hands had gone all cold.

'Yeah, he says we can try out on Sunday.'

They were all inside the Griswalds' garden by this time and making for the pine tree. As he waited his turn to swing himself into the tree, Sam heard himself say, 'I might not be able to try out.'

'What!' Jake turned and peered down out of the branches. His face was indignant. 'I've found us this great team, probably the best in Bellstone, and you're not going to try out. Why not?'

'I'm busy.'

'Busy with what?'

'Stuff.'

Sam looked away from Jake's accusing face and down at his feet instead; he kicked pine needles.

'What stuff?'

'Don't be horrible to Sam,' interrupted Elfrida. 'I expect he does all kind of things at weekends. Just because we never do, it doesn't mean Sam doesn't. All *I'm* going to do is finish reading *Blood Trail of Dracula* – it's really scary – and after that I've got another book from the library which teaches you how to hypnotise people. I'm going to practise in case I ever get a chance to hypnotise Christabel Bullock and make her my slave. And I 'spect you're just going to mess about with your skateboard –'

Jake looked offended. 'I'm going to jump it off the garage roof onto our camping mattress, doing karate kicks at the same time –'

'And Spider's probably just going to climb the town hall roof or something.' Spider nodded. 'But Sam – I 'spect he gets to do *exciting* things at the weekend, don't you Sam?'

'Err, yes,' said Sam. He thought about the coming weekend: going to the supermarket with his mother, getting his hair cut, and perhaps, if he was lucky, watching 'a nice film' on the telly with his mum. The highlight would be taking Biter for a run in the park. Then, as they all looked at him expectantly, 'Well, I might be going for a day out with my mum.'

'Where?' asked Elfrida eagerly. 'A theme park? Or Sea World to look at the dolphins? Or the beach? Or Alton Towers?'

'Abseiling?' suggested Jake enviously. 'Canoeing? Surfing? A football match?'

'A bit of shopping, most likely,' said Sam gruffly.

Their silence said it all. Sam turned crimson and stared at his feet. Then he said rather desperately, 'Well, we might be visiting an archaeological site.'

'Archaeological? What, like the pyramids?' Jake asked.

'Ancient tombs,' hissed Elfrida, her eyes gleaming. 'Curses! Mummies! Buried treasure!'

'Err, well – more likely the Roman remains they're digging up in Lower Titmarsh.'

There was another silence.

'Doesn't sound very interesting to me,' said Elfrida at last. 'And I *like* history.'

'Yeah, well,' said Sam, turning red. 'Just because it isn't

interesting to you, doesn't mean it isn't interesting to me.'

'Still, it's not going to take all weekend, is it?' asked Jake. 'You can still try out for the team. And it's time we did something about those Bullocks. I've had an idea. We'll climb into the Bullocks' garden by night and we'll –'

'I don't think I'll have time for that either,' said Sam.

After that, the atmosphere got a little strained. The Griswalds didn't say much (or rather, Elfrida would have, but Jake shushed her) but Sam knew he had gone down in their estimation. He felt they had misunderstood his character. They thought he was daring and adventurous, like them, when really all he wanted was not to be noticed. He told himself at least he would not have to pretend to them any more, but somehow it did not make him feel any better.

Soon after, Mrs Harris started calling, and Sam took the excuse to go home early. But as he climbed into his own garden, he could not help wondering if his friendship with the Griswalds was over before it had really begun.

* * *

Sam was rather quiet during tea. He had several things on his mind. One of them was that, although he understood the Griswalds' salami strategy, he still felt worried that somebody would recognise Biter and want him back. It did not help that Mrs Harris thought exactly the same thing, and kept saying, 'We'll soon have that dog off our hands,' in a bright and cheerful voice. By the time Sam went to bed, he was feeling quite depressed.

* * *

He would have felt a lot more cheerful (and his mother a lot less so) if he could have seen what Jake and Spider were doing at that moment.

'After all,' Jake pointed out to Spider, as he ripped a poster off a lamppost and stuffed it into his bag, 'Sam's kept his promise to his mum, hasn't he? He's put the posters *up*. But we don't want them to *stay* there too long, otherwise somebody really might recognise Biter. And if *we* take the posters down, then it's not Sam's fault, is it?'

Spider nodded. Being a Griswald, this made perfect sense to him.

'Mrs Harris will thank us,' said Jake confidently, 'when she finds out what a great guard dog she's got.'

Most of the neighbourhood was indoors watching TV. But one local resident was not, and that one was, unfortunately, Mrs Bullock. She was doing her regular prowl around the neighbourhood, looking for any untidiness which she could take up with those responsible the following day. As soon as she saw Jake and Spider she grabbed them and demanded to know just what they thought they were doing.

Jake was not at all abashed. 'Hello, Mrs Bullock. Well, the thing is, these posters don't look very tidy to us. Terrible, isn't it, how people go round spoiling the look of the streets? So we thought we'd take them down. Tidy the place up a bit.'

Mrs Bullock was gobsmacked. She had, after all, just

about decided that the Griswalds were the worst bunch of kids in Bellstone. On the other hand, there was nothing she hated more than people sticking up bits of paper everywhere, especially without first asking her permission; and had she seen the posters earlier she might well have ripped them down herself. All she could manage to say was, 'Humph!' Then she stalked off back to her own house.

Jake and Spider grinned at each other, then went to put the posters in the middle of Mrs Griswald's bonfire heap.

Chapter Six
Elfrida Falls to Temptation

Sam did not think he had exactly fallen out with the Griswalds, but he could not help feeling they despised him. Next morning he didn't wait for them to collect him for school but set off by himself to take the bus. Once aboard, he tried to do his invisible act, but it did not work very well. Although Christabel and Brandon were not on the bus, plenty of their friends were, including some members of the under-twelves football team. They amused themselves by recalling some of Sam's worst moments at the tryout.

Jake and Spider seemed much as usual at school (of

course, with Spider it was always difficult to tell) and they all walked home together as usual. But on Friday night something happened that convinced Sam their friendship was over. He found it hard to get off to sleep – possibly because Spider was playing his saxophone in the garden next door. He was standing on a branch halfway up the pine tree, and as the plaintive notes came drifting in through the window it seemed to Sam that the music was expressing all the thoughts Spider was never able to put into words. The sound had a mysterious, ghostly quality . . . even when it later became mingled with the less ghostly sound of Mrs Bullock, shouting at him to shut up.

When Sam eventually fell asleep, it was into a horrible nightmare, in which he was playing football against Brandon Bullock. Sam was the last defender, and Brandon scored by kicking the ball between Sam's legs. The rest of the team began to boo Sam, then he caught sight of the Griswalds on the sidelines and they were booing too; even Biter was barking in derision . . .

Sam woke with a jolt to find it was the middle of the night and Biter was indeed barking. He shushed him quickly, before he could wake Mrs Harris, then (although he could hear nothing) he got up and went to the window to see if Spider was still there with his saxophone.

There was no sign of him but as Sam was about to return to bed he saw a light. He strained his eyes: yes, he was not imagining it. It trembled, ghostly in the gloom, beyond the fence – inside the Griswalds' garden. Then it began to bob closer, through the darkness.

Sam felt as if someone had kicked him in the stomach.

Jake said he wanted to climb into the Bullocks' garden, he thought. That's what they're up to. They're going tonight. And they're going without me. A terrible pang of misery and betrayal shot through him. 'The creeps,' he muttered to himself, 'the back-stabbing creeps.' He forgot he had not wanted to go anyway. He jerked the curtains shut, jumped back into bed and pulled the covers over his head. But it was a long time before he fell asleep.

* * *

Whether or not they had spent the previous night invading the Bullocks' garden, the Griswalds did not seem particularly uneasy the next morning. Or at least, not until Mrs Griswald went on the warpath.

'Spider! Jake! Elfrida!' she bellowed. 'Come here!'

The Griswalds, being Griswalds, did not immediately race to obey their mother's command. On the contrary, Spider and Jake, who were busy setting up a ramp so that Jake could jump his skateboard off the garage roof, immediately streaked off down the garden and climbed into the pine tree. They were not sure what their mother wanted, but it was clear from her tone that *somebody* had done *something*, and they thought it as well to lie low. Elfrida had woken up with a stomachache and was still in bed. She got up and peered cautiously over the banisters.

'You kids!' her mother yelled from the hall. 'Get into this kitchen at once!'

Elfrida turned and scooted back into her bedroom. She looked around, then quickly grabbed her nun's habit from the floor. Most people, like Sam, found it rather surprising that Elfrida should own a nun's habit – she did not seem a very nun-like kind of person. But Elfrida was fond of it. She had been given it by her aunt, who had once been in an amateur production of *The Sound of Music*. It was long and warm, and it pulled easily over whatever else she was wearing. She tucked it under her arm, and grabbed a book from her bedside table.

Then she ran up to Spider's attic and went at once to the window that was cut into the eaves.

Craning out of the window, Elfrida could easily make out the way onto the roof. Spider had helpfully hammered in a series of pegs and attached a rope to hold on by, and Elfrida was almost certain that she could climb up it. She intended to try, anyway. She slung her nun's habit around her neck, and stowed the book in her pyjama pocket.

Ten minutes later she was sitting on a flat, sun-baked patch of roof with her nun's habit spread out around her, her back against the chimney pots and her book propped open against her knees.

* * *

Mrs Griswald eventually gave up looking for her children, and went back to digging her new vegetable patch. She was not unduly concerned about their absence. She knew they would reappear when they got hungry.

After a while, there was the sound of the gate swinging to and someone crunching down the path round the side of the house.

It was Mrs Bullock.

She had come to complain, of course. This time her complaint was, 'The way your dreadful children have been bullying my Brandon and Christabel . . .' Brandon's ruined designer jeans featured heavily in her account, together with Jake telling Christabel she had 'fat little legs' and Spider stealing Christabel's mobile phone. (Nobody had proved this, but it was hard to see who else, other than Spider Griswald, could have taken it from Christabel's bag in a locked and deserted classroom on the third floor, where the window was only accessible via a drainpipe. As mobile phones had been banned from school, Christabel had not been able to report the theft to any of the staff. When her phone had then gone off like a siren in assembly two days later, it had turned out to be back in her bag and she had ended up in detention for the first time ever. Where Jake Griswald had been during assembly, nobody could afterwards remember – but several people suspected the Headmaster's empty office where there was a telephone.)

Mrs Griswald listened to Mrs Bullock but was not impressed. 'If that's the best you can come up with, then you may as well go home again. My kids are not the best-behaved – I know that as well as you do. But all kids call each other names, and all kids play tricks on each other. As for those jeans – if you dress your kids in designer gear, then that's your own lookout.'

Mrs Bullock turned scarlet in the face. 'Your attitude is totally irresponsible!' she snapped. 'I demand you punish them severely!'

'Don't be ridiculous,' said Mrs Griswald. 'I have enough trouble thinking up punishments for all the crimes they *do* commit. Today, for instance, I'm fairly sure they've swiped a whole roast chicken from the fridge. I'm not wasting time on rubbish like this!'

'Well then,' countered Mrs Bullock. 'I demand you summon them at once. At least I shall give them a piece of my mind!'

'Be my guest.' Mrs Griswald raised her voice. 'Spider, Jake, Elfrida! Come here!'

Sitting above them on the roof, Elfrida had been mainly oblivious to all this. She had seen Mrs Bullock arrive. But only the occasional word or phrase had floated up to her. 'Delinquents . . . deplorable . . . wretched children . . . ought to be locked up . . .' It sounded like the usual kind of stuff, and Elfrida soon stopped listening. Besides she was deeply engrossed in *Blood Trail of Dracula*, and as she read she could not help sniffing hard, and occasionally wiping her eyes on her nun's habit. An entire village had just been wiped out by Dracula, but this was not what was distressing Elfrida. Amongst the human corpses a small dog had been found, dead. 'I don't know how people can mistreat animals,' observed Elfrida weepily to Pomfret, who had climbed up to join her. 'They ought to be shot!'

She pulled the nun's robe around her. Its warmth and length were comforting, like a blanket, and the warmth and weight of Pomfret curled up on her lap was comforting too. Animals, Elfrida thought, were much nicer than humans. Pomfret and Biter, despite all their faults (and Elfrida could not deny they had some), were a hundred times nicer than the humans Elfrida knew.

'You appreciate me,' Elfrida told Pomfret. 'Nobody else does. Otherwise I wouldn't be hiding up here on the roof.' Elfrida heaved a sigh, and allowed herself to dwell once again on the inadequacies of her family. Here she was, doing her very best for animals – trying not to eat them, for instance, and finding Biter a home – and none of her family cared, or did anything to help her. Mrs Griswald had hardly given Biter a chance before chucking him out. 'All they care about is their own stomachs!' she remarked to Pomfret. 'They just gorge themselves on meat, whenever I'm watching, and they don't care a bit how I feel. And they're human beings, Pomfret, not an animal, like you – they should know better. You *have* to eat meat, but they don't. Look at Mum carrying on this morning about that roast chicken.' She gave a sob and suddenly burst out, 'And the flesh is weak, Pomfret! I try, but the flesh is weak!'

She clasped Pomfret tightly in her arms, but he wriggled away and disappeared along the guttering, leaving Elfrida alone and forlorn.

The next thing she heard was Mrs Griswald calling her. Elfrida peered carefully over the ridge of the roof, and saw that Mrs Bullock was still there.

Elfrida decided there were worse things than feeling forlorn, and returned to her book.

* * *

Spider and Jake were not so lucky. Mrs Griswald soon worked out where they were because Elfrida's two cats, Pomfret and Arthur, were sitting under the pine tree yowling up at them. She insisted the boys come down to hear what Mrs Bullock had to say. Mrs Bullock lost no time in pitching into them, her temper in no way improved by Jake's attempt at an explanation ('It's not *our* fault that your kids are little creeps . . .'). Mrs Griswald just leant on her garden spade, listening. It took a while for everyone to notice that Elfrida's pets were behaving in a very peculiar manner.

Pomfret and Arthur had followed Jake and Spider from the pine tree, and now seemed very interested in the broken earth where Mrs Griswald had been digging. They were scratching at the soil, occasionally spitting and yowling at one another to get out of the way.

'What is that noise!' demanded Mrs Bullock, suddenly aware of the racket. 'Really, you have no business letting your animals disturb the neighbourhood like this. It is not the first time I have heard your cats yowling and fighting. I have a good mind to report you to the police – or the Public Nuisance Department!'

It was a good thing Elfrida was not down there, as she would probably have attacked Mrs Bullock for saying this. As for the rest of the Griswalds, although some of them secretly agreed with Mrs Bullock that the animals were a nuisance, they would never have admitted it to her. Noisily, Mrs Griswald and Jake defended them.

They were interrupted by an especially loud yowl. Pomfret and Arthur were confronting each other with their fur standing on end.

'Go and fetch a bucket of water!' Mrs Griswald told Jake impatiently. 'It's the only way to shut them up.' Then she looked more closely. 'What's that they've found?'

But Jake and Spider, ignoring the request for water, were already investigating. 'Wow! Look at this!' declared Jake, staring at the disturbed earth. 'Was there a mass murderer living here or something? Because somebody's been burying bodies in our garden!'

Mrs Bullock was tough – but it seemed even she drew the line at mass murderers. She turned pale, took several steps back, and looked ready to run for the gate. At the same moment, Pomfret leapt forward and grabbed something from the soil. It was not absolutely certain *what* he grabbed. It was a bone, that much was clear, but there were other things too: fleshy bits, and jellyish bits, and stringy bits, and unidentified nasty grey slimy bits. All of these were smeared with soil, which made them look even more gruesome. Carrying this revolting prize, and pursued by an enraged Arthur, Pomfret ran straight for Mrs Bullock, who shrieked. Pomfret zigzagged around Mrs Bullock's ankles, and Arthur, leaping up to race after her, landed with claws outstretched right in Mrs Bullock's stomach.

Mrs Bullock screamed very, very loudly and fell backwards.

Just then there was a bloodcurdling howl from far above

their heads. Everybody looked up to see Elfrida, balanced on the very edge of the roof, and clad in what appeared to be a nun's habit.

'It was me! It was me who did it!' she declared. 'I am the guilty one!' Her voice grew even more desperate. 'Look out! I'm going to jump!'

* * *

Of course there was a perfectly simple explanation for everything. But by the time it emerged – long after Spider had climbed up and rescued Elfrida from the roof, and Jake had separated the cats, and Mrs Griswald, and even Mr Griswald (who had come racing out of the house), had done a lot of shouting – Mrs Bullock had gone home. This was partly because Mrs Griswald had told her to leave. ('I need to get to the bottom of all this,' she had said grimly. 'And I would rather there were no outsiders present. Otherwise, I may find myself being reported for child cruelty. Possibly even child murder.') But it was mainly because Mrs Bullock herself was feeling shaky. Few things daunted Mrs Bullock but there was something about the sight of those fleshy and stringy bits, and most of all the nasty grey slimy bits, that made her feel quite funny. So she stomped back to her own house and made herself a cup of hot, sweet tea.

Mr Griswald soon went back into the house, too. Mrs Griswald was left to get to the heart of the matter.

The story that emerged went like this. Elfrida had still been reading when she heard her cats yowling. She had looked down from the roof to see what they were up to, and she had known right away what they had found. She had known because she had put it there.

She had been most alarmed at the sight – so alarmed that she had decided to climb down from the roof straightaway. Unfortunately, in her haste, she forgot to take off her nun's habit. And, of course, it is extremely difficult to do any kind of climbing in such a cumbersome garment, especially one that's far too long for you. Soon it was firmly caught on one of Spider's pegs. And there she was, stuck, right at the edge of the roof, and with a nasty drop yawning beneath her.

She had panicked. 'Suddenly,' she told her family, tearfully, 'it looked a very long way down.'

Her fingers were frozen to the roof, and her feet were

getting pins and needles. There had seemed nothing for it but to jump. Indeed, had Spider not shimmied up to the roof at lightning speed, she might well have done so.

If Elfrida had been hoping that her brush with death, and Spider's quick thinking, might distract their mother from her crimes, she was disappointed.

'What a ridiculous thing to do!' Mrs Griswald stormed. 'You could have been killed! And leaving that aside – what is all this disgusting stuff?' She pointed at the horrible little heap that Pomfret had finally been made to put down in front of her. 'These bones and – and other things? It's as I suspected all along! Your cats have been stealing food and burying the remains in the garden!'

'No! No!' moaned Elfrida. 'It wasn't them! Don't punish them! It was me! I took that chicken! I ate it! Me and Biter and Pomfret ate it all in the middle of the night! And I buried the bones in the garden!'

The whole family rounded on her.

'You ate a whole roast chicken!' raged Mrs Griswald.

'But you're supposed to be vegetarian!' Jake accused.

She turned tragic eyes on him. 'But the flesh is weak!' she cried. 'It was blood lust!' And with that she burst into tears.

Elfrida had been tempted – and she had fallen (although, fortunately, not from the roof). She had, however, started off with the best of intentions. She had not meant to eat the meat herself. She had thought that by raiding the fridge at night, and feeding her pickings to her cats, she would help the rest of her family to go vegetarian, too. By gradually reducing their meat consumption, Elfrida had reckoned she could eventually wean them off it altogether. After all, the cats could not help their animal instincts (or so Elfrida told herself). But the other Griswalds could. They just needed a helping hand.

'You would have thanked me in the end!' she wailed.

None of them showed any signs of thanking her now. 'What, for nicking our dinner?' demanded Jake indignantly.

'I couldn't understand what had happened to that chicken,' said Mrs Griswald grimly. 'I thought Jake and Spider were playing a joke –'

'And it was *you* – you ate it yourself!' declared Jake, getting to the main point.

Elfrida nodded numbly. The fact was she had grown tired of dumplings; and feeding choice morsels of roast chicken to the cats – or even leftover sausages – had made it more and more difficult not to eat any herself. Eventually, it became altogether *too* difficult.

'But I feel terrible about it!' she declared. 'Terrible!'

'Good!' her brother replied.

Elfrida's real mistake had been to bury the grisly remnants of her crimes in the exact spot where Mrs Griswald was digging her new vegetable plot. In fact, Elfrida had chosen this place precisely because somebody had already done the hard work of clearing the ground for her. It had not occurred to her that this might make her crime more likely to be discovered. Nor could she know that the cats would remember exactly where those interesting titbits had gone and would try to dig them up.

'You disgusting girl!' declared Mrs Griswald. 'Stealing food! And don't you realise that leaving decaying food around the place is sure to attract rats?'

'I like rats,' Elfrida said. 'And I've been punished for my wickedness. I've had a terrible stomachache from eating all that chicken.'

Mrs Griswald, unfortunately, did not consider this punishment enough. And she was not only furious with Elfrida, but also with Spider for climbing on the roof in the first place, and with Jake for letting him. She said that the remaining bits of bone had to be dug up now, and disposed of sensibly, and that when this was done they could dig up the rest of the vegetable plot for good measure. She doled out the shovels and trowels there and then. Only Luke, who was off rehearsing with the Horny-Nailed Toads, escaped. For once, her children were sufficiently cowed by her anger not even to think of disobeying her.

Elfrida did not much enjoy the rest of the morning. Spider and Jake were very bitter and, as they hacked at the stony earth, and disinterred disgusting pieces of smelly old bone, they grew even more bitter. They expressed their feelings to Elfrida forcibly – Jake through words ('You useless brat, what d'you think you were doing?'), Spider through grimaces and bits of soil flicked with his shovel when her back was turned. Elfrida was miserable. And the worst of it, she felt, was that nobody felt any sympathy for the pangs of guilt which were afflicting her. She knew she was a failed vegetarian, filled with grief and repentance. They just thought she was a fake vegetarian who nicked other people's food.

Nobody was speaking to her, and she had the feeling that nobody would be speaking to her for a very long time. Still, as she put her trowel away at long last, and went into the kitchen, towards the far from appetising aroma of a fresh batch of dumplings, she was able to comfort herself a little. *At least*, she thought, *I've seen the last of smelly old bones.*

She was wrong about that.

Chapter Seven
The Team

Sam spent most of the weekend avoiding the Griswalds. By Sunday morning he was so bored with mooching around the house that he started reading the new book his mother had bought for him, *Archaeology is Fun*. However, after Mrs Harris had popped her head round his bedroom door for the third time and trilled, 'Just think, Sam – archaeology means uncovering the bones of the past!' he decided to take it outside.

He sat on the front step with Biter, hoping that the Griswalds would not be able to spy him from their perch in the pine tree. But he had only read two sentences of a chapter on Neolithic burial grounds, when Jake Griswald shot past in his football kit.

He saw Sam, doubled back and proceeded to give Sam a full account of yesterday's exploits: Elfrida on the roof, the flight of Mrs Bullock and the sad fate of the roast chicken. 'You were well out of it,' he concluded bitterly. 'All that digging!' He displayed the blisters he had acquired across his palms. Sam tried to appear sympathetic, but he could not help a sneaking feeling that it was more fun than he had had, skulking about by himself. He would especially have liked to see Mrs Bullock run for home, pursued by a cat with a chicken carcass.

'Anyway, I'm off now to try out for Bellstone Rovers,' said Jake, brightening up. 'What are you up to?'

'Oh – I'm reading this fantastic book.' Sam brandished *Archaeology is Fun*.

'Right. See you then.' Jake ran off, whistling.

Scowling, Sam opened his book more or less at random.

'*A midden heap may not seem the most exciting of archaeological remains. Nothing more than a rubbish dump, yet the refuse it contains – old food, broken pots, animal bones, even dung – can help to create a fascinating picture of the past. In medieval times . . .*'

Sam shut the book with a snap, leapt up, ran into the house, and almost collided with his mother.

'Who were you talking to?' she asked anxiously.

'Jake Griswald. He's going to football practice.'

'Oh, that's all right then.'

For some reason, Sam felt annoyed. 'Actually, he wanted me to go too. It's a new team that plays on Bellstone

114

Meadows.'

'Oh Sam, I don't think so! I don't even like you to play football at school. But who knows if this coach is trained – does he know first aid? There are so many injuries in football. And sometimes goalposts fall over and hurt people! And I don't want you running around the town – and I don't have a car to drive you to practices –'

She went on and on, making Sam feel really fed up. He forgot he was not even going to try out for the team. 'You make it sound like I'm off to climb Everest! Football's not dangerous. And it's no distance to Bellstone Meadows, and I can go with Jake.'

Mrs Harris's brow creased and her eyes looked hurt. 'I don't go off and do things without you in the evenings, do I? I stay in so we can watch television together. I suppose you just want to be like your father, playing a rough game like football, where you might get hurt –'

'Oh Mum! Dad didn't even play football. It's nothing to do with him! Why do you always think it is? I just *like* football, that's all.'

Sam stomped upstairs. Biter followed him and for a while he sat and absently stroked the dog's ears. But all he could think about was what was happening on Bellstone Meadows.

'Yeah, well, you missed the boat there,' he said aloud. 'It's too late now.'

Biter gave a sudden sharp yap. It sounded oddly like a challenge. Sam started. Then he leapt to his feet.

* * *

It took Mr Hobson, the Bellstone Rovers coach, several minutes to notice the boy hovering at his elbow. He was, after all, surrounded by boys in football kit, all doing stretches and drills of various kinds, all making a great deal of noise, and one of them – that new boy, Jake Griswald – was practising volleys in a way that seemed to owe more to a Jackie Chan film than any known football technique. But when he did notice the boy he listened most attentively to what he had to say.

'We are looking for new players,' he said, when Sam had finished his explanations. 'If you like, you can try out now.'

Sam ran to join the others. Jake, spinning about in an attempt at a Cruyff turn, noticed him and waved. Then Mr Hobson set them all doing sprints, and Sam had no time to feel nervous, or to wonder if this was one of the worst ideas he had ever had.

Mr Hobson, watching closely, thought the boy looked tentative at first, but that seemed to disappear as he became more involved in the practice. When he divided them up for a game of six-a-side, Sam hung back; as the game began he was slow to move in for a tackle; then, going forward, he did not call to his team-mate, Sunil, to pass, even though he had a clear run on the goal, and even though everybody else on the pitch was yelling their head off. Mr Hobson tutted slightly to himself. Still, he reflected, it made a pleasant change from Jake Griswald, who had been one of the most confident, occasionally reckless and, beyond that, total show-offs, that he had ever seen. At least this boy, Sam, did not use a judo throw against a defender; nor did he try to use a showy bicycle kick against an easy sitter in front of an open goal, with the result that the ball shot upwards and went reverberating back off the crossbar, when a simple strike would have sent it straight into the net. Mr Hobson smiled wryly: of course he *had* to take Jake Griswald onto the team, he just hoped he would not end up crippling anybody.

But this boy, Sam, was beginning to look a bit more confident. He had just blocked the ball very neatly – chesting it down, then passing it on at once, hard and accurate – getting himself back into position – looking up all the time to see what his team-mates were doing (that boy Jake had sometimes shown signs of forgetting his team-mates altogether) – and now Greg Roylance was shouting at him and he was running forward, ready for the pass . . .

It was intercepted. Still, Mr Hobson was impressed. Sam appeared to be a steady character; he was trying hard; and Mr Hobson felt he showed some promise . . . the trouble was, could he use him? Now that he had taken on Jake Griswald, there were no places in midfield, and this boy did not seem to have the speed or strength to play up front. Furthermore, actually shooting on goal appeared to be a bit of a weakness, which was no good in a striker. His tackling was good – but they had a solid defence already . . . Mr Hobson frowned, blew his whistle, and set them to practising penalties instead.

Sam, meanwhile, was surprised to find he was enjoying himself. Certainly, it was a million times better than the tryout at school. Aside from the fact that the players seemed a hundred times nicer, and that Brandon Bullock was not playing (a huge bonus, Sam thought), he knew that he himself was playing better. He didn't know any of these boys, apart from Jake, so he felt he had nothing to prove; better yet, he knew that none of them were waiting for him to trip up, or fluff an easy pass – which meant, somehow, he didn't. He even found the fitness drills easier. Perhaps, he thought, a week of walking – or, more often, running – to school with the Griswalds, not to mention all that clambering about in their pine tree, had made a difference. He was still the slowest when it came to the warm-up jog around the pitch, but he wasn't the slowest by so much. He didn't score any goals, but then he didn't score any own goals either. He had managed several good tackles, and when for a while he was actually in goal, he pulled off a very respectable save.

He liked Mr Hobson, too. For a start he was nothing like Mr Sturgeon. He had grey hair, a rather droopy-looking face and a droopy-looking moustache to go with it; and his tracksuit looked as if it might have been in fashion the last time England won the World Cup. But when somebody miss-hit the ball and it went flying towards him, he chested it down, then stopped it very neatly with his left foot. When he barked out a command, or demonstrated a new drill, everybody paid attention.

At the end of the practice they all stood around, trying to catch their breath. Mr Hobson eyed them beadily.

'Greg, you're holding onto the ball too much. Football is a team game.'

Greg nodded.

'Beaky, you've got to come out of the goal more for corners.'

Beaky, the tall, skinny, lugubrious-looking goalie, agreed.

'Sunil, keep back more when forwards run at you. Don't be so keen to tackle. Jake –' Mr Hobson gave a groan and everybody laughed. 'Jake, keep it simple. And legal, preferably. Sam –' He beckoned Sam over for a quiet word.

When Sam was standing anxiously before him, Mr Hobson said, 'Sam, you did well today. We don't have many spaces at the moment, but one of our regular defenders, Mark Dawson, has twisted an ankle. Of course, when he comes back you may have to spend a certain amount of time on the bench. But what do you think?'

Sam gaped at him. But before he could say anything, Jake, who had followed him to listen, said, 'Sam'd rather play up front, wouldn't you Sam?'

This fresh example of Griswald cheek startled Sam out of his silence. He stood heavily on Jake's foot. Then he said, 'I'd love to play in defence. When's the first match?'

* * *

For the next week Sam was in a jubilant mood. He took

Biter for long runs on the Meadows to try to work off his nervous energy, and they would race each other, shouting and barking, along the sides of the canal. True, there was not a great atmosphere at home. Mrs Harris spent most of the time sulking in front of the TV, or doing the housework with a martyred expression – but she had not actually forbidden Sam from playing in the team.

Sam did not have much attention to spare for all the gossip about the Griswalds. Of course, Bellstone was still talking about the bus shelter. Opinion was sharply divided between those who thought the bus shelter had been a horrible eyesore, all covered in graffiti, and actually *thanked* the Griswalds for its demise; and those who had used it regularly, who did *not*. Then there was Mrs Bullock who had hated the bus shelter *and* its graffiti, but hated the Griswalds even more for daring to burn it down.

There were also all the rumours spread by Mrs Bullock, based on the roast-chicken incident: that the Griswalds had grisly remains buried at the bottom of their garden; that Elfrida, who appeared (judging from her dress) to have been carrying out some strange religious ritual on the roof ('more likely *satanic*, knowing that lot'), had tried to throw herself to the ground, three storeys below; and that the Griswald children were forced to steal food by night. Mrs Bullock (as Jake pointed out) managed to make it sound as if Mrs Griswald starved her children, *and* that the Griswalds were cannibals or Satanists, or both.

It made small matters – such as Spider and Jake

managing to nick two giant jars of assorted toffees from the top shelf of the local sweetshop, and returning them unobserved the next day with a note reading, 'Better improve your security. Best Wishes, The Griswalds' – hardly worthy of comment.

By the time of Bellstone Rovers' first match against Titmarsh Wanderers, Sam had stopped feeling jubilant and started feeling nervous. Mark Dawson's ankle was getting better, and Sam knew this match might be his only chance to show he was worthy of a place on the team before he ended up on the substitutes' bench. His nerves were not helped by Mrs Harris, who kept saying, 'It's not too late to change your mind,' and who was planning to come and watch the match with a complete first-aid kit.

When Sam arrived at the pitch with Jake he carefully tied Biter to a nearby lamppost before going to join his

team-mates for a warm-up jog.

'Hey, Jake, what you going to do to us if we win? Bury us at the end of the garden?'

Danny Myers, the Titmarsh Wanderers captain, was sneering at them. In a moment a chorus of voices had joined in, with similar attempts at wit on the subject of bodies, burials and mass graves.

Jake scowled. 'Get lost,' he snarled. Then, leaving Greg Roylance to deal with the matter, he turned to Sam. 'How do those pillocks from Titmarsh know about that?' he muttered.

Sam thought about it. 'Probably because Danny Myers is Brandon Bullock's best friend.'

'Huh! I might have known. I just wish that creep Brandon was here –'

Sam thought it as well not to point out that Brandon *was* there. He was standing by the side of the pitch, smirking at Jake and Sam in a most off-putting manner.

The whistle blew and the match began. Sam was soon absorbed in his defensive role and after a while he stopped being nervous and even forgot about the unwelcome presence of Brandon Bullock among the onlookers. Sam was marking Danny, and managed to get a couple of good tackles in against him, one of which so annoyed Danny that he shoved Sam, and ended up being warned by the referee. Just before half-time Sam managed to put in a good run up the wing as well, so that Jake could pass to him. The ball was intercepted before Sam could reach it, and he had to get back quickly as the other team counterattacked. 'That's right Fatty – run!' he heard Brandon yell from the sidelines, and his cheeks burned. But he was back in position in good time, blocking the attack, and Danny, seeing his route on goal was closed, was forced to cross the ball to one of his team-mates.

Then Mrs Harris showed up. Quite a few other parents were there, yelling things like: 'Show him, son!' and 'Put it in the back of the net!' But Mrs Harris was not yelling things like that. Sam couldn't help hearing her, although he tried not to look towards where she tottered up and down on the sidelines, dressed in high-heeled shoes which kept getting stuck in the soil.

'Do watch out dear – don't get your top dirty – that's right, brush yourself down – oh, no! The ball's hit him right in the chest – that's right Sam, kick it away – well, really! That boy's much bigger than him – he had no business taking the ball away – well really! Isn't anyone going to stop him! That boy ran right into my Sam!'

Sam felt himself growing redder and redder as he tried to concentrate on the football and not the awful things his mother was saying. Unfortunately, the forward he was marking was exceptionally big and strong and, although not actually dirty, was definitely an aggressive player. Several times he and Sam clashed, and each time Sam could hear squeaks of indignation emanating from his mother's patch of the field.

Luckily, most of the action was going on over on the

right side of the field, where Jake was amusing himself with his Ryan Giggs impersonation, and by seeing how many back passes, and dummies, and nutmegs, and little chips he could fit into one game. Nor was it all just show-off stuff: he scored once, and set up another, and soon Rovers were leading 4–2.

Five minutes before half-time, Jake tried a particularly ambitious angle, the ball went skidding off into space, and the other team's big centre-forward went loping towards it. Next moment, he was galloping down the pitch towards Sam. He wasn't a particularly quick or skilful player, and Sam made ready to stand his ground.

'Sammy!' shrieked a familiar voice from the sidelines. 'Watch out!'

Sam's head turned, before he could even think about it, to where his mother stood flapping her hands at him from the sidelines; by the time he had turned back to make the tackle it was too late, and the attacker had gone past him. Sam started running after him, but he had travelled hardly any distance before the ball went *thud*, into the back of the net. Sam felt his heart go *thud*, too – into his boots.

The half-time whistle blew. Sam was standing in a group with the rest of the team, listening to Mr Hobson, when he was appalled to see his mother coming towards him.

'I'm just checking to see if my little boy is all right,' she informed Mr Hobson in a breezy manner. Then she turned to Sam and began, 'Are you really all right Sam? That was a very nasty knock you took just now. Did you graze your knee when you fell over?'

For a moment, Sam could not even get any words out. He just grunted. The only thing he was glad about was that Mr Hobson had moved his team talk out of earshot.

'Sam, I think you did just the right thing to leave that boy alone. He was much bigger than you – I was so relieved to see him go past – you could have been seriously hurt –'

Something snapped inside Sam's head.

'Leave me alone!' he snarled. 'You're making a complete idiot of me in front of everybody. Didn't you see him score a goal? I should have stopped him!'

Mrs Harris's face took on its hurt expression. 'I'm afraid I don't think a goal matters that much in comparison to you not being injured.'

'Injured! So I get a graze – or a bruise – big deal! Nobody ever died from a graze, Mum!'

'A graze can get infected.'

'Oh right. How many eleven-year-old boys do *you* know who got gangrene from playing football?'

Sam heard a chuckle, and for a microsecond – a marvellous microsecond – he thought it might be his mother, seeing the funny side. Then he realised it was just Jake, who had come up behind him. Mrs Harris was looking hurt.

'I don't understand your attitude, Sam,' she said quietly. 'But I can see my presence bothers you, so I'm going home.'

Sam watched her go. Half of him felt miserable and guilty for hurting her feelings – on the other hand, it was a relief not having her there. He ran to give Biter a quick pat before the second half.

Mr Hobson sent them back on the pitch with a few inspiring words. 'They're getting rattled, lads,' he said, 'and in large part that's because you're doing such a good job in defence. They're frustrated. Now you have to take advantage of their mistakes and score again.' Jake, in particular, seemed to take these words to heart. He had spotted Brandon Bullock by now, and had already decided it would be his personal crusade to smash Brandon's best friend's team under Brandon's nose.

The start of the second half was scrappy. Neither side seemed to be able to build anything, and the ball went back and forth like it was stuck in a pinball machine. Jake was out to score, but his determination was getting him into trouble. First, he was warned by the referee for a dangerous challenge. Then he tried to show off by sending the ball between Danny Myers's legs. This would have been all very well if it had come off. Instead, the ball bounced off Danny's ankle and into the path of one of the other midfielders, Jamie Hill. He began to run with it towards Sam.

Sam held his ground. He knew Jamie, a wiry, skinny boy, was faster than he was. And he was remembering some of the advice Mr Hobson had given him. 'Don't go in for a tackle too soon. Once you've committed yourself, that's it: if they get past you, then half the time they're going to score. Cut off the angle and force them to pass.'

Jamie saw Sam and hesitated. He glanced up and sideways, and from his whole expression it was clear he was trying to decide whether or not to pass the ball. Across the pitch another attacker was free and calling to him to pass. But Jamie grinned, jiggled the ball with his foot and ran straight at Sam.

Sam swallowed, and forced himself to wait for the exact moment to make his tackle.

Then, just as he was about to move, he heard a terrible sound. It was a familiar sound. A barking, snarling kind of sound.

Out of the corner of his eye he saw a brown and white shape fly across the pitch and fling itself at Danny Myers. Then Danny let out a terrible yell.

His concentration shattered, Sam moved to make the tackle a split second too late. Jamie was past him. Seconds later, Sam heard the yell of triumph as Jamie beat the goalkeeper and scored. He heard it from the ground. During his mistimed tackle, his feet had caught on a divot of grass, and he had hit the ground hard.

Sam just lay there, winded and shocked. It was no comfort to know that, judging from the sound, Biter was making short work of Danny Myers. Sam knew this would do nobody any good at all.

The next sound he heard did not comfort him very much either. In fact, it was absolutely the last thing he wanted to hear.

'Sam! Sammy, darling! Are you hurt? Oh, thank goodness I decided to come back!'

Sam managed to sit up, spitting some of the grass out his mouth. His mother was kneeling down, getting mud all over her dress and screaming something about fetching a doctor, and suing Mr Hobson. Meanwhile, at the other end of the pitch, Biter was laying into the referee.

Sam shut his eyes and, like Elfrida on the day the bones were uncovered, decided this was possibly the worst moment of his entire life.

Chapter Eight
Revenge!

As Jake pointed out later that afternoon in Sam's tree house when he was telling Spider and Elfrida all about it, at least two good things came out of the whole mess. One was the bite that Danny Myers got on his left thigh, which would probably put him out of action for at least two matches. The other was the bloody nose that Brandon Bullock got when Danny Myers hit him.

'It was pretty dumb of Brandon to untie Biter like that,' Jake opined. 'He might have known he'd go for Danny, after the way Danny had shoved you earlier.'

This, of course, was what Danny thought too – which was why he had hit Brandon. Not that Brandon had intended Biter to go for Danny. All Brandon had hoped to do was disrupt the game and get Sam into trouble for not taking proper care of his dog. Brandon's big mistake was in not understanding Biter's view of the world. Sam was Biter's master, and Danny – having knocked Sam over earlier – was the enemy. And Biter knew how to deal with his enemies.

'So, it's all well that ends well,' Jake concluded. Spider and Elfrida nodded.

'That's absolute rubbish,' said Sam crossly. 'Honestly, you Griswalds! You don't care, do you – as long as there's a good punch-up! It hasn't ended well at all!'

Jake looked genuinely puzzled, but before he could say anything Sam proceeded to set out the other side of the argument.

'Firstly, Biter's in dead trouble. If Danny's parents make a fuss, he might even get put down.'

'Oh, they won't bother,' said Jake. 'Danny's tough and ugly. They're not going to worry about him getting a scratch like that.'

'Yeah, well – if they don't, Mum might. She's decided Biter's a dangerous dog. And she always thought football was dangerous, and now she might make me quit the team.'

'You'll just have to tell her you won't,' said Elfrida. Which was all very well for her to say, thought Sam crossly. It was easier said than done.

He pointed this out, then added, 'And another thing, in case you've forgotten, as I failed to stop Jamie scoring, we lost the game by one goal –'

'Yeah, that is serious,' Jake conceded. 'Still, we'll most likely play them in the Cup.'

'– and finally, I've been made to look a complete fool in front of everybody. Brandon will never let me forget it, probably for the rest of my life.'

'Yeah, well, Brandon looks a bit of a fool too, now his nose is broken,' was the only comfort Jake could come up with.

'Thanks a lot,' said Sam.

He looked down at Biter, who was sitting beneath the tree, staring up at them mournfully. He knew he was in disgrace, and even though Pomfret was walking in full view along the top of the fence, for once he could not be bothered to bark. Sam suspected the only reason that Biter had been saved was because Mrs Harris had not liked Danny Myers either, and secretly thought that anybody who shoved her Sam deserved all he got. But Sam knew that next time Biter put a foot out of line (or his teeth into somebody's leg) she was unlikely to be so forgiving.

Sam sighed, and shut his eyes to block out the sight of Biter's reproachful gaze. But this was not very comforting either, for the image that immediately replaced it was that of his mother, clasping him to her chest and crying out, 'Sammy! Sammy, are you hurt? Speak to me!' while he struggled to get free, and Brandon smirked at him from over her shoulder (this was shortly before Danny had forcibly removed the smirk from his face). And then there was the memory of Biter seizing the referee's shirt and shaking it, over and over again . . . and the way his mother had gone on and on at him, all the way home . . . and what she had said would happen if Biter ever did anything like that again . . . and the way she had cried. For a moment Sam felt physically sick.

Sam opened his eyes. 'What was that plan you said you had,' he asked Jake, 'for getting back at the Bullocks?'

Jake stopped short in the middle of the demonstration he was giving Spider and Elfrida, of how Biter had attacked the referee. 'I thought you weren't keen on that?' he said, eyeing Sam with an assessing look.

'Just tell me your idea.'

'OK.' Jake paused and leant forward conspiratorially: he looked like the leader of a group of bank robbers. (Or bandits in a Western, thought Sam. Or like a film he had seen about the French Revolution: the Griswalds looked just like a bunch of dangerous revolutionaries, preparing to storm Versailles and to march the aristocrats to the guillotine. He had a feeling that Robespierre, the revolutionary leader, might have looked just like Jake Griswald. The only thing was, he could not

help remembering that Robespierre and his cronies had themselves ended up on the guillotine.) 'It's a great plan. I got the idea when I went into our garage, and saw that massive bottle of weedkiller Mum bought. It's really lethal stuff – I saw her using some once, and it burns anything it touches right away.'

'So what are we going to do?' asked Elfrida eagerly. 'Make those Bullocks drink some?'

'Don't be stupid. In the middle of the night we creep into the Bullocks' garden, and we burn a message right into their lawn. Something like – *Buzz off Big Nose. Best Wishes, The Griswalds.* What d'you think?'

Sam thought of the Bullocks' lawn: an emerald green expanse, as level and beautifully trimmed as a bowling green. Then he imagined Jake's message, scorched across the middle of it.

Elfrida said, 'Why don't we take the weedkiller and put it everywhere – we'll turn her garden into a desert!'

'Because, little sister,' said Jake, 'this is a lot more subtle. Less work, too. Anyhow, you're not coming.'

'What!' squawked Elfrida. 'Why not?'

'Because you'll be sure to mess up, that's why. Just like you did over that chicken. You'll probably spill weedkiller over your feet or something, and we'll all be for it.'

'I am coming! I am!'

'Never mind that,' interrupted Sam. 'You haven't heard what I think about it.' He took a deep breath. 'It's a crazy idea. I'll never be able to get out of the house to do it without setting off the burglar alarm. Biter will go mad. Mum will go mad. And if she doesn't catch us we'll still get stuck on those spikes on the fence. And then Mrs Bullock'll be waiting. And if we somehow get past her, it'll be no joke I bet – writing messages in weedkiller in the dark.' He looked from face to face. 'We'd never get away with it.'

'So, you're not on for it, is that what you mean?' asked Jake, his voice disappointed but not surprised.

'I didn't say that,' Sam snapped. 'It may be the stupidest idea I ever heard. But we need to show those Bullocks – of course I'm on for it!'

* * *

Eight hours later, as Sam hung perilously from his bedroom window, a torch clutched between his teeth, and

his feet scrabbling around trying to get a grip on the drainpipe, he was already wondering if he had made the right decision. He no longer felt quite so angry with the Bullocks: what he did feel was cold, sleepy and that he was about to fall off any minute. Spider was somewhere on the wall above, trying to dismantle the Harris's burglar alarm (and probably about to electrocute himself, thought Sam gloomily) while Jake was a few feet below, shining a torch and trying to point out hand and foot holds. Sam did not feel especially grateful for their help. The only thing he was glad about was that Biter had been banished to the kitchen by Mrs Harris, who (since his behaviour at the football match) was concerned that he might take it into his head to savage Sam in the night. So at least he wouldn't wake up Mrs Harris by barking, or worse yet, come jumping out of the window after him.

Even as Sam clung there, it occurred to him how much things had changed since the Griswalds had arrived. After all, he had been living in this house and sleeping in this bedroom for the last eleven years. And it had never once occurred to him to climb out of the window, not even in the daylight when he could see his hands in front of him. At this precise moment, he was not sure it was a change for the better. He imagined being back under his duvet, with the hot-water bottles his mother always insisted on making for him, and he sighed. *I never wanted to be Spiderman*, he muttered into the ivy. *I never wanted to have adventures*.

He had more sense than to say this to the Griswalds,

however. And after a while his feet found the next hold in the brick, and things grew easier. It was only a short distance to where the back porch stuck out from the wall, and from there it was more of a slither than a climb down to where Jake was waiting for him.

'Great!' said Jake. 'Look, I've got the weedkiller.' And he brandished an enormous bottle.

'Don't spill it!' said Sam quickly. 'It's not *my* garden we want to destroy.' He glanced around. 'Where's Elfrida?'

'We told her we were going tomorrow. Then we crept out after she was asleep. She'd just mess things up. Anyway, she's too young, really, to be mixed up in something like this.'

Sam nodded. A few minutes later all three boys were sitting on top of the fence, peering down into the darkness of the Bullocks' garden. It seemed as if nobody was about. There were no lights, and no sounds, other than the occasional rustle of the wind passing through the leaves. After a while, Spider, who had been staring into the darkness with the acuteness of a cat, nodded to signify that all was clear.

Jake turned and said to Sam, 'Come on. You and I'll get going with the weedkiller.'

'Why? What's Spider going to do?'

'Never you mind,' said Jake mysteriously.

Sam grabbed the fence – and Jake's jacket – determinedly. 'Oh no you don't. I want to know what's going on. I'm not going to get mixed up with poisoning their cat, or burning down their house, or anything like that.'

'What good ideas,' said Jake, grinning. Then, as Sam shook him, 'It's nothing like that. Spider, give me those.' Jake turned on his torch, to reveal something pink and voluminous in his hands.

'What's that?' Sam asked.

'Mrs Bullock's knickers.'

'What!' Sam nearly fell off the fence. When he had recovered he grabbed at the knickers (which appeared to be covered in pink roses) and then, thinking better of it, shoved them back at Jake. 'Where – I mean what – I mean *where* did you get them? And – *what* are you going to do with them?'

'Spider nicked them off her washing line, didn't you Spider? As for what we're going to do with them – you just wait and see.'

'Well, as long as you're not going to smother her with them, or anything,' said Sam dubiously, 'I suppose it's all right. Come on. Let's get this over with.'

They leapt down into the garden, and soon found a nice flat piece of lawn. Then they got going with the weedkiller. It was much harder than they had expected. The bottle was heavy, the moon had gone behind a cloud, making it difficult to see, and both of them were secretly nervous about what would happen if they slopped the weedkiller on their feet. After all, according to Jake the liquid destroyed everything it touched.

There had been a lot of debate about what they would write. Sam had persuaded Jake, eventually, that it would be madness to sign their names, and in the end they had decided on:

TRY TIDYING THIS, TWERPS

They had not even finished the first word when Sam felt something soft and sinuous sliding round his ankles. It gave him quite a shock. Then he heard a hissing sound.

'Jake,' he whispered urgently. 'It's Delilah.'

'So what? She's only a cat.'

Sam swallowed. Of course, Jake had not actually witnessed the horrible way in which Delilah had dispatched Morris. Meanwhile, the hissing was getting louder.

Suddenly, there was a spitting noise and Sam felt a sharp pain in his leg.

'Oww! She scratched me!'

'Shut up!' Jake hissed. 'They'll hear you!'

As if Delilah had understood him, she began to yowl. The noise was bloodcurdling. Inside the Bullock residence lights snapped on, first upstairs, then downstairs.

'We've got to run for it!' Sam said, desperately trying to fend off Delilah. His jeans were flapping around his ankle: Delilah had cut right through the denim with her claws.

'No! We've got to finish this!'

At that moment lights appeared across the lawn. The back door had been flung open. Sam and Jake, in the shadows beyond, froze.

'What's out there, Clarence? Can you see anything?' demanded an all too familiar voice.

'Not really, dear,' replied the milder tones of Mr Bullock. 'It's too dark. Perhaps there are some cats on the lawn.'

'It will be those Griswald cats,' returned Mrs Bullock grimly. 'Picking on poor Delilah again. Well, I'll sort them! I've a good mind to put down poison!'

'Oh, I wouldn't do that dear –'

The voices receded. In any case, Sam was too busy trying to shut Jake up to really notice what was going on. 'She'd poison our cats, would she?' Jake was muttering to himself, making snarling noises. Meanwhile, Delilah was still yowling, and getting in the odd jab at Sam's ankles. From across the fences that separated their territory, the Griswald cats heard Delilah, and joined in. The noise was truly terrible. Sam thought he could even hear Biter, barking faintly.

Suddenly, the back door was flung open again.

'Out of my way, Clarence!'

'Really, dear, I don't think –'

'This will make them shut up.'

Sam turned towards the door. He was not sure what he expected, but he would not have been surprised to see Mrs Bullock brandishing an axe, or even a machine gun. Instead, he was just in time to receive a bucketful of icy cold water, full in the face. He sat down abruptly from the shock, then realised he was probably sitting in weedkiller and got up hastily. The only good thing was that Delilah had been caught by some of the water, too, and had fled, silenced at last, into the bushes.

Satisfied, Mrs Bullock slammed the door shut. But the lights did not go out.

'Just answer me this,' said Sam, as the water ran down his neck. 'Why, whenever I do anything with you Griswalds, is it *me* who ends up getting scratched, *me* who ends up getting bitten, *me* who gets soaked to the skin by icy cold water?'

'Put a sock in it,' said Jake. 'Let's get finished before she comes out again.'

Sam could see the point of this. The only problem was that neither of them could remember where they had got to in their message, or where exactly the letters had been. Jake suggested that they feel around and try to work out where the letters were by touch, but Sam did not feel this was a sensible approach with a weedkiller that burnt away everything it touched. Then they realised that in the confusion they had put the bottle down, and in the darkness they could not find it.

'Put the torch back on!' hissed Jake.

'No! They'll see it from the house.'

They felt around desperately. After a pause Jake said, 'I think I've found the bottle.'

'Then get a move on!'

'I think I've knocked it over.'

They were just beginning to quarrel about whose fault

this was, when the door was flung open again. Once more they froze. This time there was complete silence, but somehow both of them were sure that Mrs Bullock was standing on the back steps, looking for them. Either she had not believed they were really cats at all, or she had heard their voices from the house. Both of them felt that those eyes were boring into them as powerfully as the weedkiller could ever do. Worse yet, she had a flashlight. A beam of light was now roving around the garden, picking out first the garden shed, then the birdtable . . . and it was getting nearer. Sam felt like a prisoner-of-war, trying to break out of a camp in a World War II film. He knew that any moment now the searchlight would catch his face or body, then everything would be over. The light was getting nearer . . . it had almost reached his left foot . . .

'Run for it!' hissed Jake suddenly, grabbing Sam's arm. Together they turned and raced for the fence, expecting at any moment that Mrs Bullock would catch them with her light. From behind them there was a terrible cry. Mrs Bullock had heard them, and even if she could not see them clearly, she was pretty sure that the two shadows speeding towards the fence were not cats.

They were certain that all was lost, when suddenly there was a huge splash from the direction of Mrs Bullock's ornamental lily pond. Mrs Bullock gave a cry of alarm and the light beam turned away. Sam and Jake made it to the top of the fence, and paused for a moment before they jumped into Sam's garden, trying to make sure they avoided the compost heap and the brambles at the bottom.

'Hey, wait for me!'

They looked round and saw Elfrida peering up at them from the Bullocks' garden, Pomfret in her arms.

'What are you doing here?' her brother hissed.

'Why shouldn't I be here? You pigs, you never tell me anything, you sneak out and think I won't notice!'

'Well, it just serves you right –'

Sam had a feeling this argument could go on for a long time. He also felt it would be better conducted somewhere that wasn't the Bullocks' garden. 'Here, Elfrida,' he said, reaching down a hand.

She jumped and he pulled. And a few minutes later, they were all safely over the fence.

'You should be grateful,' Elfrida told her brother. 'If I hadn't distracted Mrs Bullock, you would have been caught.'

'Why, what did you do?' he asked suspiciously.

'I chucked that ugly stone jar into Mrs Bullock's duck pond.'

'You did what!' Jake yelled.

'Shut up! I had to do something! It was the only thing I could think of!'

'If you mean Mrs Bullock's Grecian urn, it cost a thousand pounds,' Sam stated glumly. He knew it had, because Mrs Bullock had told his mother, who had told him.

Even Jake was shaken by this news. 'Did it float?' he

asked Elfrida hopefully.

Elfrida said nothing. They immediately knew that it had not.

And then they all felt somewhat gloomy. Messing about with weedkiller was one thing, but destroying thousand-pound garden ornaments was a very different matter.

'It's not like Mum's had a chance to get over the bus shelter, yet,' said Jake.

Sam sighed, and thought of all his own mother still had to get over from that afternoon.

Jake and Elfrida scrambled over into their own garden. Sam went back towards his own house, relieved to see that there were no lights showing; clearly, even if Biter had been barking, it had not wakened Mrs Harris, or if it had, then she had not gone to check on Sam. Otherwise, thought Sam, she would probably have called the police by now.

It was only as he stood beneath his bedroom window, peering up, that he realised what he should have realised before. He could not get up by himself. He needed somebody to at least give him a leg up, so that he could grab onto the first handhold and get up onto the top of the back porch.

He stood for a while cursing the Griswalds and their bright ideas. Then he tried to work out what he should do. He could go next door and ask Elfrida and Jake to help him; but he could not see how to do that without waking Mr and Mrs Griswald. And the only other alternative he could see was spending the night on the cold, dark floor of the tree house, being crawled over by spiders – and that was not very appealing either.

He was just about to go and brave the spiders when someone laid a hand on his shoulder. Sam almost jumped out of his skin. But once he'd got over the shock, he was quite glad to see Spider Griswald. Spider had not forgotten that Sam could not reach his room unassisted, even if everyone else had. In another moment, Sam found himself gently easing up his bedroom window and climbing in; and the last thing he saw that night was the ghostly form of Spider waving farewell, before he went abseiling gently down through the ivy and out of view.

Chapter Nine
Spider Gets Mrs Bullock's Knickers Down

Almost the first thing Sam saw the next morning was Mrs Bullock's knickers, flying gently in the breeze from the top of the Bullocks' poplar tree.

The second thing he saw was Mrs Bullock, standing underneath the tree. She was scarlet with anger. Sam pulled his head back in through the bedroom window and slammed it shut before she should see him. Then he collapsed onto the bed and laughed and laughed and laughed.

The Griswalds did not live close enough to view the effects of their handiwork from their bedroom windows.

Being Griswalds, however, they did not let that stop them. Even before they had eaten breakfast, they went down the street to have a look.

Mrs Bullock was still there and she turned puce with anger when she saw them.

'You disgusting – revolting – despicable –'

'Hello, Mrs Bullock,' said Jake. 'Do you realise there are some knickers caught in your tree?'

Elfrida peered upwards and observed solemnly, 'I don't think it looks very tidy, Mrs Bullock. I don't know what your neighbours will say.'

Spider doubled up with silent laughter.

Mrs Bullock looked as if she was going to throttle them, only she didn't know which of them to throttle first. She made a snarling sound, which sounded a bit like Biter at his least friendly. Then she said, 'Wait until I speak to your parents!' and charged back into the house.

The Griswalds remained where they were, chuckling amongst themselves, and were still there when Christabel and Brandon appeared.

'You Griswalds are disgusting!' declared Christabel. 'We're never going to live this down!'

'You're too right,' said Jake. 'Anyone got a camera? It might make a nice shot for the school newsletter.'

'Just you wait!' declared Brandon furiously. 'We'll get you for this!'

* * *

The Griswalds eventually went back to their own house.

To their surprise, and relief, Mrs Bullock did not call their parents to complain. For the moment, it seemed, they were off the hook.

The knickers, however, were not. During the course of the day various Bullocks could be seen trying with various ladders to climb the tree. But reaching the knickers, they soon discovered, was no easy matter. None of the Bullocks' ladders were anywhere near long enough, and the branches at the top of the poplar tree were very thin, which made climbing difficult. Mr and Mrs Bullock were too heavy, and Brandon was scared of heights. At last, Mrs Bullock managed to chivvy Christabel up a few branches, but she snagged her tights on a branch and refused point-blank to climb any higher.

Then Brandon suggested Mrs Bullock call the fire brigade. Mrs Bullock replied that she did not want to become the laughing stock of the whole town, at which point Brandon pointed out that they were going to be the laughing stock of the whole town anyway, if they did not do something soon. The Griswalds and Sam, who could hear all this from Sam's tree house, almost killed themselves laughing. They were eating a box of toffees that Spider had mysteriously produced from somewhere and enjoying themselves enormously. Elfrida and her brothers had forgotten their differences in their triumph over the Bullocks.

Next morning the knickers were still there, although now looking rather bedraggled. The Griswalds, setting out with Sam for school, stopped to peer upwards into the branches, then grinned at each other smugly. They looked less smug when Mrs Bullock appeared from behind the hedge and stood, hands on hips, barring their way.

'You Griswalds,' she barked. 'I know very well that you put my – that you put *them* up there! And –' she looked straight at Spider – 'I know *you* can get them down. Now I'll do a deal with you. Go up there and fetch them, and promise me it never happens again, and I will agree not to mention the matter to your parents. What do you say?'

'What's the alternative?' asked Jake.

'The alternative is that I pay good money to chop this tree down, and you get into the worst trouble of your lives!'

Spider turned and looked at the others with raised, enquiring eyebrows. They grinned back at him. They were feeling rather pleased with themselves. None of them had ever imagined that Mrs Bullock might be reduced to bargaining with them, and now that she was, they were not minded to give way easily.

'What's more,' added Mrs Bullock grimly, 'if you fetch them, I will also overlook the matter of the large hole that has been burned into my back lawn, apparently with some kind of powerful weedkiller. I have arranged for some workmen to come and dig a new flower bed on that spot, and provided my – *you-know-whats* are restored to me, I shall not send the bill to your parents.'

This put a different light on things. Reluctantly, Jake

nodded, and while Mrs Bullock watched stonily, Spider went to the tree and hoisted himself up. In a matter of seconds – or so it seemed to his spectators – he had reached the top.

That morning, Sam and the Griswalds were all in trouble for being late for school. But the glorious memory of watching Spider present Mrs Bullock with her own flower-patterned knickers more than made up for it.

* * *

As it happened, the Griswalds' triumph was short-lived.

They were sitting around the dinner table, eating their usual meal of beans and dumplings, this time served with sausages and boiled cabbage. Mr Griswald, for once, was eating with his family. He was staring into the distance, preoccupied with his own thoughts. Mrs Griswald, on the other hand, was right on the ball.

'You lot have been looking very smug recently,' she remarked to her children, with obvious suspicion. 'Are you up to something?'

'Nothing!' – ''S'not fair!' – 'We aren't planning anything!' – 'You always think the worst!' These, and similar declarations, issued from the lips of her two youngest children with Spider nodding in vigorous agreement. Only Luke looked sceptical, but he soon disappeared – to write an essay he said, although almost immediately they heard the sound of his guitar.

'Humph.' Mrs Griswald pushed her empty plate away, but she looked thoughtful. 'The trouble with this family,' she said suddenly, 'is that we don't do enough together. If we did more things together, maybe you wouldn't get into so much trouble.'

Her children looked distinctly wary.

'We eat dumplings together,' said Jake.

'And that's no fun at all,' Elfrida pointed out.

Mrs Griswald turned to her husband. 'Alfred!' she barked. 'It's time to do something as a *family*. What shall we do? And I don't mean watch television! I mean something *together*.'

Slowly, Mr Griswald's eyes left the middle distance, and focused on his family. 'Something together? With the children?' he asked, as if this was a truly amazing concept. Then he frowned gently. It seemed he was having difficulty thinking of anything.

'Yes, with the children,' said Mrs Griswald crossly.

'I know, Dad,' said Jake. 'Let's play darts.'

'Or poker,' said Elfrida eagerly. 'You once said you'd teach us how.'

'Or we could set up that pool table in the attic –'

'Or arm-wrestling –'

'No, no.' Mr Griswald pondered for a moment. 'Well, I suppose we could make up verses.'

His children's faces fell.

'Yes, I need some for an Easter card –'

Mrs Griswald snorted, but was distracted by the doorbell. Moments later, Mrs Bullock was among them. And something about her face, which was red and glistening; her hands, which were alternately clawing and shaking; her eyes, which were bulging and rolling; but perhaps most of all her teeth, which were bared and wolf-like, immediately informed the younger Griswalds that, bargain or no bargain, they were in deep trouble.

'Your children,' began Mrs Bullock at once, addressing Mr and Mrs Griswald, 'are total barbarians! They are demented, evil and possibly possessed! I do not doubt that they will end up in prison – I only wonder if they will not end up somewhere worse!'

Mr Griswald gazed at Mrs Bullock with a mildly puzzled expression. 'Do I know you?' he murmured at last. 'You do look familiar –'

Elfrida said, 'Nicking someone's knickers 's'not *satanic* –' but Mrs Griswald interrupted her.

'My children are not the best behaved,' she told Mrs Bullock. 'But they are not evil. At least,' she added, rather spoiling the effect, 'most of the time they're not.'

Mrs Bullock looked like a volcano about to erupt.

'Oh, aren't they? Well, what do you say to this?' And she produced a carrier bag and emptied it onto the table. Something large and heavy fell out with a *thud*. The table shook, making the plates dance about, and Spider's plate of cabbage and dumplings went flying into the air and landed on the floor. Ignoring the mess, the Griswalds stared at the object. Even Mr Griswald managed to look quite interested.

'What is it?' asked Mrs Griswald.

'What does it look like?' screeched Mrs Bullock, startling everyone. 'It's a bone! A horrible, disgusting bone! It's dead too!' (As Jake later pointed out, it would have been very surprising if it wasn't.) 'Isn't it enough that your horrible, disgusting children are dismembering dead things, and burying them in *your* back garden, without them coming and doing the same thing in mine! What did they kill this time? A horse?' (And truly, the bone did look as if it came from something horse-sized, or even bigger.) 'Or a *person*?'

'That,' Mrs Griswald stated firmly, 'is going too far. How did you find this bone?'

'I'll tell you how I found it! I was watching the workmen digging my new flower bed, when suddenly this – this – this object appears! And it wasn't the only one!' And she slammed down another carrier bag on the table. A couple of smaller bones escaped

and bounced out into Mr Griswald's dumplings. 'Your children have some explaining to do!'

'And why exactly do you think *my children* are responsible?' Mrs Griswald shot a glance at her children, who were doing nothing to dispel the impression of guilt. They were scowling at each other in a horrible manner, and none of them were saying anything to deny Mrs Bullock's charges.

'Isn't it obvious?' Mrs Bullock retorted. 'How many children in Bellstone do *you* think occupy themselves burying dead bodies – or *bits* of them – at the bottom of the garden? Don't you remember I was present during the first discovery in your garden! Furthermore I know for a fact they have been in my garden – and by night too! And don't you dare deny it!' Here she turned a truly ferocious scowl upon the younger Griswalds.

'All right – what if we were?' asked Jake.

'What if you were? Well! Personally, I think it is time the police were called in – because you lot definitely need locking up!'

Mrs Griswald held up a hand.

'Spider, Jake, Elfrida,' she said, in a grim voice. 'I want an honest answer from you. Were any of you responsible for burying this bone in Mrs Bullock's garden?'

Her tone told them she meant business, and her eyes narrowed as she scrutinised them one by one. Nobody would look her in the face. Jake shifted his feet uncomfortably, Elfrida glared at the floor, and Spider tried to whistle, which he only did when he was nervous (and which was always spooky for other people, because it never made a sound).

'I see,' said Mrs Griswald, at last. 'Guilty, all three of you. I suppose this was your idea of a joke. Well, let me tell you, it is a joke you will all regret. And for a start, you can make good whatever damage you've done.'

Before they could protest, Mrs Bullock intervened, her nostrils quivering with rage. 'If you think I would let your horrible brats anywhere near my garden, you can think again!' she declared, and she continued like this for some time. At last she left, still ranting about the dreadfulness of the Griswalds, but this was not much of a relief. For as soon as she had gone, Mrs Griswald let loose.

It was a great pity, she said, that it was no longer legal to beat one's children with heavy objects or to lock them up in damp rat-infested cellars with no food. She was beginning to think that only measures of this kind would make any impression on them. But as it was, she was forced to content herself with banning all visits to friends and imposing a six o'clock curfew.

'Nor is that all,' she concluded grimly. 'This crime requires a particularly severe punishment. I'll let you know when I've thought of one. Now go to your rooms! And take these disgusting objects with you!' She shoved the grisly collection of bones towards them.

As they disappeared towards the stairs, it was Mr Griswald who had the last word.

'I can see it will be a long time before this family spends a quiet evening together,' he observed sorrowfully.

He was right.

* * *

Sam, meanwhile, had arrived home from school that same afternoon to find a note from his mother, saying she was lying down with a headache. As Biter was barking loudly, Sam decided to take him for a run around Bellstone Meadows.

The leaves were turning on the trees, and some of them had already fallen onto the paths. Sam and Biter had a wonderful time chasing through them, diving into them, and kicking them around. Sam felt on top of the world. Together with the Griswalds, he had humiliated the Bullocks; he had Biter to keep him company; and he had the next Bellstone Rovers game to look forward to on Saturday. All things he would never have dreamt possible a few weeks ago. To add to his good mood, as he raced Biter across the grass he discovered that he could run further and faster than ever before. Maybe he would be able to make that run up the wing he had always dreamt of . . . maybe he would be able to outrun their defence . . . maybe he would be able to score that goal. He could already hear the rest of the players cheering . . .

He decided to take Biter home, then find Jake and chat about tactics for the next match. But when he got home, he saw the breakfast things were still sitting on the table; he looked in the fridge (which was empty) and then caught sight of Mrs Harris's bag, full of papers which she had brought home from the travel agency where she worked. Then he remembered how she kept bringing work home and sitting up late doing it on the kitchen table, and how she always looked tired and harassed. And suddenly he changed his mind. After all, his mum had been pretty nice lately: she had stopped going on about the incident with Danny Myers, or about finding a new home for Biter, *or* about how Sam should give up football and take up archaeology instead. So, instead of going to see the Griswalds, he raided the jar of loose change and went to the corner shop. By the time Mrs Harris finally came downstairs, the washing up was done and the kitchen sparkling; and the table was laid with a pot of tea, a jug of milk and a jar full of flowers, picked from the garden. As soon as he heard her footsteps, Sam turned the grill on and put the cheese-on-toast underneath.

Mrs Harris saw none of this. She sat down heavily in a chair and said in bleak voice, 'Mrs Bullock came round today. I am very unhappy about what she told me about you and those Griswald children.'

'That's not fair!' burst out Sam, without thinking. 'She promised she wouldn't say anything if we got her knickers down.' Then he realised what he had said, and snorted with laughter.

Mrs Harris did not laugh. 'I don't know what you mean, and I'm not sure I want to. But it seems to confirm what Mrs Bullock said. Which is that those children are running wild and that you seem to be caught up in it. I have to say I didn't really believe her, but now I'm not so sure. She told me they have been banned from using the buses! You know perfectly well that I thought you were taking the bus to school each morning – not running amok through the town! How could you deceive me, Sam?'

'It's only walking to school!' Sam protested (conveniently forgetting the outlandish routes the Griswalds used to get there).

Mrs Harris sighed. 'And then there's the matter of Biscuits. As Mrs Bullock very sensibly points out, goodness only knows where he came from, and he has already given that friend of Brandon's a very nasty bite. It's only fortunate that the boy's parents decided not to sue.'

'Mrs Bullock's trying to make them, I bet,' Sam said bitterly.

'And it was the Griswalds who landed this dangerous

dog on us in the first place. Mrs Bullock also said – although I can hardly believe it – that she saw those two Griswald boys ripping down all the posters you made to find Biscuit's owner. No wonder we've had no telephone calls! And their own animals are causing all kinds of problems. Apparently their cats go into the Bullocks' garden, and fight with Delilah, and yowl, and apparently they – well, they pee all over Mrs Bullock's best rose bush, right beside the Bullocks' front door. So the whole porch smells of cat pee!'

'Good! I'm glad!'

'It's not funny, Sam. I have enough trouble at work, without having to worry about you running wild when my back is turned –'

'I'm not running wild! And why don't you just look for another job, if you hate this one so much?'

'That's easy to say! You don't know how difficult it is to find a job where I can be home when you get back from school –'

'But you don't *have* to be home. If you don't want me to be by myself you know I can always go next door.'

Mrs Harris's mouth set in a thin, determined line. 'To the Griswalds, I suppose! As if I would permit that! After all I've heard!'

'But I'm going next door tomorrow evening,' Sam remembered. 'You were going to that talk on boring old Roman villas.'

'You mean the talk on *Archaeological and Antiquarian*

Aspects of Bellstone, at the public library,' said Mrs Harris stonily. 'Oh, that's quite out of the question. I shall just have to stay home, and work, as usual.' Mrs Harris's face took on its familiar martyred look. And Sam could feel the rage boiling up inside him.

'That's not fair!' he yelled. 'You're punishing me because you won't go out!'

'I am not punishing you, Sam, I'm trying to take care of you. And another thing. After all this, I've finally made up my mind. Biscuits has to go. He's dangerous. We'll take him to the Dogs' Home in the morning.'

Sam stood up, his face crimson. 'If Bite— I mean Biscuits goes, then I go too!' He was about to rush out of the door when the smell hit him. Mrs Harris noticed it too. Black smoke was belching out of the oven door.

Mrs Harris quickly removed the grill pan. The slices of cheese-on-toast that Sam had so carefully prepared were now charred, smoking lumps.

'Oh really, Sam! This is too much!'

Sam yelled something very, very rude. Then he turned and fled into the garden. It wasn't fair. None of it was fair. His first thought was to go and see the Griswalds, but he did not feel he could tell them what his mum thought about them. He sat for a while on the swing, with Biter leaning against his legs, but after a while Biter wandered off to snuffle around in the compost heap. Sam clambered up onto the platform of his tree house. He felt utterly miserable and alone.

He was sitting there, lost in a despondent silence, when he became aware of something strange. First, there was the odd creak from the wood behind him, then he heard soft, smothered noises, and a scuffling. He was almost certain he could hear something breathing. *Something* – not *someone* – because the quick, heavy breaths sounded more like an animal than a person.

The hairs on the back of Sam's neck rose. His hands were cold. *Something was there, something was in the tree house behind him*.

Slowly, he twisted round and squinted at the open doorway of the tree house itself. Inside, all was shadow. But was that something in the shadow? Was the darkness *too* dark, right at the back, in the far corner?

He got to his feet and, heart thudding, crept into the tree house.

Next moment, he went flying – right over the sobbing figure of Elfrida Griswald.

Chapter Ten
A Bone of Contention

When they had been sent upstairs by their mother, the Griswalds had immediately made for Spider's bedroom, which was not only the largest but also the furthest from their parents' ears. And there they proceeded to have things out in true, spectacular Griswald fashion.

'You pig, Jake!' Elfrida burst out, as soon as the door was closed. 'You didn't have to keep looking at me like that! You know very well it was you who made that hole in the Bullocks' lawn!'

'Yes, but I didn't bury a load of bones in it!'

'Of course you did!'

Jake turned crimson with anger. 'I like that!' he yelled. 'There's me and Spider, just sitting there, taking the rap for you, not saying anything, not grassing you up, and now you turn round and accuse us!'

'But, but – I was protecting *you*!'

'Yeah, right! You buried the first lot of bones, didn't you? And you were mooching around in the Bullocks' garden that night we were there – you know you were – and now I see why!'

Elfrida turned and looked at Spider, but he was glaring at her every bit as fiercely as his brother. Jake was beside himself. It had been bad enough, he declared, the first time round, with Elfrida stealing their food, and burying the remains in their *own* garden. That she should be doing the same thing again – and burying the leftovers in Bullock territory – was almost beyond belief. It was treacherous, it was sneaky, it was downright unforgivable . . . and on top of everything, she had even had the nerve to pretend that she was in the Bullocks' garden simply to find out what *they* were doing – and had then tried to take the credit for rescuing them by chucking that urn in the pool. And now this evening, when she was found out, she just sat there and let her brothers share the blame . . .

Elfrida listened as Jake yelled all this at her and then, most untypically, she burst into tears. She could not help it. She felt quite overwhelmed.

'Don't think you'll get round us that way!'

'I don't want to get round you! I don't want to cry!' she squeaked. 'I hate you! I'm angry with you!'

'You're crying because you know you're a nasty little

sneak, and you've got what you deserve!' yelled Jake. 'We're not talking to you, and we're not walking to school with you, and we're not having anything to do with you –'

Elfrida began to make strange noises. Jake, rashly, ignored them.

'– and if you want to go off and gnaw on some more bones you've nicked, that's fine, just don't get us involved –'

Elfrida threw up all over him. She was so worked up she couldn't help it. Bits of regurgitated dumpling splattered all over Jake and Spider. It did nothing to improve their mood. They chucked Elfrida into the corridor and the bones after her. Then, once they had cleaned themselves up in the bathroom, they went into Spider's bedroom and slammed the door behind them. Elfrida hammered with her fists, but they would not let her in.

She went back to her own room, and tried not to cry, but she could not help it. She tried cuddling her gerbils, but they did not want to be cuddled, and nor did the white mice or the budgies. There was nowhere in the house she could go where she would be met with anything other than anger and insult. And she did not want her brothers to know she was still crying, but she couldn't stop crying, and she was afraid they would hear it through the ceiling.

Then she had an idea. She picked up her bag of bones, and sneaked out through the house.

* * *

'So I came here, and I've been waiting for you for ages!'

Elfrida concluded, having told Sam the whole story. 'Where've you been?'

'I don't *live* in the tree house, you know,' said Sam crossly. 'How was I supposed to know you were here? You Griswalds – you'd think you owned this tree house, the way you're always turning up. And when you do, why is it always me who ends up with bits missing?' He held his palms out for her to inspect their skinless state. 'And anyway, why didn't you say anything? That's another thing about you Griswalds – you're always *creeping up.*'

'I wanted to make sure it was just you. Not Spider and Jake too. I *hate* Spider and Jake! I don't know who I hate more. Jake and Spider – or Mrs Bullock – or Mum. None of them'll believe me!'

'And *did* you put all those bones in Mrs Bullock's garden?' asked Sam sternly.

'No I didn't! Why would I want to do that? I haven't even taken any more food from the fridge –' Sam stared at her hard and she suddenly blushed. 'Well, all right, just one leftover sausage, just one – but it didn't *have* any bones.' Elfrida wiped her nose on her sleeve. 'I thought you'd believe me, Sam, that's why I came here, because I thought you'd believe me and help me and I needed to get away from *them* –'

'Hmm.' Now that Sam's eyes had adjusted to the darkness he could see that she certainly did look woebegone. She was sitting with her arms wrapped around her knees and her carrier bag of bones beside her. He felt

himself softening. Nobody had ever turned to him for help before. Besides, it seemed to him that both he and Elfrida were in the same boat, misunderstood and mistreated by their respective families.

Under the tree, Biter began a gentle and melancholy howling, something he often did at the close of day. It matched their moods perfectly. For a while, Sam and Elfrida maintained a mournful silence.

At last, Elfrida said dolefully, 'It's not easy being a Griswald, you know. Everyone always thinks the worst of us. They always think we're to blame for everything. That's why it's so bad now, with Jake and Spider against me. It means nobody's on my side.' She stopped, and looked at him hopefully. But he said nothing so she continued, 'Sometimes I wish I wasn't a Griswald, but just ordinary.' She paused. 'Like you, f'rinstance.'

'Oh.' Sam was not sure whether to be pleased or put out. 'What's so ordinary about me?'

'Well, you've got an ordinary name – Sam Harris, you can't get more ordinary than that – and you don't wear funny clothes, like we do – so you look ordinary – and you like playing football, and all boys like playing football, s'far as I can see – and you get in trouble a medium amount, instead of all the time, like us. And –'

'All right,' said Sam quickly. 'I get your point. But why would you want to be me?'

'Lots of reasons – 'cos your mum's a normal mum, she's nice to you, and she doesn't make you eat dumplings all the time. And she cares if you get hurt playing football. And your house is always nice. And even if you don't have a dad, at least it's not like having our dad, who doesn't remember we're there most of the time. I'm tired of being a Griswald. D'you know what I would like more than anything?'

'No,' said Sam.

'I'd like a school uniform,' said Elfrida in a wistful tone. 'I'd like one just like Christabel's, always pressed, with a tie, and a crest on my blazer and everything. And I'd wear it to school every day.'

Sam was amazed. If she had said she wanted a bomb-making kit, or a pet iguana, or a highwayman outfit, he would have believed her . . . but a *school uniform*. 'But I thought – I thought you liked being different.'

'You won't tell anyone, will you?' said Elfrida, suddenly anxious. 'You wouldn't tell *Christabel*, would you?' Sam hastily promised that he would not, and she continued. 'I'd like a more ordinary name, too. Elfrida's a stupid name. Everybody always stares when I tell them.'

'Why *are* you called Elfrida?' asked Sam curiously. 'I never heard of it before.'

'It was Great-Aunt Elfrida's name. Stupid old bat,' she added. 'And now I'm stuck with it! And my middle name's Agnes, after Granny, and that's horrible too. D'you know what I'd like to be called?' Sam shook his head and Elfrida continued dreamily, 'Ann. I think Ann's a nice name. Ann Griswald. That's ordinary, isn't it? Ann Griswald might wear a blazer, mightn't she?'

Sam agreed that she might, although privately he doubted whether anybody bearing the name Griswald was likely to be that ordinary. 'Still,' he added, 'I wouldn't worry about it too much. I think you Griswalds have a lot more fun on the whole. Even if you're not ordinary.' Elfrida looked unconvinced, and he continued, 'It's no fun being ordinary, you know.'

'Why isn't it?' asked Elfrida.

'Well – look at me. My mum's all right, but ever since my dad left she fusses over me, and won't let me do anything, and says she has to look after me all the time, even when I don't want her to. And if I tell her I don't want her to, she makes me feel terrible, but if I let her, then all the other kids laugh at me, and Brandon Bullock, and kids like that, start picking on me.' He swallowed. 'The truth is, it wasn't much fun round here until you lot moved in next door.' He looked away quickly. He had never said it out loud like that before, even to himself. And he had never expected to be confiding in Elfrida Griswald.

'Still, we did move in,' Elfrida argued, 'so now you have the best of everything.'

'That's what you think.' Sam found himself telling her all about what had happened that evening. Elfrida stopped snuffling and listened. 'And the worst of it is,' he concluded, 'Mum says Biter has to go. And I don't know what to do. If we take Biter to the Dogs' Home, I'm sure nobody's going to want him, the way he is, and maybe he'll be put down.' Sam swallowed, hard.

'He musn't go to the Dogs' Home,' said Elfrida firmly. 'He'll just have to come back to us until your mum changes her mind.'

Sam blinked at her. 'But what about *your* mum?'

'Mum won't send Biter to the Dogs' Home. I won't let her.'

'Thanks, Elfrida!' Sam felt so grateful that he wanted to do something for her in return, but he couldn't think what that might be. Then he remembered that she had her own problems. He picked up one of the bones and considered it.

'Hey, this bone's huge!'

'I know,' said Elfrida glumly. 'Mrs Bullock said it looked as if it came off a horse.'

'It would have to be a horse's leg, or something.' Sam considered. 'How could Jake and Spider think you had got hold of a whole leg? I mean what do you Griswalds eat?'

'We don't eat horse's legs, of course we don't. The only thing we eat lots of is dumplings.'

'And another thing, this bone is really old. Look how crumbly it is – and there's no fleshy bits stuck to it.'

'So it couldn't be me,' said Elfrida, looking considerably brighter. 'I've only been vegetarian for a couple of months.'

'And you haven't been living here very long. It's strange though, isn't it, that there should happen to be an old bone like this, just where Jake and I put that weedkiller –'

'Unless Mrs Bullock was lying,' said Elfrida doubtfully.

'But she seemed really cross, like she really had found it there. And she said there were workmen there, too. But it's funny, isn't it? That they should have dug up a bone there, in that very spot.'

'Unless,' said Sam, 'unless that garden is full of bones. Then it wouldn't be funny at all.'

They both looked at each other and shivered. They thought of that huge expanse of lawn, and imagined it covering bone after bone, skeleton after skeleton. It didn't bear thinking about. Why, the Bullocks' garden must be practically a graveyard.

Elfrida leant forward and whispered in a conspiratorial tone, 'Have you ever thought that Mrs Bullock, if she got really, really angry – I mean she looks very strong – and if she had a knife . . .?'

Sam swallowed. He would not put anything past Mrs Bullock. Then again, if she really *was* murdering people, it was hardly likely she would dig up the remains and bring them round to show the Griswalds. Much more likely she would be making sure the Griswalds were among them. He pointed this out to Elfrida.

'She might have shown us,' said Elfrida stubbornly. 'She might want to gloat over her victims and her cleverness in not being caught. Some murderers do that. I saw a programme about them on telly. She might be biding her time, until she can do the same thing to us.'

Sam felt quite cold. Then he said sensibly, 'But that bone looks too big to be human to me. Unless it's

170

somebody's whole leg or something.' He reached out to the carrier bag, and emptied some of the smaller bones onto the floor. Unfortunately, neither Sam nor Elfrida were expert enough to know whether or not they might be human.

'We need to investigate this,' Elfrida said in distinctly sinister tones.

* * *

When Sam returned to the house, his mother was sitting staring into a cup of tea, her lips pursed together in a determined kind of way. 'You were right, Sam,' she announced. But before Sam could feel more than a first rush of relief, or ask whether she meant about Biter, or the Griswalds, or both, she continued, 'I *don't* get out enough. It's quite true. So I've decided that I will go to that talk tomorrow after all.'

'Oh,' said Sam.

'Yes, and you're going with me.'

Sam did his best to change her mind, but she was adamant. And so the following evening, Sam found himself sitting in the library, listening to *Archaeological and Antiquarian Aspects of*

Bellstone. It was every bit as boring as he had feared. A small panel of experts took it in turns to address the small audience on Ancient Britons in Bellstone, what the Romans had done in Bellstone (not even any good battles, Sam noted sadly), animal husbandry in medieval Bellstone and the sewerage system of Victorian Bellstone. Sam yawned, and spent most of his time thinking about Bellstone Rovers.

When they turned the electric light back on after the slide show about medieval ploughs, Sam, blinking up at the panel, recognised Mr Hobson. True, he was not wearing his usual faded tracksuit, but an ancient tweed suit that looked at least thirty years out of date, but there was no mistaking that droopy moustache. He was the speaker who was going on about Ancient British tribes near Bellstone – and the stuff about medieval Bellstone as well. Sam regretted now that he had hardly listened to it.

At the end of the evening, Sam went up to Mr Hobson. 'Hello,' he said shyly. 'I didn't know you were an archaeologist.'

Mr Hobson looked surprised to see him, then he smiled. 'And I didn't know you were interested in local history, Sam. But sadly, Bellstone's past is only a hobby of mine – although a very time-consuming one. I have an antiques business – you've probably noticed it, on the High Street. That's how I first developed my interest in ancient artefacts.'

'Oh right,' said Sam. He knew the antiques shop of

course, but he had never really paid it much attention. He couldn't help finding it strange that someone who knew as much about football as Mr Hobson should want to bother with old stuff.

Mrs Harris, who had followed him over, had a different question. 'Why would somebody like you, Mr Hobson,' she said, 'who knows so much about local history, want to give your time to a football team?'

'Breadth of interest is the key,' Mr Hobson said. 'People focus too much on one thing. Personally, I get exactly the same pleasure watching a well-executed goal as I do from a piece of ancient pottery. And speaking of football, make sure you're there on Saturday, Sam. Mark Dawson is still not fully fit, so we really need you.'

Sam looked at Mrs Harris, who was looking as if she had just swallowed a toad.

'Well,' she began, 'I *had* been thinking about taking him to see the archaeological remains at Lower Titmarsh –'

'Oh, don't do that,' said Mr Hobson cheerfully. 'I'm taking my nephew to see the remains soon. Sam can come with us.'

Mrs Harris was forced to give way. Sam grinned. It seemed talks on local history had their uses after all.

* * *

Despite the fact that he was still on the team, it was the beginning of a difficult time for Sam. For a start, he missed Biter. Sometimes, when he lay in bed at night, he could hear Biter barking from next door (probably because he had Elfrida's cats trapped up a tree again). Feeling as if a solid lump of ice was wedged in his chest, he would hide his head under the pillow to block out the sound. After a while he would hear Mrs Bullock shouting over the fence at Biter to shut up (no pillow could block that out) and threatening to report him to the Council, and all his hatred for Mrs Bullock would well up, more strongly than ever. At times like that he felt almost certain that Mrs Bullock *was* a murderer. He would puzzle away, trying to think of a plan to unmask her.

He was no longer allowed to visit the Griswalds. It would have been difficult to go round there anyway, as Elfrida had told Mrs Griswald she was looking after Biter while Sam was away on holiday (it was the only excuse she could think of to make her mother agree to have the dog). Every morning Mrs Harris would walk Sam to the bus stop herself, and wait until he had got onto the bus. (At least, thought Sam, she no longer insisted on travelling on it with him.) Sometimes Sam would see the Griswalds, hurrying back and forth from school, but he could do little more than wave at them as the bus swept by. At least he still saw Jake and Spider at school.

Of course there was the team. Mark Dawson's ankle was still not right, and Sam was part of the starting line-up for both the next matches. He did not set up any goals, never mind score any, but he knew he was becoming a better player: his tackling was more accurate, and he was getting stronger and faster. He was enjoying practices as well, and he even started going for secret runs in the morning before school to improve his fitness. It helped him to forget how lonely he was feeling. He went down the back lanes and alleyways so that people like Brandon Bullock would not see him.

The Griswalds were not having such a great time either. The Bullocks had lost no time in spreading the news of the bones, and they attracted strange looks and nasty comments wherever they went. 'Vandals – ruffians – young tearaways – hooligans –' and even 'cannibals' were some of the comments that were flying around the town. They kept clear of Mrs Griswald, too – she was rumoured to be a former member of MI6 or the SAS. Only Mr Griswald escaped suspicion. 'Quiet fellow,' the gossips said. 'Works from home. Seems to be some kind of artist.'

Sam himself was curious about Mr Griswald: he could not help remembering seeing him sitting in front of a picture of fluffy bunny rabbits. But whenever he tried to bring the matter up, Jake always changed the subject.

The next Bellstone Rovers game was against Greavesby F.C. Mark Dawson was back on the team, but was not back to full fitness; Sam came on for him at half-time, and managed to kick away a direct shot on goal, almost from the goal-line. Better yet, Mrs Harris had not come to watch – she had an appointment at the hairdresser. All in all, Sam was in a good mood as he sat next to Jake at the end of the game and undid his shin pads.

Elfrida and Spider had both come to watch, but as her

brothers had still not forgiven Elfrida over the matter of the bone, they were standing on opposite sides of the field. Elfrida had Biter with her – although she was careful to keep him on his lead.

'Maybe I'll be able to take Biter for a quick run round the park,' said Sam to Jake, interrupting a reliving of Jake's goal in the second half.

'Yeah – Mum's started complaining about him, by the way. Yesterday, he was chasing Arthur and they got into Dad's studio and destroyed two weeks of work. She's beginning to wonder when you're coming home.'

Sam was so alarmed by this, that he did not think to ask what Mr Griswald's work might be. 'Can't you distract her?' he asked.

'We did our best. We asked if she'd decided how to punish us. You remember I told you she was thinking of an especially evil punishment to serve us right over the bones in Old Bullock's garden? Well, guess what? She's decided. We've got to join Mrs Bullock's Tidy Bellstone Campaign.'

Sam winced in sympathy, his bad temper entirely forgotten. 'That's bad. My mum's always trying to make me join, too. How are you going to get out of it?'

'We're not going to try and get out of it.' And, as Sam stared, he added, 'Don't you see? We're going to join that campaign, and destroy it from within. I mean: sabotage!' Jake's eyes were gleaming, with an evil glitter that meant he was full of plans. While Sam listened, he went waffling on about Lenin, and forming 'cells' and 'infiltrating from below' and 'bringing the whole thing down'. Sam did not understand him exactly, but he had the strong feeling that Lenin could have taken lessons from the Griswalds, when it came to causing mayhem.

Jake saw he was confused, and reverted to simpler language. 'Don't you see? Mum thinks she's punishing *us*, but it was us who put the whole idea into her head! We kept going on about how it was our worst nightmare, when we knew she could overhear us. But if we join the Tidy Bellstone Campaign, there are a million ways to get back at Big Nose Bullock. And you can join too. Even your mum would let you join something like that. I mean, what could possibly happen to you? Unless you got attacked by a sweet wrapper or something. Of course, she won't know we've joined the TBC too.'

'She'll be suspicious. I've always said I'd rather die than join that stupid campaign.'

'You'll just have to convince her you've had a change of heart. That you've seen the error of your ways.'

Sam was torn. It would be great to do something other than being at home, staring at the walls and listening to his mum go on and on about him looking peaky, and how she wanted him to give up football and take up archaeology. And it would be great to do something with the Griswalds. On the other hand, he could not escape the sneaking suspicion that the Griswalds, combined with the Tidy Bellstone Campaign, almost certainly spelt disaster.

'I'm going to join too.' Elfrida had appeared, with Biter,

who had flung himself at Sam.

'That's what you think,' said Jake. 'You'd just ruin everything. Get lost!'

Elfrida went red. 'I hate you! I don't want to do anything with you either!'

'That's good then – isn't it?'

Elfrida stalked off in high dudgeon. Biter remained with Sam, barking, worrying at his shin pads, and demanding that sticks be thrown for him. It took Sam and Jake a while to notice that a large and familiar four-wheel-drive vehicle had pulled up at the edge of the Meadows. A moment later, Mrs Bullock and her children emerged. It was only when Mrs Bullock marched off across the grass, ploughing her way through the remaining team members and spectators like a ship surging through the sea, that Jake suddenly said, 'Hey – what's *she* doing here?'

'Oh, blimey,' said Sam, watching as she went up to Mr Hobson. 'I expect she's trying to get us thrown off the Meadows. She's been trying to get sport banned from here for ages.' And certainly, Mrs Bullock was very deep in conversation with Mr Hobson about *something*. 'Maybe you're right,' Sam added. 'Maybe we *should* try sabotage.'

'Of course I'm right,' said Jake. 'Come on. Let's try and overhear.'

But Sam had noticed something else. A small group of people, including Brandon and Christabel Bullock, had gathered under some trees. In the centre of their circle stood Elfrida. Something in the way Elfrida was standing made her look both defiant and desperate.

Obviously Sam was not the only person to think so. Even as he watched, Spider was racing over to join her.

'Hey,' Sam nudged Jake. 'I know you're mad at her, but don't you think –'

Jake needed no persuasion. He took one look, and was off across the grass like a jet-propelled missile. 'Hey!' he yelled, skidding to a halt in front of Brandon. 'What are you doing to my sister?'

Sam followed more slowly, being careful to keep a tight hold of Biter. He could see now that several of Brandon and Christabel's friends were present, including Danny Myers.

Brandon was sneering. 'I'm not doing anything to your sister.'

'Yeah, we're just having a chat with her, aren't we Brandon, which is more than you can be bothered to do,' put in Christabel. 'Poor little girl.'

There was a low snarling noise. Nobody was sure if it came from Elfrida or Biter.

'I suppose I'd better tell you, before you start bullying her again,' Brandon said. 'Poor little girl, we see her walking to school each day, all by herself, wearing her funny clothes –'

Jake broke in. '*What's going on?*'

'Oh, we were telling Elfrida here about how our mum has just been round to visit yours. She was delivering a letter from her solicitor. It's about our very valuable Grecian urn, worth a thousand pounds *at least*, which got broken when *somebody* pushed it into our pond. My mum is demanding full compensation. And I can't think why – but somehow, for some reason, she thinks you Griswalds are responsible.'

'Your mum wasn't too pleased when she heard,' put in Christabel, with an amused little laugh.

Jake glanced at Elfrida who was looking white and tense. The Griswalds had all pretty much forgotten about the Grecian urn, and they had assumed that Mrs Bullock had done the same. If they had thought anything about it, they had assumed it was part of the bargain by which Spider had agreed to rescue her knickers. It was a very mean trick to drag up the whole thing now.

Jake pointed all this out, forcefully. There was tide of

laughter – but not at the Griswalds' expense. Brandon's friends had not heard about the knickers episode before, and they thought it extremely funny.

'Hey, Brand, what's this then – who put them up a tree – why didn't you tell us?'

'Would I have loved to see that –'

Brandon flushed angrily. 'It was just a stupid joke. It wasn't even funny.'

'Yeah right,' Jake said. 'I'll tell you what was funny, watching all you Bullocks trying to get up that tree and falling down again. Only you didn't even try, did you Brandon? You had to get Spider to do it for you.'

'Shut up!' Brandon glanced uneasily around the circle of faces, suddenly aware that the mood was turning against him.

Danny said, 'Climbing that tree's pretty amazing. I mean, it's higher than the house. Hey, Spider, do you go rock-climbing ever?'

Brandon sneered triumphantly. 'You're not expecting him to *answer* that, are you?'

Danny looked puzzled: he did not go to Bellstone High, and had never met Spider before.

Christabel said, 'And another thing. We *know* about your dad.'

'What d'you mean, you know about him?' demanded Jake.

'I mean we *know*.' Christabel and Brandon exchanged malicious looks. 'He makes *greetings cards*. That's his job.'

She held one up. It showed two fluffy kittens, wearing pink and yellow bows. 'Listen:

May All Your Hopes And Dreams Come True
On This Very Special Day For You
You Are Always Close To My Heart –'

'Yeah, well, he doesn't write what's inside,' Jake interrupted.

They all stared at him. 'So is it true?' asked Danny Myers in a tone of disbelief. 'That's what your dad does? He paints pictures of kittens?'

'And teddy bears,' put in Christabel. 'And hedgehogs –'

'What's wrong with that?' demanded Elfrida bullishly.

Jake had gone very red. For the first time since Sam had known him, he seemed uncertain. He hesitated, as if he was thinking exactly what to say, then burst out, 'Yeah, well, he only does that since he got let out of prison, and promised Mum to go straight. Before that he was a top criminal!'

'A criminal? What kind of criminal?'

'He used to forge things – bank notes, mainly. He had a gang.' He stared round their disbelieving faces. 'They were famous in East London!'

There was a pause, while everyone who wasn't a Griswald exchanged looks. Only Sam stared hard at his feet. 'Yeah – right,' said Danny contemptuously. 'So he was a master criminal. And now he paints kittens. D'you really expect us to believe that?'

'It's not easy painting kittens,' said Elfrida indignantly. 'I 'spect it's just as hard as bank notes.'

'Honestly.' Christabel sounded amused. 'What a family! A dad who draws kittens – a mum who shouts her head off – a girl who only gets on with animals – one brother living in a fantasy world – and another who can't even speak!'

Before anybody else could say anything, Danny said, 'What d'you mean, can't speak?'

'Oh, didn't you know?' She pointed at Spider. 'He never says a word. We don't know if he's actually dumb, or mentally subnormal. But he's definitely not all there. My mother says he ought to be at a special school – or even in an institution.'

Her words fizzled away into silence. Somehow, everybody knew that this time the Bullocks had gone too far. The silence had a scary feel to it, as if something was about to happen. Spider's face was completely blank, it might as well have been a mask. It was impossible to tell what he was thinking. But his siblings were white with fury. Jake's eyes and hair looked as if they were sparking electricity, he was so angry.

Sam looked from one side to the other. He knew he needed to do something, before everything got out of hand.

But before he could think what this might be, Elfrida launched herself at Christabel. She was yelling and shouting, but she was also kicking and pummelling so hard, it was only possible to make out the odd word of what she said. But the message was clear enough.

'You – pigs – hate – beast – kill you!'

Biter leapt after her, and it was all Sam could do to restrain him. Next moment, Jake had gone for Brandon, and they were both on the ground, kicking and punching.

'Stop!' yelled Sam. He looked desperately at Spider, who was about to enter the battle on his siblings' side. 'No, don't! Stop them!'

Already, heads were turning. A growing murmur was coming from nearby parents. Clearly, if they did not get things under control soon, there would be all manner of consequences. Sam swallowed, thinking what these would be: they might all be banned from the Meadows for life; the fight would be reported to the school; and Jake and Sam would be kicked off the team. Worse than all that, somebody might be seriously hurt, and while that somebody might be the Bullocks, then again, it might not.

To his relief, Spider was trying to separate Elfrida and Christabel. Sam grabbed Jake with one hand (he held Biter's leash with the other) and tried to haul him away from Brandon. It would have been hopeless, but help came from an unexpected quarter. Danny stuck out a foot just as Brandon was going after Jake, and sent Brandon flying; then he grabbed Elfrida by the scruff of the neck, and Spider grabbed Christabel, and they pulled them apart as if they were two warring cats.

'Thanks!' Sam gasped. But at that moment Biter managed to pull himself free. He hurled himself towards the Bullocks with a rising crescendo of barks. Brandon and Christabel yelled and tore off to their mother. Sam threw himself forward at full stretch and just managed to grab the end of Biter's lead. He would have liked to have let Biter loose on the Bullocks, but he knew for Biter's own good it would be best if he did not.

Danny Myers helped him up. 'They shouldn't have said – you know,' he said gruffly, looking at Spider with an apologetic sort of look. Spider grinned slightly in acknowledgment. Danny disappeared, and the various people across the Meadows who had been staring at them with disapproval, and thinking about going to intervene, returned to their own business. Luckily, Mr Hobson and Mrs Bullock were too deep in conversation to have noticed what was going on.

It seemed a good idea to remove themselves before

anything else happened. They all walked back to Thistle Lane together. For the time being, Sam did not care whether he obeyed his mother's orders or not; and Jake and Spider had forgotten their grievance against Elfrida. She, on the other hand, had not forgotten her grievance against them.

'I think you should say sorry!'

'What!' Jake glowered at her. 'You get us into all kinds of trouble, with your horrible, bone-gnawing ways, then we have to pile in to rescue you, and now that we're nice enough to actually think about forgiving you – you expect us to say sorry!'

'There was no way I had anything to do with those bones! Tell them, Sam.'

'She's right,' said Sam. 'That bone was ancient. And it was too big to come off a chicken.'

'Hmm! Probably Old Big Nose gnawed it herself. All right, Elf, I take it back.'

It was a while before Jake could be persuaded to reword this in a way that Elfrida would accept. But when peace was made at last, Jake added, 'It's very strange – all these bones. Makes you wonder what the Bullocks are up to. Probably burying people in the back garden!'

Sam shivered, and managed to turn the conversation back to how they were going to infiltrate the Tidy Bellstone Campaign.

As he said goodbye to the Griswalds and Biter, and turned in at his own gate, Sam realised something was puzzling him, besides the matter of Mrs Bullock's bone. He would never have thought Jake Griswald would have made up a lie like that about his father. Of course, it must be embarrassing to have a dad who painted birthday cards for a living, especially soppy ones of kittens and bunny rabbits, and even more especially if you were a Griswald. But imagine telling everybody he was a *master criminal*! As if anybody would believe that!

Sam smiled rather pityingly. Still, it was nice to know that even Jake Griswald had his weaknesses. Sam had never noticed any before, and it made Jake seem more human, somehow. So, if he wanted to spin tall tales about his unremarkable father – well, Sam wasn't going to say anything.

As he went into the house, he put the matter out of his mind, and began wondering how he was to convince his mother of his sudden, new-found interest in tidiness.

Chapter Eleven
The Griswalds Tidy Up

Mrs Griswald was absolutely furious about the Grecian urn.

'You kids have really gone too far this time. Breaking into her property! Vandalising her property! I tell you, I'm so angry, I'm going to tell your dad, that's what – and we'll see what he has to say!'

Her offspring were not concerned. Everybody knew Mr Griswald was too gentle to hurt a fly – and, unlike the rest of the family, never, ever lost his temper. Besides, he was probably too absorbed in his latest picture (of five Easter bunnies sitting in a basket) to notice anything Mrs Griswald had to say.

'And as for the money! A thousand pounds she says that urn is worth! We don't have a thousand pounds. We don't have a spare fiver, come to that! All the money we've had to spend on the move, and on this house – I'll tell you something, at this rate, I'm not sure if we shall be able to stay in Bellstone. I'm not sure we can afford it. And I'm not sure I want to stay. You haven't exactly made us popular. I'm sick of getting dirty looks in the street.'

This was more worrying. They were getting plenty of dirty looks on the street too, but they still liked Bellstone and wanted to stay there. They exchanged anxious glances.

'Maybe we should try to make people like us?' Jake suggested doubtfully after their mother had stormed upstairs.

'That's all very well,' said Elfrida. 'But how? I mean, hardly anyone ever does. I don't see how we can make them.'

It was a good point. The Griswalds were not used to seeking popularity. They had no idea where to start.

* * *

They had still not found a solution by the time of the next meeting of the Tidy Bellstone Campaign. The Griswalds met Sam secretly in a back lane, so Mrs Harris should not see them, and as they walked to the meeting, Jake and Elfrida told Sam what Mrs Griswald had said about the possibility of the Griswalds leaving Bellstone. Sam was immediately worried. The Griswalds were the only friends he had; and besides, what would happen to Biter?

'Why would you have more money if you moved away?' he asked.

'Well, I suppose Old Big Nose wouldn't be there to send us nasty letters demanding a thousand pounds –'

'No,' said Sam, 'but somebody else would. Somebody else whose property you'd destroyed.'

'But I'm not sure it's the money. I think it's more this feeling Mum has, that everybody in Bellstone knows who we are and thinks we're the Forces of Darkness.'

'Young hooligans,' agreed Sam, quoting remarks he had heard in shops and the library. 'Delinquents in the making. Tearaways. Off their heads –'

'All right,' said Jake. 'Anyway, you see the problem.'

'*I* think,' said Elfrida, 'if people here liked us, then Mum wouldn't want to leave.'

Sam sighed. He knew that Bellstone's far from flattering view of the Griswalds would not be easy to change. At least, he suggested, getting involved with the Tidy Bellstone Campaign might help. It might make the Griswalds look more public-spirited.

Jake disagreed. 'The whole point is we're going to *sabotage* the TBC. I don't think that's going to make us look public-spirited.'

Sam frowned slightly. 'Maybe we shouldn't do it then. I mean, it's just not worth it, not just to upset Mrs Bullock.'

'What? You must be joking!' Jake stopped short and stared at Sam. His eyes were sparkling with anger and his voice was passionate as he demanded, 'Don't you see? It's not just about getting at Old Big Nose. It's about stopping *her* getting at us, squashing us up like an old Coke can somebody dropped on the street. She thinks kids should be all neat and tidy and well behaved, like her rows of marigolds in the park. And we're not. We're the blot on the landscape as far as she's concerned. She'd like to get rid of our old house and our apple trees and she'd like to get rid of us too. She doesn't like our games or our pets or our jokes or our noise – and she doesn't like *us*. She wants all kids to be the same – doing their tests at school, or sitting at home in front of the TV.'

'Exactly!' said Elfrida, nodding vigorously.

Sam said no more, and they soon reached the town hall, which was where the Tidy Bellstone Campaign met. Lots of well-scrubbed children with keen, eager faces were filing in; Sam and the Griswalds, in their old jeans and jumpers, attracted some rather disdainful glances as they went past.

They had intended to slip into the back of the meeting to avoid any chance of Mrs Bullock spotting them and throwing them out. But she saw them immediately and came charging down the central aisle like an enraged bull.

'What are you lot doing here?' she demanded.

'We are here to work for a better, brighter Bellstone,' said Jake, piously. 'Also,' he added, 'our mum made us.'

It was a wise admission. Mrs Bullock had been looking extremely suspicious, but now she snorted in a self-satisfied manner. 'Hah! Punishing you, is she? Well, just you make sure you behave.' Then she went charging off back to the platform. The four of them grinned at each other, and Jake gave a small thumbs-up.

Sam looked around with interest, curious to see who actually chose to spend their weekends being bossed around by Mrs Bullock. He recognised several people from school: Anthea Roberts, Elaine Bennett, Peter Philpotts and Iain Dawson. They were the kind of kids who did community service in their spare time – when they weren't busy with Girl Guides, or choir practice, or taking their next batch of piano exams. Or just bossing other people around (Elaine Bennett was head girl). They had a smug, self-righteous air about them – even their jeans were pressed, and their trainer laces neatly tied. The others, he reckoned, were either older kids who needed something to put on their university application forms – or younger kids whose parents wanted to get them out of the house.

There was a scattering of adults too: Mrs Pierce, the deputy head teacher; Mrs Appleby, who was on the Council and was Mrs Bullock's best friend; the vicar; and (much to Sam's surprise) Mr Hobson.

The meeting began with a greeting from Mrs Bullock, then moved on swiftly to the TBC song.

'Tidy, tidy, tidy!
Bellstone will be tidy!
Clean and bright and nice for everyone!
We will keep it tidy!
Bright and clean and sparkly!
That is why we sing this happy song!'

Not everyone, Sam was pleased to see, joined in. Mrs Pierce looked embarrassed, and Mr Hobson just fiddled with his moustache. Jake, on the other hand, flung himself into it with gusto. This was unexpected, until Sam realised that Jake had a rather unusual gift. He had a strong and musical voice, but he was also able to sing totally out of tune. This was very off-putting for everyone else. The people nearby started singing out of tune too, then they stopped singing altogether, and the song petered out in a horrible, discordant wailing. Only Jake was left singing strongly.

'That is why we sing this batty song!' he concluded cheerfully, winking at Sam. Anthea Roberts, the leader of the school orchestra, and who had written the song specially, turned round and scowled at him.

Sam was paying more attention to Spider. He listened

hard, trying to work out if Spider was actually singing. But although Spider's lips were moving they made, so far as Sam could tell, no sound at all.

'Dear, dear,' observed Mrs Bullock, looking round the hall in a menacing manner. 'I see we can all do with some practice. But now, to business! As you know, this campaign has only one aim: to make Bellstone the acknowledged Tidiest Town in England. Last year we narrowly missed the title, but this year we will not be defeated!'

She continued like this for quite a while, and soon Sam found he was only catching one phrase in three: '. . . need to prevent litterbugs . . . chewing-gum to be eradicated . . . gardens weeded regularly . . . flowers of uniform height . . . trees chopped back . . . dogs and children banned from public places . . . no ball games . . . graffiti eliminated once and for all . . .'

Jake nudged Sam. 'We did eliminate some graffiti once and for all,' he whispered, 'when we burnt down the bus shelter. Shall I point that out?'

Sam snorted and shook his head.

Mrs Bullock had finished the first part of her speech and started listing the tasks for the day, when someone in the audience raised their hand and, when Mrs Bullock ignored it, actually stood up.

Mrs Bullock glared. 'Excuse me, Mr –'

'Hobson.'

'Mr Hobson, what seems to be the trouble?'

'I wanted to ask a question.'

'*You wanted to ask a question!*' Mrs Bullock's eyebrows shot right up into her hair. Everyone else turned to stare in amazement at Mr Hobson. He, however, did not look intimidated.

'Well, not so much ask a question as make a point. Which is, that admirable though all this tidiness is, there are other ways in which we can work to improve our wonderful town. As you know I am President of the Bellstone Local History and Antiquarian Society, as well as an acknowledged expert on antique stonemasonry, and I think it would be very valuable if we could do some work to restore some of the neglected remains of early eighteenth-century Bellstone, as they are described in my book: *Bellstone, A Town with a Past*. There is the matter of the old coachman's lodge, which could be restored –'

Mrs Bullock barged in. 'That coachman's lodge, as you call it – filthy old shack, *I* would say – is a complete eyesore. I've already suggested to the Council that it be demolished.'

'Demolished! It's over two hundred years old!'

'Then high time it was replaced with something more modern. Did you have any other points you wished to raise?'

Mr Hobson glared at her, and pressed on.

'Yes, the matter of Bellstone Public Park. Valuable archaeological remains are thought to exist beneath the bowling green. Possibly relating to the Ancient British Bellebriggan tribe. My own research suggests –'

Mrs Bullock had gone very red. 'Mr Hobson!' she barked. 'I couldn't care less about any archaeological remains. And digging up the park would hardly make the place look tidy, would it?'

'Well, not in the short term, no –'

'Exactly! Tidiness is our aim, Mr Hobson. Tidiness, tidiness, tidiness! Now, we need to get started on our tasks for the day. Elaine, I want you and your team to go on litter patrol –'

Mrs Bullock droned on, dividing everybody into groups, and giving them different jobs to do – picking up crisp packets, weeding flowerbeds, painting the park railings – and taking no more notice of Mr Hobson. Eventually, he got up and left. Mrs Bullock took no notice of the Griswalds or Sam either, and for a time it seemed she had forgotten them. Then she assigned Elfrida to a group that was going to scrape bits of old chewing-gum off the pavements. Elfrida protested but was overruled.

'You are too small to work with your brothers,' said Mrs Griswald. And she turned to them with a look they did not much like. 'Yes, I have a lovely job for you!' Mrs Bullock's voice was sugary now, almost honeyed (or as honeyed as Mrs Bullock's voice was ever likely to get). 'You're really going to enjoy it. I want you to go with Iain and clear out all the mess that's blocking the upper river. Iain will tell you what to do. The water is quite low at the moment, so it won't be dangerous. Just a little wet. And perhaps smelly. But that won't bother you, will it?' She laughed as she said it: it was probably meant to be a tinkly laugh, but it sounded like an electric drill. 'Now, everyone, please be back here by four o'clock sharp. The mayor is coming to hear about our work, and the *Bellstone Gazette* will be taking photographs.'

'Typical,' Sam told Jake, when they had said goodbye to a bad-tempered Elfrida and were trudging after Iain Dawson towards the river. 'Everyone else gets weeding or picking up sweet wrappers, but we have to dredge the river. We'll get filthy!'

'I'd rather dredge stuff out of the river than pick up sweet wrappers. And this is about sabotage – remember?'

'Huh,' said Sam. He did not see how Jake proposed to sabotage a river. He thought it more likely that *it* would sabotage *them*. This was probably why Mrs Bullock had given them the job in the first place – because they could not ruin it. And Jake could say what he liked, but he would not have to listen to Mrs Harris carrying on about how he might have drowned and what had he done to his clothes.

They joined the river near Thistle Lane, but then they had to walk much further upstream, through Bellstone Meadows, until they reached a place where two channels of water joined together. Or rather they were meant to join together, but one of them was clogged with all kinds of rubbish so that the water did not rush into the river, but instead formed a pool or trickled away at the sides. Not surprisingly, it had turned the ground all around into what looked and smelled more like a swamp than the field it was supposed to be. Under the grey autumn sky, it was not an appealing sight.

'Aren't people disgusting, dumping all this?' said Sam, eyeing the mound of rubbish.

'Yeah,' Jake agreed. 'I mean, it looks like good stuff.'

Sam sighed. It was at moments like this he knew he would never understand the Griswalds. A rusty old bike-frame, two car tyres, a supermarket trolley and an old oil drum, among other things, were not Sam's idea of 'good stuff'. And dragging them out of the river was going to be a nightmare. Mrs Bullock really had been incredibly mean.

'We'd need a bulldozer to clear this lot,' said Sam glumly.

'Nonsense, Sam,' said Iain Dawson, overhearing. 'A little hard work, a little elbow grease, is all that's required. Although I'm rather surprised you boys haven't worn waders. You're going to get wet.'

Iain Dawson did not seem a natural TBC sort of person. He was Mark Dawson's older brother, and until recently he had been most famous at school for throwing up during biology. But rumour had it that he was now going out with Elaine Bennett, and no doubt this had had a bad effect on his character.

Jake did not care about this. Nor did he care that Iain Dawson was several years older than him. 'Now listen,' he snarled. 'Unless you want to go down there in person, and show us how to do it, you can just shut up. Otherwise *your* feet might be getting a bit on the damp side too.'

Iain started to protest. Although he was older than they were, there was only one of him and three of them. Besides, like everybody else at school he had heard enough about the Griswalds to treat them with respect. He shut up.

'Right,' said Jake. 'Let's get cracking.'

They lowered themselves into the river.

The first few moments were absolutely horrible. Cold water seeped through their shoes and around their ankles; clammy mud squelched beneath their feet and oozed slowly up beneath their jeans. But after those moments had passed, there was something wonderful about getting so gloriously, utterly dirty. After all, once you were that wet, and that muddy, there was simply nothing to worry about any more. Sam had not been allowed to get so filthy for years – if ever. By the time he had shifted just two branches and an old pram from the heap of rubbish, he was streaked with mud to his eyebrows, drenched with river water, and had a huge piece of weed draped from one shoulder. He was also thoroughly enjoying himself.

There were some minor irritants, it was true. In particular, Iain Dawson, standing on the bank in his immaculate jeans and leather jacket, squawking out orders, was getting on everybody's nerves. So nobody (other than Iain) was very sorry when Jake nudged him with one of the rescued supermarket trolleys, accidentally-on-purpose, sending him with a tremendous splat into the very deepest part of the mud. Iain tried to scramble back up the bank, but his shoes would not grip, and he kept sliding back in. Jake and Sam yelled encouragement – when they weren't laughing – and Spider came and gave Iain a helpful boost, which resulted in Iain losing his balance altogether, and belly-flopping into the water. When he picked himself up, dripping with mud, he was far from happy, and his mood was not improved when Jake pointed out that all he needed was a positive attitude.

'Yeah – and a wet-suit,' shouted Sam, rather pleased with his own wit.

Iain glared. When he finally climbed out he announced that he was wet through and was going home to change.

'*We've* been wet through for ages,' Jake pointed out, but Iain paid no attention.

As soon as he had left, the sun broke out from behind the clouds and shone down with unexpected strength. The boys no longer felt cold and clammy, but warm and cheerful. They set to work with a will. Soon the rubbish heap on the bank was steadily rising.

The Griswalds had the idea of setting up a pulley system. Spider went clambering up a large willow tree, looped some ropes over its biggest branches (Spider carried rope everywhere), attached a hook (he carried hooks too) and soon they had the perfect way of winching up the larger items and getting them over to the bank. At least, they would have done, had Jake not pointed out that they also had the perfect way of swinging out across river, at least once they had attached a sturdy branch to the rope.

For a time they took it in turns to swoop out in a great arc over the water, then back to a feet-tingling landing on solid ground. Of course it was Jake who suggested that they all swing out at once. For a few dazzling moments, as they swooped giddyingly over the muddy water, it seemed like a great idea; then, all of a sudden, it did not. There was a rending, splitting noise; Sam and Jake yelled; and next moment they were all sprawling in the muddy water. Once they had picked themselves up and wiped themselves off they realised that they had had enough swinging. It was time to get back to work.

'The water's getting deeper,' said Jake, after a bit. It was true. They had removed enough rubbish to let some of the water flow through, and it was now well up above their knees.

'Whoever owns this field,' said Sam, 'should pay us for draining it for them.'

Half an hour later, the water had risen even higher, and they had had enough. They stood on the bank and surveyed the results of their salvage operation. Rubber tyres, a pram, some dustbin lids, umbrellas with most of the cloth missing, old paint tins, an empty TV set, somebody's old go-cart, saucepans with holes in, old crates and a supermarket trolley. Most of these things were so battered and mud-covered as to be almost unrecognisable.

'What shall we do with it?' Jake asked.

'Leave it here, I suppose,' said Sam.

Spider frowned and shook his head. Jake said, 'You must be kidding! Some of this stuff could be useful.'

Sam was about to say that if the Griswalds could tell him a use for a bunch of old dustbin lids, he'd carry the whole lot back himself: but then he thought better of it. Knowing the Griswalds, they probably could. So he said, 'We can't carry it all.'

Spider looked at the pram. Jake, understanding, said, 'We'll load up the pram and the go-cart with as much as we can, and then come back for everything else later.'

Sam agreed, and they were soon ready to go, Sam and Spider with the go-cart, and Jake with the pram. All three were in a very good mood by this time; tired, but feeling proud of a job well done. All three had totally forgotten that their plan had been to sabotage the tidiness effort, rather than to assist it.

It so happened that the street back into Bellstone was long and straight. It was a quiet street, too, with few cars until it reached the centre of the town, and with a gentle downwards slope.

Nobody afterwards could remember whose idea it had been. But at some point somebody spoke the fateful words: *Why don't we have a race?* And next moment they were all sitting aboard their piles of junk, and careering down the road.

Nobody who was on the scene that fateful day in Bellstone would ever forget it.

Helter-skelter, the chariots of destruction swept into town, scattering pieces of junk as they went, their three riders perched precariously on top. All three were so plastered with mud as to be completely unrecognisable, as if they were each some terrible monster or prehistoric beast that had arisen from the mire. And all three were almost totally out of control of their vehicles.

Jake had the advantage in this respect. At least his pram went more or less straight. Spider and Sam's go-cart lurched drunkenly from side to side, so that every few minutes they would be forced to leap off, in order to avoid some disastrous collision. Sometimes they leapt just that tiny bit too late. Then they would pick themselves up, collect the go-cart and push it back to the centre of the road, and race behind it until it had built up speed, before leaping aboard again. And all the time they were yelling at each other (or rather Sam and Jake were) in encouragement and defiance.

Clang! Two of the salvaged saucepans went clattering down the road. *Yowl!* Somebody's cat fled for its life. *Crunch!* An unattended skateboard ended up tangled around the front of the go-cart. *Crash!* Somebody's dustbin, sitting by the side of the street, went rattling and rolling down the hill, spreading its contents as it went.

Sam was no longer aware of the destruction all around him. All he was aware of was the blood singing in his veins, the wind racing past his cheeks, and the cold metal in his hands, as he and Spider careered down the street in hot pursuit of Jake. It was one of the most glorious moments of his life.

With Jake's vehicle being easier to steer, he soon got ahead. So it was he who first realised the magnitude of the disaster that was looming. As he sped into the home-straight he saw a small clutch of people gathered next to the town hall. They were all watching the mayor of Bellstone, who was climbing out of his Jaguar. A photographer from the local paper was taking pictures.

There was nothing Jake could do. Spider and Sam, just seconds behind, were equally helpless, although both tried, desperately, to swerve.

Crunch!

Jake's pram hit the Jaguar, with a terrible rending of

metal. The go-cart hit the kerb at speed, and went toppling. Agile as a cat, Spider leapt from his vehicle and somersaulted neatly onto the pavement. He would have been fine had the photographer from the *Bellstone Gazette*, in his eagerness to get photos of Jake, not cannoned straight into him, sending him crashing into a lamppost. As Spider's arm made contact with it, there was a sickening crunch. But Sam met the worst fate of all. Sam hurtled straight into Mrs Bullock.

There was no doubt about it. The Griswalds and Sam between them had just sabotaged Mrs Bullock's Tidy Bellstone Campaign more effectively than they could ever have imagined.

Chapter Twelve
Suspicions

The crash outside the town hall was an absolute sensation in Bellstone. 'I would never have thought it – not even of those kids,' the town gossips said to each other. 'As for that Sam Harris – such a quiet lad I always thought he was. Whatever's happened to him?'

Even those people who had not been anywhere near the town hall at the time had a good idea of what happened from the photos in the *Bellstone Gazette*. The photographer, despite his collision with Spider, had managed to get some wonderful shots. The one of Jake perched atop the pram, as it ploughed into the side of the Jaguar, was particularly striking. It appeared on the front page, under the headline, *Crazy Kids Cause Mayhem in Bid for Tidiness*.

Jake liked the photo so much he hung it on the wall.

One of the results of all this was that the Griswalds – and even Sam – became celebrities for a while. Of course, the Griswalds always attracted a fair amount of attention, but they were not used to being asked for autographs – as now happened at school. The rumours of buried bodies at the end of the garden were all forgotten as everybody crowded round Sam and the Griswalds and asked to know exactly how it had felt, slamming into the mayor's car like that. Melissa James, who was the best-looking girl in the school, asked to sign the plaster cast around Spider's broken arm; and several members of the under-twelves approached Jake and Sam to say how much they wished they were on the team.

On the other hand, most of the adults in Bellstone agreed with Mr Sturgeon that the whole thing had been 'a further example of flagrant recklessness by those hooligans'. And although the police had announced that they were not going to press charges, this did not alter the fact that the two Griswalds and Sam were in terrible trouble at home.

Mrs Harris had hysterics when the policeman brought Sam to her front door, dripping with mud and covered in grazes. Later, she told him it was the worst day of her entire life. Unfortunately, although she heaped plenty of blame on Sam himself, the main people she held responsible were the Griswalds. 'You were a gentle, loving boy until *those children* got at you!' she shrieked. And she immediately forbade him from playing football for the Bellstone Rovers. 'I will not let you play in a team of which any of those children are members,' she announced. 'My nerves will not stand it. Either you find yourself a nice, peaceful hobby, or you stay home.' Nothing Sam could say would make her change her mind. Sam was inclined to think it had turned into the worst day of his life, too.

Mrs Griswald thought up a particularly nasty punishment for Spider and Jake. She made them go and visit Mrs Bullock in hospital, where she was being treated for a broken ankle, to apologise in person. Or rather, Jake apologised, while Spider handed over the bunch of flowers and box of chocolates he had been forced to buy with his own money. ('If only we'd saved some of that weedkiller,' Jake said regretfully afterwards, 'we could have made sure they were the last chocolates she ever ate.') Mrs Bullock was not grateful, and wasted no time in expelling them from the Tidy Bellstone Campaign for ever.

'I thought she was actually going to attack us at one point,' Jake told Sam. 'Good thing she had that broken ankle. She couldn't get out of bed. By the way, she's booted you out, too.'

In fact, Mrs Bullock had good reason to be angry. The incident had just about wrecked her Tidy Bellstone Campaign. Although most people blamed the Griswalds for what had happened, plenty of them held Mrs Bullock responsible too, for letting kids like the Griswalds loose on the town. These included the mayor, who was very unhappy about the dent Jake had made in his Jaguar, and who sent Mrs Bullock a nasty letter talking about 'inadequate supervision'. He also sent a copy of it to the *Bellstone Gazette*, whose photographer had been very shaken up by his collision with Spider.

Tidiness is not the be all and end all, the *Gazette's* editorial commented. *Whether or not Bellstone is chosen Tidiest Town in England is unimportant, compared to the old-fashioned virtues of courtesy, good citizenship and respect for other people's property.*

Mrs Bullock felt under pressure. Unlike the Griswalds, she was not used to being unpopular on such a scale. She stayed in the hospital longer than she really needed to, having an ingrowing toenail removed. When she came out it was to find that membership of the Tidy Bellstone Campaign had dwindled: parents rang up to say that their children were too busy with exams (even though it was not the exam season). Things were not looking good for Bellstone's bid to become the Tidiest Town in England, and Mrs Bullock and her children had no doubt who was to blame.

They blamed the Griswalds.

* * *

A couple of weeks later, Sam woke up early. As usual, his first feeling was that he missed Biter. In all honesty, most of the things Biter did in the morning were not so great: sitting on Sam's stomach and breathing heavily into his face, his bad breath much in evidence; or waking the whole house with savage barking, because he had glimpsed one of Elfrida's cats out of the window; or scattering unidentified bits all over the carpet because he had chewed up Sam's slippers, or his homework, or his new football socks, in the night. 'But I do miss him,' thought Sam stubbornly. He scowled around the room, which no longer smelled of dog but of the peaches-and-blossom air freshener his mother used, and which Sam hated. Then his eye fell on his Bellstone Rovers kit, sitting uselessly on a shelf, and he felt even worse.

The whole thing reminded him of the weeks after his father had left. He had found himself sniffing for the smell of bacon sandwiches on Sunday mornings, or listening for the sound of the sports reports on the radio. But there had been nothing: just dull emptiness. Mr Harris lived in London now and Sam virtually never saw him.

Sam shook this thought away, then determinedly pushed back the covers. In the last match for Bellstone Rovers, he had decided he was still not fast enough whenever he was running forwards up the wing. Well, if by chance he did ever play for a football team again, he could at least do something about that.

As he dressed in his running clothes he noticed they were a lot looser than they had been. His legs looked more muscular too. And he remembered what the doctor had said, when Mrs Harris had rushed him there after the crash in front of the town hall, convinced (despite Sam's protests) that he must be bleeding to death inside from some terrible internal injury. 'There's absolutely nothing wrong with him,' said the doctor wearily (she knew Mrs Harris well). 'In fact – he's looking more fit and healthy than I've ever seen him.' Mrs Harris had been furious about this, but Sam, contemplating himself with some surprise in the mirror on the landing, was inclined to think she had been right.

He managed to creep out of the house without waking Mrs Harris. She would not have liked Sam to go running before breakfast. For her, the early mornings were not full of dew and bird song, but mad dogs and axe murderers and speeding cars and child molesters. It did not make any difference that all these things (with the exception of Biter, who was mad enough) were rarely found in Bellstone.

Outside, there was a chill in the air. His breath rose up in clouds as he jogged down Thistle Lane. Then he spotted Biter, snuffling around in the Griswalds' garden. Quickly, Sam opened the gate.

'Good boy!' whispered Sam, as Biter came out to join him.

Feeling a great deal more cheerful now that he had a companion, Sam set out. Pursued by Biter he ran through back ways, behind high hedges, down alleys and over stiles, keeping out of the way of any nosy neighbours (in particular Bullocks) who might report his presence to his mother. For a while he ran beside the river, which was covered in a sheen of silver in the early morning light, and practised sprints and doubling back.

Sam had seen and heard some interesting things on these runs of his. There had been, for example, the time he had seen Christabel Bullock throw an empty can of Coke into a hedge, chortling as she did so. Sam had wished he had a camera on that occasion.

This time, as he turned away from the river and into the

winding alleyway that led round the back of the Bullocks' garden, he heard the sound of voices. He immediately stopped, signalled Biter to heel (not that Biter took much notice), then edged his way, slowly and silently, towards the sound. As he got closer, he noticed a burning smell.

'But my dear, do you really think this is a good idea?' (It was Mr Bullock's voice.)

'For heaven's sake, Clarence!' (This was Mrs Bullock.) 'Will you just do as you're told!'

'But dear, do you really think *burning* these things is the answer?'

'Of course I do! We have to get rid of them somehow.'

'But what about the smell? I mean, can't we just throw them out with the rubbish?'

'Of course we can't! Somebody might find them . . . those pesky children . . . this way there will be *no remains*.'

By this time, Sam was close enough to the hedge to be able to make out Mr and Mrs Bullock as they stood next to the smoking pile of rubbish. The first thing he felt was astonishment, partly that they should be up so early, but mostly that they were tending a bonfire. Mrs Bullock was dead against bonfires; she claimed they were untidy. She spent a lot of her spare time patrolling Bellstone, finding people who were having bonfires, and making them put them out.

But then his astonishment turned to absolute horror. Mrs Bullock was holding *a bone*. As Sam watched, transfixed, she hurled it into the fire.

Some of the smoke caught in Sam's throat, and he coughed.

'What's that?' said Mrs Bullock. 'Did you hear something?'

Sam hardly dared breathe. He glanced sideways at Biter, who could not always be relied upon at times like this, and who was already shaking his head in dislike of the smoke.

'I don't think it was anything, dear,' said Mr Bullock mildly.

'Maybe you're right. But I've told you, Clarence, nobody must know about this . . .'

As she spoke Mrs Bullock hobbled forward (clearly her ankle was still giving her some trouble) and emptied a carrier bag into the fire. It looked like more bits of bone. Sam frowned. What on earth was Mrs Bullock up to now?

Mrs Bullock tutted. 'Some of these bits just won't burn,' she complained. She leaned forward and fished a roundish, brownish object out of the fire.

At that moment, the smoke got up Biter's nose, and he sneezed. Sam did not wait to find out if the Bullocks had heard. He grabbed Biter's collar, and went scrambling and slithering away from the hedge, in the direction of his own house.

As there was no sign of pursuit, Sam let go of Biter and slowed down to a jog. He was loping around a bend in the lane, when he ran slap-bang into Elfrida Griswald.

'Ouch! Look where you're going, why can't you!'

They picked themselves up off the ground and glared at

each other. As usual, Sam had come off worse in the encounter. His palms and knees were bleeding.

'You Griswalds,' he declared bitterly. 'They shouldn't let you out by yourselves. What are you charging about the lanes for?'

'Huh! I like that!' Elfrida drew herself up indignantly. 'Charging about the lanes, indeed! I've been searching high and low. Somebody's stolen Biter!'

She looked genuinely upset, and Sam felt a twinge of guilt. He had not thought any of the Griswalds would be up early enough to miss Biter. Just then, Biter himself came trotting around the corner, and Sam explained.

Elfrida seemed too relieved that Biter was all right to give Sam much of a hard time. They turned to walk home together, and Sam told her what he had seen and heard in the Bullocks' garden.

Elfrida's eyes immediately began to gleam. 'They're up to something,' she announced. 'Why else would they be burning bones in the middle of the night?' Sam pointed out that half-past six was not the middle of the night, but Elfrida dismissed this as a mere quibble. 'They're doing it when nobody can see them. It's all very suspicious. I say,' and her voice dropped to a conspiratorial whisper, 'they're *murderers*. Or *worse*.'

Sam could not see what they could be doing that was *worse* than murder, but he did not point this out. Basically, he agreed with Elfrida. It was all very suspicious.

'What we should do,' said Elfrida eagerly, 'is investigate.

After all, we said before that we would.'

'If we do she'll report us to the police this time. I know she will.'

Elfrida tapped her nose in a knowing manner. 'I don't think she'll want the police involved. Leave it to me. I'll think up a plan.'

Sam was not reassured. But he saw no point in arguing. With any luck she would forget all about it. 'All right then,' he said, and left her and Biter at their own garden gate.

* * *

Elfrida did not forget. She ambushed him that afternoon as he walked into Thistle Lane.

'Look at this!' Elfrida glanced round to check they were not overheard, then produced something from under her jumper.

'What is it?'

'It's Brandon's new computer game, *Super-Matrix Destructor Five*.'

'What, the new one he keeps boasting about? You mean – you stole it!' Despite everything Sam had learnt about the Griswalds, he was shocked.

'I did not steal it!' Elfrida sounded so indignant that Sam felt ashamed of his suspicions. 'Spider stole it,' she added.

Sam stopped feeling ashamed. 'What! Spider nicked Brandon's new computer game –'

'Oh, do shut up,' interrupted Elfrida. 'I asked him to take it and he did. He loves stealing things – he can't help it. He usually puts them back afterwards,' she added, as if that made it all right. Sam snorted but she ignored him. 'Don't you see? Now we have the perfect excuse for snooping round the Bullocks' garden.'

Sam did not see. He pointed out that being in possession of Brandon's computer game was in no way an excuse for trespassing in the Bullocks' garden; it would simply get them into even worse trouble if they were caught. Elfrida did not agree.

'If the Bullocks catch us, we'll just say we found Brandon's game and were bringing it back to him. After all, if we'd nicked it, we wouldn't be hanging around the Bullocks' garden, would we? Stands to reason.'

'But we *did* nick it.'

'No, we didn't. Spider nicked it.'

'No – I mean yes – I mean you know what I mean! The point is it's nicked! And we know it's nicked.'

'Yes, but *they* don't know we know. I mean, the way *they* see it, if we *knew* it was nicked, then trespassing in the Bullocks' garden would be a stupid thing to do.'

Sam gave up. Her logic, or perhaps the lack of it, defeated him.

The Bullocks appeared to be out. When nobody answered their knock, Sam and Elfrida hurried around the side of the house.

The Bullocks' garden looked as depressing as ever; and not improved by the remains of the bonfire which was still smoking gently. They investigated this first but found nothing, only charred lumps which might be anything, and ash. Then they went to look at the new rose bed, planted where Jake and Sam had messed up the lawn, and where Mrs Bullock had found the original bones. She had even managed to find an ugly rosebush, Sam thought. It stood up like a soldier on guard, and boasted an abundance of long, lethal thorns.

Elfrida, looking smug, produced two trowels from her satchel, and they began to dig.

They did not mean to disturb the rosebush, but they found digging around it was more difficult than they had expected. First of all Elfrida stuck her trowel through half its roots by mistake. Then Sam lurched accidentally against it, and the whole plant tipped over.

'Blimey,' said Sam, surveying the capsized plant. 'She's sure to notice this.'

'We'll just have to prop it up with lots of earth,' said Elfrida, burying away like a mole.

At that moment they heard the gate slam shut. Swallowing, they stared at each other, then at the lopsided plant.

'Oh no!' Elfrida squeaked.

'If they go inside they won't even see us,' said Sam sensibly. But the sound of footsteps on gravel at the side of the house put paid to this notion.

'Quick,' said Sam. He grabbed Elfrida's arm and pulled her towards the conservatory on the side of the house. To his great relief the door was open. He pulled her down behind some garden furniture.

'Ow, that hurt,' said Elfrida crossly, rubbing her arm.

'Shut up!'

'I'm not scared of those Bullocks, anyway.'

'You were ten seconds ago!'

'Well, obviously I don't especially want to see them . . . what's happened to *Super-Matrix Destructor Five*?'

'Oh great,' said Sam, disgusted. 'You've lost it.'

Elfrida turned her back on him. And as she did so, she caught sight of a strange object, tucked away behind a garden umbrella. It did not look as if it belonged in Mrs Bullock's neat-as-a-pin conservatory. 'What's that?' she asked, pointing.

Sam turned, without much interest; then he took another look. 'Hey! I think that was in the bonfire, but Mrs Bullock took it inside.'

They stared at it for a moment. 'It's not very pretty is it?' said Elfrida, disappointed. 'And it's not a bone.' She prodded it. 'It seems to be some kind of pot.'

It was, Sam had to admit, the kind of object that nobody would look at twice in ordinary circumstances. 'Oh well,' he said. 'Maybe we should make a move. It's all quiet outside.' He poked his head cautiously into the garden. 'I can't see anybody. We'd better go over the fence, just in case.'

They were halfway there, congratulating themselves on their escape, when a figure stood up unexpectedly. It was Mr Hobson, and he had been kneeling down, apparently examining the lily pond.

'Hello,' he said, eyeing their flushed, surprised faces. 'Have I got the wrong house?'

'Err, I don't know,' said Sam. 'I mean, the Bullocks live here.'

'Yes, that's the place,' said Mr Hobson cheerfully. 'How's your left foot, Sam?'

'Oh, all right,' said Sam, rather surprised that Mr Hobson should have forgotten he was right-footed.

'Good, good. You know, Sam, you've made great strides with your game. You're twice the player you were. In fact, it's a great pity you won't be playing this week –'

Mr Hobson was interrupted by a screech from Elfrida. She was kneeling to pick something up from under the rosebush. Sam, who had felt he was turning all colours of the rainbow with pleasure and embarrassment, was half relieved at the interruption and half disappointed.

'Look!' said Elfrida. She brandished *Super-Matrix Destructor Five*.

'A computer game,' observed Mr Hobson gloomily. 'I don't know what you young people see in them. There are so many more interesting things in life. Which reminds me, Sam – I am taking my nephew to see the Roman remains at Lower Titmarsh this week, if you would still like to come.'

'Yeah, great,' said Sam, trying to sound enthusiastic.

'Can I come too?' asked Elfrida eagerly.

Mr Hobson looked at her with interest. 'Now you must

be a little Bullock –'

'I'm not a little Bullock,' said Elfrida indignantly. 'I'm a Griswald. Elfrida Griswald.'

'A beautiful and unusual name. Tell me, are you from Bellstone originally?'

'No. We just moved here.'

'I see. I only ask because I wondered if you had been named for Queen Elfriga.'

They stared at him. '*Queen Elfriga?*' Sam echoed.

'Yes. She was the leader of the Ancient British tribe that lived in this region, during the Roman invasion. The Bellebriggans, they were called. Elfriga led the Bellebriggans against the Roman invaders. Hopeless, of course. She died in battle and is said to be buried close to Bellstone, but her grave has never been discovered.'

'Wow, Mr Hobson,' said Sam, into the silence that followed. 'I've lived in Bellstone all my life and I've never heard that.'

'Haven't you, Sam?' Mr Hobson's moustache twitched with amusement. 'Funny that – I mentioned it the other day in my talk.'

'Was there *treasure* buried with her, do you know?' asked Elfrida eagerly.

Mr Hobson smiled. 'Quite possibly. And rumour has it she was buried with her horse.'

Elfrida's eyes were gleaming. Sam, looking at her, was suddenly aware of something strange about her. He grabbed hold of her arm. 'Well, we'd better be off now,' he said quickly. 'Goodbye, Mr Hobson.' And he marched Elfrida towards the gate. As soon as they were out of sight he made a grab for her jumper. 'What are you doing with this?' he demanded furiously, uncovering the strange object from the conservatory.

'Well, I thought we should have a closer look –'

'Stealing!'

'Borrowing, that's all –'

They were so intent on their argument they didn't hear the sound of a powerful four-wheel-drive pull up on the other side of the hedge. The first they knew of it was when the gate clicked and an irritable voice snarled, 'Get a move on, you two!'

Sam just had time to stuff Elfrida's booty under his shirt before Mrs Bullock appeared, closely followed by Brandon, wearing football kit (it was the kit for Titmarsh Wanderers, Sam noticed with surprise), and Christabel, lugging a violin case.

'What are you doing here?' demanded Mrs Bullock, as soon as she set eyes on them.

Elfrida did not flinch. 'We came by to see Brandon and Christabel,' she said, as Sam tried to hide his bulging front behind her. 'Only nobody was in.'

'You what?' Mrs Bullock scowled. 'Why would you do that?'

'Well, because we're neighbours, of course.' Elfrida was doing a good job of sounding surprised and innocent. 'We want to be friends. Of course, as me an' Jake'n'Spider are new, really *they* should have come round to visit us. But we thought they didn't mean to be rude. We thought perhaps they were shy.'

The idea of the Bullocks being shy caused a bubble of laughter to rise up inside Sam. He snorted, and tried to turn it into a cough.

'That's rubbish, Mum,' said Brandon furiously. 'They know we don't want to be friends. And what's Sam doing here? He's lived here for years and years – and he definitely knows we don't want to be friends with *him*.'

'Yeah, well, I don't want to be friends with you either,' Sam began, but Elfrida laid a hand on his arm. She put on an extremely sorrowful expression and remarked, 'Now Sam, there is no need to sink to their level. It's just sad, that's all. After you and me brought round Brandon's game and everything. We were afraid he might be worried.'

She produced the computer game from behind her back. It was all covered in dirt, from where she had dropped it earlier.

'Give that me!' Brandon seized it, his face red and furious, and began examining it tenderly. 'What have you done to it? It's filthy!'

'Not surprising, really. We found it on the street,' said Elfrida sadly. 'Tossed aside, unwanted. Or perhaps lost. And then Sam said that you had one –'

'Really, Brandon! That computer game cost a lot of money. I told you to take care of it!' Mrs Bullock sounded ferocious.

'I did take care of it! They must have stolen it. Go on – admit it!'

Elfrida looked solemn. 'I promise you that neither Sam nor I took your game from you. I swear on the memory of my dead hamster,' she added. 'The one your cat ate.'

There was a brief glint of anger behind the innocence, as the real Elfrida shone through, like the tiger under the fluff of a Persian kitten. Sam watched her nervously. He knew Elfrida pretty well by this time and wondered how long it would be before fists were flying. Certainly the silence that followed was very tense. Brandon, it was plain, thought they were lying, but Mrs Bullock looked less convinced.

'Come on Brandon,' she said at last. 'Take your game and let's get inside.'

Sam tugged Elfrida's arm but she ignored him. 'Aren't you going to say thank you for bringing back your toy?' she asked Brandon.

'Toy!' Brandon went scarlet with indignation.

'And aren't you going to invite us in for tea?' asked Elfrida who, being a Griswald, never knew when to stop. 'I mean, that would be a nice gesture. Especially if there's cake.'

'No!' chorused Mrs Bullock and Brandon.

Sam grabbed Elfrida with his free hand. He felt she was pushing her luck. As he frog-marched her down the garden path, he was painfully aware of their eyes upon him – and of the illicit takings stuffed up his front. As they scurried along Thistle Lane, Mrs Bullock's voice came floating over the hedge. 'That boy really does have a weight problem. I *had* heard he was getting thinner – but really, did you see the belly on him!'

'Imagine him waddling around the football pitch,' Brandon sneered. 'It's a pity he's not allowed to play any more. My new team's playing his soon.'

Elfrida wanted to go back and attack the Bullocks for these statements, but Sam wouldn't let her. She had other grievances too. 'I think they were very ungrateful. I mean, the least they could do, after we returned that valuable computer game, is to offer us refreshments. Some cake, f'rinstance – we never get any cake at home.'

'You stole their computer game. And you dug up their garden. And you got out alive. And now you want cake?'

'Yes, but *they* didn't know I stole it. *They* thought we were bringing it back. Anyway, I didn't steal it – Spider stole it – so we *were* bringing it back – so they *should* have been grateful –'

Sam groaned. 'Never mind that. At least we got away. Now you take the loot and hide it somewhere nobody can find it.' He paused. 'I wonder what Mr Hobson was doing in their garden?'

'Perhaps he was casing the joint before breaking in,' suggested Elfrida hopefully.

'Don't be stupid! Mr Hobson, a burglar! Not in a million years!'

'They don't always look the way you'd expect,' said Elfrida darkly.

'Oh, don't start that again!'

'Start what again?'

'About your dad.'

'But my dad's not a burglar!'

'Exactly. Now shove off, before my mum spots you.' He put his head to one side. 'Anyway, I can hear Hobson talking to Old Big Nose from here, and they sound perfectly friendly. So there must be an innocent explanation.'

'Oh well.' Elfrida was disappointed but philosophical. 'I'm looking forward to that trip to Lower Titmarsh, anyway. Our mum and dad never take us anywhere.'

'I can tell you've never been to Lower Titmarsh,' said Sam glumly. But she had gone.

Chapter Thirteen
Sam Makes a Stand

By the time the weekend came, Sam found he was quite looking forward to the trip to Lower Titmarsh. Anything, he felt, to get away from his mother. She kept fussing and clucking over him and was reluctant to let him out of her sight – but even she could not think of a good reason why he should not go and look at Roman remains with Mr Hobson. In fact, she was quite pleased about it and kept saying, 'I *told* you archaeology was interesting if only you'd give it a try. I was right, wasn't I? It's much more fun than football, isn't it? I told you –' over and over again. She was so happy about the idea that she didn't even insist on coming with him – which was a good thing, as it meant she would not know that Elfrida was going too.

Elfrida was remarkably well behaved. She splashed around cheerfully amongst the ruins, asking Mr Hobson questions about Roman settlements, while Sam followed, grimly trying to ignore the rainwater running down the back of his neck. Mr Hobson's nephew was of no interest: a weedy specimen with huge spectacles, he made no response to Sam's attempts to start a conversation about England's prospects in the next World Cup. Inside the museum, Elfrida seemed very interested in all the exhibits, although rather disappointed to find that nothing on display had ever belonged to Queen Elfriga. As he stood next to her, looking at a reconstruction of a Roman sewage system, Sam discovered the reason for her interest: Elfrida had decided that she was a direct descendant of Queen Elfriga herself.

'But that's ridiculous!'

'No, it isn't. Mr Hobson said so himself.'

'No, he didn't, he only asked if you were named after her. Anyway, you told me you were named after your Great-Aunt Elfrida.'

'Elfrida's an old family name,' she said. 'So there. It's probably been handed down through the generations and changed from Elfriga to Elfrida over time. Have you ever thought, Sam, that I have the look of an Ancient British princess?'

'No,' said Sam, 'I haven't. Come on, they're waiting for us.'

But as they turned to go, Elfrida caught sight of something in a glass case. 'Look!' she hissed. 'Isn't that like our pot?'

Sam considered the exhibit carefully.

'Well, it's the wrong size and shape, and the colour is different. But apart from that,' he added sarcastically, 'yeah, it's an exact replica.'

The exhibit bore a label which read, *Religious or Ceremonial Artefact, found in vicinity of Bellstone, first century AD*.

'Maybe our pot is a religious or ceremonial artefact belonging to Queen Elfriga!'

'Maybe. And maybe I'm a Roman centurion. This one is years older!'

'No it isn't!' Elfrida was not backing down. 'Ours looks ever so old. You couldn't buy something like that in Woolworth's!'

'I know that! It's a bit of old rubbish. But that doesn't mean it's *Ancient British* old rubbish. There's centuries and centuries between then and now.'

Their argument was interrupted by Mr Hobson summoning them to the car. He dropped them off at the end of Thistle Lane, and they hurried back through the rain, still arguing about Queen Elfriga. When they reached Sam's gate, they were about to say goodbye when Elfrida said, 'Isn't that Biter barking?'

He sounded as if he was in Sam's back garden. Sam went hurrying around the side of the house; and Elfrida followed. They found Biter sitting under the tree house, peering up into it. Sam knelt down to pat him, and as he did so something came flying out of the branches above. Spider landed, catlike, just in front of him; and Jake landed, a little more heavily, just behind.

'Hah, gotcha!' yelled Jake.

Sam jumped about two feet into the air. He scowled at Jake. 'What are you doing here? Mum will kill you if she finds you.'

'So let's get up into the tree house so she doesn't see us.'

Sam glared, but it seemed simplest to agree. Once they were all aloft (Biter howling reproachfully below) he asked, 'What are you up to?'

'It's what *you're* up to,' said Jake, looking from Sam to his sister. 'Skulking about the place with bones, disappearing on mysterious trips, hiding things, going into the Bullocks' garden . . . Yes, Brandon told us about that. And that's another thing. We came to warn you. He reckons you've wrecked his *Super-Matrix Destructor Five*, as well as all of us wrecking the Tidy Bellstone Campaign – and what with everyone laughing at him about his mum's knickers – well, he's after revenge. He says he's got plans, and we'd better look out!'

'Oh great.' Sam groaned.

'So what are you and Elf up to?'

'Well –' Just as Sam was about to tell Jake everything – the bonfire, the strange pot, the visit to the Roman remains – they heard the back door open.

'Sam!' called Mrs Harris querulously. 'Are you there?'

They all stayed silent but it was no good. Mrs Harris was coming towards them, keeping up a steady stream of complaint as she did. 'What *is* that dog doing here – you know, I *keep* hearing him – and I *thought* you'd taken him to the Dogs' Home – I think I'll take him there now – and I've such a bad, sick headache – I *know* you're in that tree house, Sam, there's no good pretending you're not –'

'It's all right, Mum!' Sam was so eager to get down from the tree house – both to stop his mother from taking Biter to the Dogs' Home, and from spotting the Griswalds – that he slipped. He came crashing through the autumn leaves, with a great rending and splitting of twigs, and landed with a thud.

'Sam!' Mrs Harris shrieked. 'My baby!' She immediately had hysterics – which were not helped by the three Griswalds, dropping out of the tree, almost on top of her, 'like a posse of panthers on their prey' as she described it later.

'It's all right,' said Jake, striking an attitude. 'We know first aid.'

Elfrida looked from Sam – who was fending off a delighted Biter, but was otherwise unharmed – to Mrs Harris. 'I think it's her who needs the first aid,' she said.

* * *

The Griswalds and Biter were sent home in disgrace. Mrs Harris insisted on taking Sam straight to the doctor – and the things the doctor had to say (about 'over-protectiveness' and 'wasting valuable time') did not improve her mood. *She* was sure that Sam was unwell after his fall and being caught in the rain, and she made him drink a hot lemon drink, then go and sit in front of the television with a hot-water bottle for his feet. Sam felt miserable and fed-up. It did not seem much of a way to spend the weekend: trailing around a soggy Roman ruin, then sitting indoors, being fussed over by his mother.

It was, he realised with a sudden shock, just like the weekend before the Griswalds had arrived. Nothing to do, being kept in, his mother coddling him, nothing to look forward to . . . It was as if all the changes that had taken place since then counted for nothing.

Mrs Harris disappeared for a while, and when she came back she was rather muddy herself, and there were twigs in her hair. She had, Sam discovered, been putting a padlock on the tree house. She had also removed the ladder up to it and fixed a large sign to the tree trunk saying 'Keep Out'.

Sam didn't think any of that was likely to deter the Griswalds, but he said nothing.

'I've never been happy about that tree house,' said Mrs Harris, 'ever since your father built it for you. And those children use it as an excuse to come and hang about in our garden. Well, enough is enough! We shall have a lovely time, just the two of us. I've a chocolate cake in the oven, and there's some nice gardening programmes on the telly. Perhaps we'll watch a film later. The important thing is for you to keep warm. If you're not better by Monday I might keep you home from school, and hopefully by next weekend you'll have recovered and we can go for a nice trip.' She settled herself in an armchair. 'Perhaps we can go to a museum – I've heard there is an interesting collection of fossil tools at Greavesby. You know I'm so pleased you've developed this interest in archaeology. I was wondering if I'd been entirely fair, making you give up Bellstone Rovers. But now I can see it was all for the best.'

Something happened then: it was as if a firework went off in Sam's head.

'What!' he yelled, shoving off the blanket Mrs Harris had tucked around him.

'Don't do that Sam – you'll get cold –'

'No I won't! Because I'm not ill!' Everything was suddenly clear to Sam. He didn't want to sit about, watching TV; he didn't want to eat cake; and he certainly didn't want to go and look at collections of fossil tools. And the more he went along with it, the worse it would get. The Griswalds, he thought, would never stand for this. And he musn't either. He leapt up and chucked the hot-water bottle onto the sofa.

'Sam! What are you doing?'

'I'm going out.'

'But you can't! It's raining!'

'No it isn't. It's clearing up.'

'But look at those clouds! It's going to start again any minute.'

'Well, it won't kill me, will it?'

'But you're ill! Sam, I forbid you –'

Bang! The door slammed behind him, and he went running down the path. He knew his mother wouldn't follow him immediately: she would need to put on her outdoor shoes and find her keys (that usually took at least ten minutes) and turn off the oven (in case of a fire) and lock up behind her and put on the burglar alarm. Half of him felt mean and guilty, but the other half felt relieved. He could do with some time on his own.

He ran in the direction of Bellstone Meadows, and it was only when he heard the shouts and yells of spectators that he remembered Bellstone Rovers were playing that afternoon. He hesitated – so far he had avoided watching them; avoided anything that might remind him he was no longer on the team. But he couldn't help it; he found himself being drawn towards the game.

The second half had just started. Jake was playing in midfield as usual, and Mark Dawson had taken what Sam still thought of as his own place at the back. Two things were immediately obvious: one, that Jake was playing superbly well, and the other that Mark was doing a good job in defence. He made a couple of tackles that even Sam had to admit grudgingly to himself were pretty good. A little later, Mark passed the ball across the field into space, and Jake ran on to it. He dodged a defender, wrong-footed another, and the next moment, as if from nowhere, the ball was flying into the back of the net.

It was not the most cheerful thing in the world: standing

in the rain without a coat, water dripping down the back of his neck, watching somebody else play in his place, and play very well indeed. And yet somehow, when the goal was scored, Sam forgot his grievances. He leapt into the air and cheered.

From the field Jake spotted Sam, grinned and waved a V-sign. Sam waved back. Then he stuck his hands in his pockets and remembered he was no longer a member of the team and that Mark had set up the goal. Still, the sting had gone. Somewhat surprised, he realised he was looking forward to the rest of the match.

'Here, take this, or you'll catch your death.' Mr Hobson was handing Sam a jacket. 'And I want a word with you,' he added, 'after the game.' He strode away, down the touchline.

Sam sat down and watched as Beaky, making a desperate bid to save a goal, collided with a goal post; as Greg Roylance, with easy nonchalance, scored Rovers' second goal; and as Sunil and Jake, with the security of a two-goal lead, amused themselves by flicking the ball to each other, back-heeling and attempting to nutmeg their opponents. Strangely, all this paid off, and when Jake casually rolled the ball to his right, Sunil ran on to the pass and hammered it into the bottom corner. Ten minutes later Mark scored too, from a penalty. Sam cheered, and tried to ignore the part of his mind that kept imagining Mark being stretchered off the field and himself coming on to win the match in a blaze of glory. Then the final whistle went.

'Oh well,' said Sam aloud. He had known it could not happen really. He reached down and gave Biter's chest an absent-minded rub. Then he did a double-take, looked round and saw Elfrida standing beside him, holding Biter's lead and looking melancholy.

'How are you?' she asked, and then, not waiting for an answer: 'Biter had a massive fight with the cats, so I thought it was best to get him out of the house. Mum was really cross, and she said you seemed to have been on holiday for a very long time, and when were you coming back.'

'Oh no! She won't send him to the Dogs' Home will she?'

'Of course not!' But Elfrida did not sound altogether sure.

Sam was distracted from this new worry by Jake and several other of the Rovers players rushing up to say hello and to ask what he thought of the match. They asked when he was going to play again, and Sam was forced to shake his head and say that he did not know.

Then Sam heard the voice which he had been trying to forget.

'Sam! How could you? How could you rush down here when I specifically told you not to go out?' Mrs Harris, wearing a pink plastic raincoat and a hurt expression, stood behind him. There was rain dripping down her nose, and her face was creased and reproachful.

With unexpected tact, Elfrida, Jake and the rest melted

away. Sam stood and confronted his mother, the embarrassment and misery rolling over him in a great wave. He breathed in, cleared his throat, and suddenly felt immensely angry.

'It's not fair!' he shouted.

'Sam!'

'You never wanted me to play football in the first place.'

'That's not true –'

'Oh yes it is!' snapped Sam. 'You won't let me play football, and you won't let me have a dog; you won't even let me walk to the bus by myself, or see my friends, and now you won't even let me out of the house. I haven't done anything so terrible. You're punishing me, and I don't even know what for! Just leave me alone!'

Mrs Harris was very white. She looked as if she was going to say something, but instead she turned round and walked away. Sam watched her go, a hammering noise in his head. He had no idea what to do next.

He started off in the opposite direction, then realised he was still wearing Mr Hobson's jacket, so he went over to return it to him. Mr Hobson was lecturing Jake and Sunil on 'showing off' – although not very sternly, given that Rovers had won the match 4-1.

'Ah, Sam,' said Mr Hobson benevolently. 'I was glad to see you today. It really does you credit, coming to support us like this in the rain. Some boys, if they're not actually playing, just don't bother.'

Sam stared at his feet and said nothing. The praise made

him almost as uncomfortable as Mrs Harris's ticking off had done.

'Now – how is that left foot of yours?'

'Huh?' Sam gaped at him.

'It must be a lot better by now. Mark's been playing well, but there's still a space in the team for you as soon as you're fit. You're a hundred times the player you were at the start of the season. And as Mark may not be able to play next weekend – his family are visiting relatives out of town – it's doubly important that you can.'

Sam was astonished, first that Mr Hobson should feel that he had improved so much, and second that he did not seem to realise that Sam was out of the team for good. Then he caught Jake's eye over Mr Hobson' shoulder. Of course, it was *Jake* who was supposed to have told Mr Hobson that Sam could not play any more . . . only he hadn't. He had told Mr Hobson that Sam had injured his left foot instead. Jake grinned and winked.

Mr Hobson was still talking. 'Now, this is a very strong team we're playing – we've already played them once this season – the match in which your dog unfortunately intervened . . . Anyway, this time we're playing them in the Cup.'

Sam did a double-take. 'You mean we're playing Brandon's team!' he burst out. 'Titmarsh Wanderers!'

'Yes, and whoever wins goes through to the semi-finals.'

Jake said gloatingly, 'Wouldn't it be great to score a couple of goals, right under Brandon's nose!'

Mr Hobson looked pained. 'How many times must I tell you, Jake, it's not the winning but the taking part? You really have a most unsporting attitude.' Jake grinned, unrepentant. Mr Hobson turned back to Sam. 'So can you play?'

Sam swallowed. A lot of different things were passing through his mind: that he might speak to his mum and talk her round (not that this would be easy, especially after today's events) or sneak out without her noticing, or that she might have a sudden change of heart. But, the sad truth was, he knew he could not take part. He would have to say no.

He opened his mouth to explain.

'Actually,' he heard himself say, 'my foot feels just fine.'

'Fantastic!' Mr Hobson beamed. 'We'll see you then!'

Chapter Fourteen
Catnap!

As he was already in deep trouble, and likely to be in still deeper soon, Sam thought he might as well go the whole hog and walk home with Jake and Elfrida. Jake was in high spirits, both because Bellstone Rovers had won, and because Sam was rejoining the team. 'If Mum doesn't put the boot in,' Sam muttered, but Jake paid no attention. He was now explaining why the goal he had created, and Sunil had scored, had been exactly like Brazil's classic goal in the 1970 World Cup.

'Have you ever seen that old footage? Well, I was just like Pele, setting it up, then Sunil came charging in from nowhere, just like Alberto Carlos, to score!'

Elfrida was more interested in Queen Elfriga, and had

managed to corner Mr Hobson after the game for another chat about her. 'Mr Hobson says some people think she doesn't even exist – like King Arthur. But legends say she had healing powers and vast wealth.'

She went on talking about her and after a while even Jake took notice. 'What's all this about Queen Whats it?'

Elfrida explained. Jake snorted contemptuously. 'How can she possibly be an ancestor? You know you were called after Mum's aunt who lives in Weston-Super-Mare.'

Elfrida explained her theory about how the name Elfriga had been passed down over the centuries, changing eventually to Elfrida. Jake was no more impressed than Sam had been. 'Great-Aunt Elfrida's not even a blood relation,' he pointed out. 'Anyway, she was Danish originally.'

Elfrida launched herself into an account of how there might have been trading links between Denmark and Bellstone in ancient British times (a theory she intended to check with Mr Hobson in due course). Sam and Jake were so busy contesting this that none of them had much attention to spare for their surroundings. So it was a complete shock when Brandon Bullock suddenly leapt out in front of them.

'Hey you! Just stop there! You're not going anywhere!'

Brandon had his henchmen with him: Christabel was at his shoulder, her mouth pursed up into a threatening pout; while lurking in the shadow of the hedge were the Biggerstaffe twins. Nobody could ever remember which was which, but it didn't matter, as they were both exactly the same: big for their age, and mean.

'What do you want?' asked Jake. He moved closer to Elfrida and Sam, and they moved closer to him. It felt as if they were positioning themselves against attack. All of them were suddenly aware of the absence of Spider, who was the biggest and the oldest of them. And while Jake might be good at martial arts, the Biggerstaffe twins were larger, and certainly excelled at anything in the kicking, punching and mauling line.

'To get you,' snarled Brandon. 'You've gone too far, this time, Griswalds!'

'Oh yeah? How's that?'

'You know how! You've taken Delilah! You've taken our cat!'

Sam, watching, thought there was something strange in Brandon's expression. But he had no time to consider it. 'I wouldn't take your cat if you paid me,' said Jake contemptuously. 'Anyway, we've plenty of our own. Much nicer cats than that flea bag.'

'Yes, our cats don't murder kind, gentle old hamsters,' added Elfrida.

'I'm glad Delilah ate your hamster,' hissed Christabel. 'Just imagine how he felt when her jaws closed round him, and her teeth snapped his neck. Or maybe he was still alive when she started eating him –'

Elfrida gave a howl and launched herself at Christabel. But Jake and Sam grabbed her and hauled her back. They had both seen the smirking faces of the Biggerstaffe twins, dying to get stuck in. Sam swallowed. Had he been alone, he might have made a run for it to his own house which was only a short sprint away. But if they tried that, then Elfrida, the youngest and smallest, might get caught; anyway, he doubted Jake and Elfrida would follow.

'You'd better give Delilah back,' Brandon said in a soft voice. 'Or else we'll get you!'

'I'd like to see you try!' Jake was clearly getting himself into what Sam recognised as a fighting stance.

Sam said, in a sensible voice, 'Why d'you think they'd take Delilah? Where would they put her?'

'Oh, we know what they've done with her all right! And that means you too, Harris! What did you do with the body, Griswald? Did your little sister bury it?'

'What?' Jake stared at him.

'Or did she eat it?' said Christabel sweetly. 'Yes, we all know about the little darling's habits. What did you do, Elfrida? Roast it? Fry it? Have you still got it laid to one side, so you can go and have a gnaw at it, whenever you feel like it?'

'You're disgusting,' said Jake. He took a step forward, but Brandon stepped forward at the same time, his face set in a menacing sneer. Christabel was just a step behind.

'Maybe we'll take one of your cats –'

'And lock it up –'

'Somewhere you can't hear it cry –'

'And we'll set fire to its tail –'

'We'll starve it to death –'

'We'll pull out its fur –'

'You're sick!' shouted Jake.

'Leave us alone!' yelled Sam furiously. He could feel an immense rage welling up inside him against the mocking, taunting Bullocks.

'Oh, Sammy, I don't think you're supposed to be here at all, are you?' Christabel looked at him in pretend concern.

'Yes, you're not supposed to go to nasty, rough football games either,' said Brandon. 'Which is a shame – because we're going to destroy Bellstone Rovers next week –'

'And your mummy doesn't think the Griswalds are very nice friends for you. Perhaps we'll have to tell her you were here. Don't you think so, Brandon? I mean, we don't like to tell tales, but I really think it's our duty.'

Sam had never been one for fighting, but at that

moment it was all he could do not to hit somebody. The only thing that stopped him was that he could not decide who to punch first: Christabel or Brandon. Before he could make up his mind, Elfrida Griswald, who had never had a reputation for holding back, launched herself at Christabel. She was hissing and spitting like a cat herself. She only managed to get in one good thump before Sam and Jake grabbed hold of her, but she was still spitting and clawing.

'You Bullocks are disgusting! Just you wait! I'll lock you up and I'll set fire to you too! But first I'll pull out all your hair – and your eyelashes and eyebrows – and your toenails and fingernails – and all your teeth! And when there's nothing but bones I'll gnaw on them – yes I will, however horrible they taste! I hate you Bullocks! I hate you!'

'Stop it, Elfrida!' yelled Sam. But Elfrida lunged at Christabel again, and this time she broke free from her captors. She flew at Christabel, her hands stretched out before her like claws; and Christabel screeched and flew to meet her. Sam and Jake flung themselves at them, but already they could see the Biggerstaffe twins charging out of the hedge. They looked as if they meant business. Jake hurled himself at them, and Sam followed, hoping Elfrida would be able to look after herself.

'STOP!'

Sam practically froze to the spot. For Mrs Harris had appeared amongst them, her face white with anger. The Biggerstaffes fled down the road, leaving Brandon and

Christabel standing there, looking as meek and harmless as anybody could be. Even Christabel's curls seemed to have returned to their usual, immaculate position. The Griswalds looked far less innocent. Jake, who had slipped to the ground while trying to bash one of the Biggerstaffe's heads against a lamppost, was covered in mud; and Elfrida was still itching to get at Christabel. She looked and sounded like a wildcat as she flung herself again at Christabel with a bloodcurdling shriek.

'Elfrida!' Mrs Harris grabbed Elfrida by the scruff of her neck.

'You see what she's like, Mrs Harris,' said Christabel, retreating quickly. She didn't wait for an answer, but grabbed Brandon, and the two of them disappeared into the Bullocks' garden.

Sam started to explain, but Mrs Harris ignored him. 'Be quiet! Jake, take your sister home. I shall be coming round later to speak to your parents.'

Sam's heart fell. He might have known how his mother would look at things. He would try to explain the truth to her, but he doubted she would understand. Meanwhile, Jake had decided, for once, not to argue. He took hold of Elfrida and led her, still protesting, down the street.

Mrs Harris marched Sam back to the house and into the kitchen. When he turned to face her he actually felt quite scared. All the blood had drained away from her face, and her freckles stood out like patches of ink against the white. She was beside herself with fury.

'Look Mum, it wasn't the way it seemed –'

'Those children are despicable!'

'No, they're not. You don't understand. See, what happened –'

'There is no excuse! Evil monsters! And the things she said –'

'Yes, but you see –'

'Whatever else she may be,' Mrs Harris announced, 'I cannot imagine that Elfrida Griswald would ever hurt an animal! She may be without manners – and totally lacking in self-control – but the idea of her harming an animal is ridiculous! Why, she even manages to be fond of Biscuits! And her brothers are a bit uncouth, but their hearts are in the right place, which is more than can be said for those diabolical children!'

It took a while for this to sink in. 'D'you mean – you're on our side?' Sam asked at last. 'The Griswalds' side? Not the Bullocks'?'

'Sam,' said his mother reproachfully, 'why did you never tell me what those Bullock children are really like?'

Sam sat down heavily. And although there was quite a lot he could have said, in the end he just croaked, 'Well, I did try.' He felt dazed. He tried to gather his thoughts while his mother charged round the kitchen, ranting and raving about how disgusting the Bullocks were, and how she had never in all her life heard anything so revolting and outrageous as what they had said.

'You see, Sam, I was so angry when I got back to the

248

house – but then, it *was* still raining, and I remembered that you didn't have your jacket, so I set out to meet you. I was walking along when I heard those – *fiends* planning something. They were behind the hedge so they didn't see me. Something seemed strange about it, and I heard your name, so I went back behind the bend in the road and waited to see what happened.'

'So you heard everything?'

'Oh yes! I heard everything the little dears had to say.' Mrs Harris practically gnashed her teeth. 'My goodness! I was so angry I could hardly speak! The things I would like to do to them –'

'So what happens now?'

'Well – I – I don't know.' Suddenly, Mrs Harris stopped looking fierce and became her usual uncertain self. She sat down abruptly at the kitchen table, and reached for a cigarette.

'Mum!'

'Sorry – sorry, love.' She pushed the packet away, then fidgeted nervously, all the anger gone. 'Well – I could go and speak to Mrs Bullock, I suppose. And I will do if you want me to.' For a moment, her chin lifted and her shoulders straightened. But then she sagged again. 'Only I don't think she would take any notice of me. And the trouble is, the Griswalds *did* start the fighting. That's what she would say.'

'I know,' said Sam gloomily, 'even if the Bullocks did have their bully boys all ready and waiting. Still,' he added, awkwardly, 'thanks Mum. It was great of you – to rush to the rescue like that.'

'It was the least I could do,' said Mrs Harris. She was blushing, and sounded strangely formal, not like his mother at all.

'I'll tell you what, you looked great, storming in – really frightening, more frightening than Mrs Bullock –'

Mrs Harris laughed. 'She *is* frightening, isn't she? It's a terrible thing to admit, but I'm scared stiff of her. And I'm the same age. I don't know how she must seem to you.'

'Like a mad rhinoceros,' said Sam. 'That's how she seems. I think everybody's scared of her. Except the Griswalds.'

'She's always been that way. But I didn't know those children of hers were so vicious. I really had no idea.' Mrs Harris hesitated, looking down at her hands, worrying at a broken nail. Then it burst out of her: 'Do they bully you, Sam? If they do, then I'll go round and complain, even if she does terrify me. I'll go round and pull her hair out. And I'll go round and talk to the school, too.'

Sam was so surprised that at first he did not know what to say. At last, he said slowly, 'I don't think it was me they were really after. Not this time. It was the Griswalds. I think they're furious because the Griswalds made fools of them. Although I suppose I helped,' he added, in a very surprised voice. Then he went on, 'I mean, Jake is better at everything than Brandon is, so they hated that, and the Griswalds make fun of their car and their mobile phones and the Tidiness Campaign, and that. But I think what really made them mad is when Spider climbed the tree in their garden and he – well, everybody laughed at the Bullocks then – and when we had that crash, outside the town hall, and got in the paper, everybody was on *our* side. The Bullocks are used to being boss you see. They're not used to being laughed at.' He stared hard at the salt and pepper pots. He swallowed. Then, his cheeks burning, he said: 'But – but – I suppose before the Griswalds came, they did bully me. I mean, they said I was fat, and no good at sport, especially Brandon, and that I was a baby –' He stopped short.

'A baby?' said Mrs Harris quietly. 'Because of me, I expect. Because I would never let you do things on your own.'

Their eyes met, then glanced away. Mrs Harris studied the ceiling and Sam found he was staring very, very hard at the saltcellar. He had never found it half so interesting before.

'I'm sorry I went off like that,' said Sam at last.

'Well. I shouldn't have kept you in.'

'It's just – you don't ever let me do things. And they're just ordinary things – things that everybody does.' He could not look at his mother. He was afraid she would be wearing her martyr look; or worse, that she might be going to cry.

'I suppose I do fuss too much,' said Mrs Harris. Her voice sounded shaky but not at all martyred. Her eyes were

251

still on the light fittings. 'It's just, since your dad left, you're all I have.'

'I know that, Mum.'

'But that's no excuse. I shouldn't have stopped you playing football. And Biscuits – well, he never did much harm. And you did so enjoy looking after him.' She took a deep breath. 'I'm sorry, too.'

'That's all right,' said Sam.

Mrs Harris brought her eyes down from the ceiling and Sam stopped scrutinising the saltcellar.

'I'm glad we've had this chat, Sam,' said Mrs Harris. She reached over and squeezed his hand and he squeezed back. They grinned at each other. Then Sam remembered something. 'Err – Mum? You know you said just now you shouldn't have stopped me playing football?'

'It was a mistake,' agreed Mrs Harris warmly.

'I'm glad you think that. Because, well – the thing is I've told Mr Hobson I'll play next week.'

'What!' Mrs Harris let go of Sam's hand. She stopped looking warm and smiley and dewy-eyed, and instead looked thoroughly put-out. And then, unexpectedly, she laughed.

'You've a nerve. All right. I don't see why not.'

'Thanks Mum!' Sam was so delighted he got up and gave her a hug. Then he put on the kettle to make them both a cup of tea, and fetched out the chocolate cookies with the double chocolate chunks, which were kept for special occasions. While he was fetching the milk from the fridge something else occurred to him.

'Mum? You know that other thing you said, about how you shouldn't have made me give Biscuits away? Well – I can't remember if I told you this – but he's living next door with the Griswalds. And, the thing is – I happen to know he doesn't get on with their cats.' He paused, and held his breath.

Mrs Harris picked up a cookie and looked at it pensively. Then she gave a big sigh. 'All right, Sam. You can have Biscuits back.' She read the question in his eyes. 'For good.'

'Oh, Mum! That's fantastic!' Sam suddenly felt on top of the world. He picked up a cookie and bit into it with great gusto. As he chewed, something else occurred to him. 'Just one more thing you should know,' he added, through a spray of crumbs.

Mrs Harris looked wary. 'Oh, yes? What's that? I suppose you've signed up for a course in abseiling, have you, or you're adopting a tarantula?'

'Oh nothing like that. It's just – his name's not Biscuits. It's Biter.'

* * *

Mrs Harris had been so nice about everything that Sam did not like to ask her if she was lifting the ban on seeing the Griswalds, too. On the other hand, if he was going to get Biter back, he needed to go next door to fetch him. When, at last, he pointed this out, Mrs Harris surprised him by saying they would both go round. And when Mrs Griswald

came to the door, his mother surprised him even more by presenting Mrs Griswald with a home-made chocolate cake and explaining that as well as coming to take Biter off their hands, she had also come to welcome the Griswalds to the neighbourhood.

Mrs Griswald was delighted. Part of this might have been because she was thrilled to be getting rid of Biter at last, but Sam thought she was simply pleased to find a friend. She invited Mrs Harris and Sam inside and summoned the entire family to welcome them – and to get stuck into the cake. Mrs Harris was offered home-made dumplings (which she declined) and a glass of wine (which she accepted). Mr Griswald kindly showed her his latest picture, of Easter chicks, while the younger ones sprawled on the floor and ate cake and played Monopoly. What Mrs

Harris thought about the housekeeping (or lack of it), or the multitude of cats that wandered in and out, or the way everyone bawled 'Get off Biter!' whenever he tried to nab somebody's cake, she did not say. Perhaps, after her second glass of wine, she did not really care.

As for Sam, he found that the Monopoly board (and both dice) had been chewed so badly by Elfrida's pets that it was almost impossible to work out which square (or side) was which; the Griswalds were fiercely competitive, and tried to sneak money from the bank when they thought nobody was watching; and Spider spent half an hour relentlessly driving everybody into bankruptcy at the end, and everybody hated him.

It was the best evening Sam had spent in ages.

Chapter Fifteen
Conference in a Caravan

Next day, things went rapidly downhill. True, Sam spent several blissful moments after he woke up, with Biter sitting heavily on his feet, imagining the glories of the coming match against Titmarsh Wanderers (himself passing the ball through an astonished Brandon's legs, and watching it thud into the back of the net). And his mother let him walk to school with the Griswalds (although as it was still raining, this was not as much fun as it might have been). But once there, he reckoned he and Jake were lucky not to get lynched.

The Bullocks were to blame, of course. They had told everybody that the Griswalds and Sam had kidnapped their cat.

All the respect and popularity the Griswalds had won for their various escapades had vanished. Burning down bus shelters was one thing, as was smashing into the mayor's Jaguar: but cruelty to animals was quite another. The whole school was united in hostility. Christabel sat near the railings, in a huddle of her friends, and wept for poor Delilah; Brandon sat pale and stony-faced through every lesson, and everyone knew that he was suffering inside. And everyone knew who was to blame.

'We all know you hate the Bullocks,' they told Sam and Jake. 'Everybody knows you'd do anything to get at them.'

'I reckon the Bullocks have hidden her,' said Jake. 'It's a set-up.'

'But Mrs Bullock's reported her lost to the police,' they replied.

Jake thought the Bullocks perfectly capable of hiding their own cat, and then reporting the loss to the police, and said so. But nobody else was convinced. They were even less convinced when it became known that Mrs Bullock had offered a two hundred pound reward for Delilah's return.

'If only we had the Foul Fiend From Hell, we'd give her back like a shot for two hundred pounds,' said Jake, but this cut no ice with his classmates.

And it was alarming to learn that the police were involved. 'After all,' said Jake, 'there is such a thing as being framed.' He was sitting with Sam on the roof of the school boiler-house, which was the only place where they could be sure of being left alone, as nobody else (except Spider, who had discovered it) knew the way up. It was wet, admittedly (the weather had been terrible recently), but they preferred that to the accusations below. 'Still,' Jake added, 'Mum used to be in the police, so maybe that will count in our favour.'

'It didn't with the bus shelter.'

'Oh, I don't know – we're not in prison, are we? Although,' Jake added gloomily, 'Mum's still talking with the Council about whether we'll have to pay for a new shelter. That's another thing she keeps going on about.'

Sam thought of something else. 'How come your mum and dad ever got married, if he's a criminal and she's a policewoman?'

'It was their work that brought them together.' Jake ignored the sceptical look on Sam's face. 'I don't like the way things are going, Sam,' he said darkly. 'We Griswalds don't care too much for public opinion, but at this rate we're going to be the lepers of Bellstone. And we have to do something about those Bullocks. I think we should get together with Spider and Elfrida, and make a plan.'

Sam agreed readily enough. They were all feeling the burden of Bellstone's disapproval. An article had appeared in the *Bellstone Gazette* about Delilah's disappearance (describing her, with complete inaccuracy, as 'a gentle good-natured tabby'), and although it did not mention the Griswalds, local gossip soon decided who was to blame. Neither Sam nor the Griswalds were welcome in the local shops at present.

Nor was this the Griswalds' only problem. The mayor had sent Mrs Griswald a very nasty letter about his Jaguar, saying that he was thinking of going after the Griswalds for damages. The prospect of this, on top of the thousand pounds that Mrs Bullock wanted for her urn, and  possibly having to find the money for a new bus shelter, did nothing for Mrs Griswald's mood. She started talking about moving away from Bellstone again.

But by the time they held their meeting, something much worse had happened. Spider, sneaking into the Bullocks' garden to see if they were hiding Delilah in their shed, had closed his hand around barbed wire. It was wound all around the spikes at the top of the fence that separated the Bullocks' garden from Sam's, and Spider, who was not expecting it (and who was not as quick as usual with one arm in a sling), had caught hold of it. Sam sneaked his mother's first-aid kit out into the garden where the Griswalds were doing their best to patch up Spider's hand. They were livid.

'Putting up barbed wire is disgusting!' said Elfrida fiercely. 'It's the most evil thing I ever heard! And it's not only Spider. It might hurt the cats.'

'They'll pay for this,' Jake snarled, battling with a roll of gauze. 'We shall be revenged!'

They all retired to the Griswalds' pine tree, which Spider, despite his injuries, still managed to climb twice as quickly as anybody else. It was a bit damp in the drizzle and Jake suggested they decamp to the tree house, but Sam vetoed this. Mrs Harris's padlock was still in place, along with her 'Keep Out' notice; and although the Griswalds did not consider these to be obstacles, Sam wanted to humour his mother – after all, she had been so good about everything else.

'She won't know we're there,' Jake pointed out.

'Yes, she will,' Sam said. 'Biter will sit underneath us and bark. You know what he's like. Actually, he's been doing it even when we're not there.'

They soon turned their attention to more important matters.

'As we all know, those scum have accused us of taking Delilah,' Jake announced. 'I say the Bullocks have hidden her themselves.'

'But how could they?' Sam asked. 'After all, she's the noisiest cat on the planet. She yowls like anything. You haven't seen or heard anything, have you Spider?'

Spider shook his head.

'Maybe she's in their house,' Elfrida suggested.

'But if they hid her in the house,' Jake said, 'or even the garden, then Mrs Bullock would hear her, and then I don't think she would have gone to the police. And Spider's looked at school, haven't you, Spider? On the roof, and in the outhouses, and the cupboards and everywhere.'

'But you're the one who thinks they hid her,' Sam pointed out.

'Yeah – but not necessarily alive,' said Jake grimly. 'If they've killed her, she could be anywhere. I reckon they've buried her at the end of the garden, with all the other bodies. That's probably what they do with their pets, when they get fed up with them. That would explain all those bones.'

They all shuddered. Nobody had liked Delilah, but if she had fallen victim to a serial cat-killer – well, it was a very grisly thought.

'Probably they'll dig up more bones and say it's her and we did it,' said Sam.

'I expect that's their scheme,' said Jake. 'After all, they have already accused us of burying bones in their garden. Although it might cause questions to be asked. I mean, *why* is their back garden more stuffed with skeletons than Bellstone Cemetery? You and Elf went in there, didn't you Sam? What did you find out?'

Sam related how he had seen the Bullocks burning something on a bonfire, then how he and Elfrida had successfully infiltrated the Bullock residence.

'Mr Hobson was there,' Elfrida added. 'Maybe he's suspicious too.'

'No doubt,' said Jake darkly. '*Burning things* – that's very suspicious – and *burning things secretly* – that's very suspicious indeed. And they looked like bones, you say?'

'Yes,' said Sam, 'only we didn't find any when we poked around in the ashes.'

'So what did you find?'

'I've got it,' said Elfrida. 'I'll show you – only you'll have to come to the caravan. I don't think I could carry it up here.'

The caravan was dangerously close to Mrs Griswald's territory of kitchen and vegetable patch, but they decided to take the risk, and were soon sitting in a circle, staring at the strange object Sam and Elfrida had found in the Bullocks' conservatory.

'It looks like an old pot of some kind,' said Jake at last. 'Sort of beaten up, and not very interesting. What is it?'

Sam coughed. 'Well – I think that's it,' he admitted. 'It's an old pot.'

'It's an ancient bowl belonging to Queen Elfriga! And don't you dare laugh like that, Jake Griswald!' Elfrida's face was red and indignant. 'It is so! I saw one just like it on display with the Roman remains!'

Spider raised his eyebrows, and Elfrida made haste to fill him in on her theory about Queen Elfriga being a Griswaldian ancestor – while Jake snorted contemptuously from time to time. Sam didn't think much of her theory either, but he said nothing. He knew Elfrida was attached to her fantasy, and he saw no reason to ruin it for her. The Griswalds all had powerful imaginations – and it was really no worse claiming a semi-legendary queen as a distant ancestor than claiming a twentieth-century master criminal as a direct one. (Or even, he admitted to himself, imagining twenty times a day how he would score the goal which would win Rovers the Cup.) Her brothers were less sympathetic. Spider shook his head, and Jake said, 'What a load of drivel. *I* reckon it's the Bullocks' old washing-up bowl. And anyway – it doesn't matter. The important thing is: is Old Big Nose a murderer? I reckon she is. And I reckon it's not just cats, either. I reckon she goes creeping around Bellstone, and if anybody's not tidy enough, then it's curtains for them.'

Suddenly, it seemed very dark and cold in the caravan. The rain dripping on the roof sounded like sinister fingers, tapping. And they all had the same mental image – Mrs Bullock, red-eyed, creeping along through the alleys of Bellstone, wielding a dagger or even a machete.

Sam swallowed. In a slightly higher voice than usual he said, 'She'd never get away with it. Not in Bellstone. People would notice if she was going about killing people. Besides, there's no way she'd go round to your place with the evidence, if she really *was* a murderer. It would be stupid.'

'She was trying to blacken Elfrida's name,' said Jake. 'And divert suspicion. It was a cunning double bluff.' Elfrida and Spider nodded.

'But if she *was* killing people, surely she'd have finished you lot off long ago.'

Jake considered this, eyes gleaming. 'Probably she's still
planning it,' he said ghoulishly at last. 'Preparing the way.
She's going to make everybody hate us first, then they
won't care when we go missing.'

Sam said, 'If you really think that, why don't you go to
the police?'

'The police! They'll never believe us. Not after that
smash-up at the town hall. Of course, we *could* ask Mum –
they'd believe her – but the mood she's in, she'd probably
be quite happy for Big Nose to do us in.'

'So what are we going to do?'

Jake and Elfrida immediately burst out with a stream of
ideas which Sam, for one, found more blood-curdling even

than the thought of Mrs Bullock as a mass killer. Elfrida was the most vengeful: she wanted to kidnap Christabel, and lock her in the caravan, and torture her until she admitted the truth. Jake was less extreme. He suggested destroying the entire Bullock garden with weedkiller, sending them anonymous letters accusing them of cat murder (this, he said, would reduce them to quivering wrecks and lead them to confess); breaking into the Bullock household to search for evidence or imprisoning the lot of them in the house with quantities of barbed wire. Spider, of course, suggested nothing. But his eyes were gleaming, and he kept cracking his knuckles.

As he listened, Sam became paler and paler. Two thoughts were going through his head. The first (sensible) thought, in the topmost part of his mind, was that the Bullocks could not *possibly* be murderers, either of pets or humans: the notion was just one more fantasy of the Griswalds' overactive imaginations. The second (more secret) thought was that if the Bullocks really *were* murderers (and somehow he could not get the image of Mrs Bullock and her dagger out of his head) then the *last* thing they should do was antagonise the Bullocks with weedkiller and barbed wire or by breaking into their house. Or they might all end up buried in the garden, alongside Delilah.

Sam swallowed. He did not want to admit his second, secret thought. The only thing to do was to convince the Griswalds that the Bullocks were definitely not murderers.

But he did not see how he could do that.

Then he had an idea.

He coughed for attention. They ignored him. He raised his voice. 'Umm, aren't we rather jumping to conclusions?' he said loudly.

'How d'you mean?' asked Jake.

'Well, I think Elfrida might be right. I mean what if that pot is – err – Queen Elfriga's bowl?'

'What are you on about?' Jake and Spider stared at him.

'I mean, the fact is, I have been doing a lot of archaeological research of late. And it seems to me quite likely that the Bullocks' garden *could* be a burial site of some kind. Even if it's not Queen Elfriga's, it could still be of historic interest.'

'Huh?' Jake and Spider were puzzled. It did not sound very convincing, even to Sam. But one person at least was convinced.

'Of course it's Queen Elfriga's!' Elfrida was beaming. 'And that bone – the huge one, that Mrs Bullock found – it belongs to Elfriga's horse! Mr Hobson said her horse was buried with her. And maybe that was why he was snooping round the Bullocks' garden! He thinks it's her burial site too.'

'So, you're saying all those bones – they belong to dead people from centuries and centuries ago?' Jake sounded undeniably disappointed. And Sam could see the problem. It was much more *fun* (for the Griswalds, if not for Sam) to think that Mrs Bullock was a murderer. He searched for ways to attract Jake's interest.

'Treasure!' Sam burst out. 'There's bound to be treasure! People back then were buried with loads of stuff. Gold and jewellery and – and – things! If there are bones in the Bullocks' garden, then most likely there's treasure too!'

Jake and Spider were suddenly looking a lot more alert.

'And if Queen Elfriga was a Griswald – which I'm sure she was,' added Elfriga, 'then all the treasure belongs to us! I'm sure Mr Hobson could help us prove it, if we traced our family tree.'

Neither Sam nor her brothers thought this sounded the least bit likely, but nobody was inclined to argue. Once they got their hands on the treasure, then they could worry about establishing ownership.

'Well – it's certainly a possibility,' said Jake thoughtfully. 'I mean – archaeology sounds dull and everything – but if you're right – it could be interesting.' He turned to Spider. 'D'you remember *Indiana Jones and the Temple of Doom*?'

Spider nodded.

Sam said, 'Exactly. It'll be just like that.' Then he added quickly, 'Although there'll be lots of careful research to be done first.'

Jake nodded. 'You know Sam,' he added magnanimously, 'I'm glad you're with us. We'd never have thought of all that ourselves. All this reading about old things and visiting museums – it's worth doing after all.'

Sam blushed with pleasure – and embarrassment. But deep down he felt uneasy. He had convinced the Griswalds that the Bullocks' garden was a site of archaeological interest, bursting with buried treasure. He just wished he had managed to convince himself.

Chapter Sixteen
A Dog and a Match

Soon the new interest in archaeology had to take second place to the coming Cup match with Titmarsh Wanderers.

'I really wonder if this match is a good idea,' said Mrs Harris. Sam looked up, from where he was stuffing his boots and shin-pads into a kit bag, and glared at her so hard that she turned round quickly and began making a great clatter with the washing-up. With great difficulty, she managed not to point out that Sam did not look as if he had slept, that he had eaten hardly any breakfast, nor had he done any homework, and although it was no longer raining the ground was sure to be extremely wet. Sam, who knew all this only too well, was relieved when the door bell rang. He went to open it, expecting to see Jake, come to collect him for the match. To his amazement, he saw Christabel Bullock. She was wearing a shiny pink raincoat, and looking very pleased about something.

'What d'you want?' asked Sam. He could not help adding hopefully, 'Has Delilah come back?'

'I'm afraid not. No, I just thought you'd like to know that Brandon and I saw your dog earlier. He was running in the direction of the river.'

'What d'you mean? Biter's been in the garden all morning. He couldn't have got out.'

Christabel shrugged. 'It looked just like him.'

Sam scowled at her suspiciously. 'Of course, if somebody opened the gate –'

As he spoke, somebody else opened the gate – Jake, come to collect Sam for the match. Christabel looked meaningfully towards him. 'With these Griswalds around, you never can tell. I don't expect people who'd burn down a whole bus shelter would be very good at shutting gates.' And she went skipping past Jake and away down the path.

Sam began calling Biter, trying to keep the panic he felt out of his voice.

'What's going on?' asked Jake.

Quickly, Sam explained. 'I'm going to look in the back garden,' he concluded. He had a feeling Biter might be sitting under the tree house. He often sat there, despite Sam's attempts to dissuade him, barking loudly and annoying Mrs Harris, because that was where Sam and the

Griswalds used to hang out. But Biter was nowhere to be found.

'D'you think the Bullocks have done this?'

'Of course,' said Jake. 'This is their way of making sure we miss the match.'

Sam stared at him, dismayed. Jake must be right. But there was nothing to be done. Sam had to find Biter before anything happened to him, even if it meant he missed the match.

By this time Mrs Harris had appeared and Sam told her that they were going down to the river immediately.

'Oh no! The river is so high with all this rain we've been having.' Mrs Harris looked distinctly nervous. 'I mean – it could be dangerous –'

'We must find Biter,' said Sam fiercely. 'We're going now!'

Mrs Harris hesitated. Then, to Sam's amazement, she did not forbid them, but instead said that she would follow along shortly. They set off, calling loudly, along the towpath by the side of the river. But there was no sign of Biter.

'This is stupid,' said Sam, half an hour later. 'The match is going to start soon. And we're going to miss it.' He took a deep breath, then said slowly, 'It doesn't need two of us to look for him. And you're more important to the team than I am. You should go and play.'

Then he looked away quickly. It was the right thing to do, he knew that – but, he discovered, he didn't much enjoy being noble.

Jake frowned. 'All right,' he said at last. 'But only because I don't want to give Brandon the satisfaction. Hah! I'm going to kick him right off the field!'

'Don't do that – you'll get sent off. Just score goals.'

'All right. And then I'll knock his block off. See you later.'

Jake set off across the grass, and Sam felt mournful and alone. It was all very well being team-spirited, he thought crossly, kicking at some grass, but at that moment he hardly cared if Titmarsh Wanderers *did* win the Cup. He walked on, calling for Biter as he went. He had almost reached the place where they had cleared all the rubbish, but the water was much higher than it had been, rushing past, full of mud and stones; soon it was coming over the banks, and the path was impassable.

Sam was forced to turn back, and as he did he was struck by a new and terrible thought. He paused for a moment, then went on more quickly. Eventually, he came upon his mother, hopping over puddles in her unsuitable shoes.

'Oh, there you are, dear. I was getting terribly worried, with the water so high. Do you know, I really think the most sensible thing is to go back. Somebody may have found him and handed him in to the police.'

Sam swallowed, then put his terrible thought into words. 'Mum, what if he's fallen in? What if he's been washed away?'

Something about his pale, tense face must have affected Mrs Harris. For she made an immense, heroic effort and, for perhaps the first time in her life, managed to look on the bright side. 'Biter won't have fallen in! Dogs are sure-footed. And even if he has – well, he can swim. All dogs can swim. At least I think they can. And if he has fallen in, he'll be downstream, so that's the place to look for him.'

They turned back together, Mrs Harris struggling to keep up a flow of bright and cheerful chatter. It did not come naturally to her, and fortunately she did not have to struggle for very long. As they entered Bellstone Meadows, they saw three shapes hurrying towards them. One was unmistakably the tall and lanky form of Spider Griswald; the other the smaller figure of Elfrida, scurrying and skipping to keep up; and the third –

'Biter!' Sam yelled.

The next moment Biter hurled himself joyfully through the air, and landed with his muddy paws on Sam's chest.

'Jake ran back and told us what happened,' Elfrida explained, after Sam had picked himself up. 'And we were coming to help look. But then Spider heard something, so we went to see. And sure enough, *somebody* had locked him in our caravan. With a big bone to keep him quiet.'

'My goodness!' said Mrs Harris, very shocked.

'Yes,' Elfrida said darkly. 'It must have been those Bullocks – trying to frame us. It's lucky Spider's got hearing like a cat.'

Spider nudged Sam and pointed across the grass. Sam had forgotten all about the match. He left Biter with the others to follow on more slowly, and ran. As he came

closer, his heart thudding painfully inside him, he saw that
the pitch was empty. The two teams were huddled around
their respective coaches. It must be half-time. Sam forced
himself to run harder. If he got there in time, perhaps Mr
Hobson would put him on for the second half. With a final
burst, he reached the pitch. But even as he approached, the
huddles broke up and the players streamed onto the pitch.
Before Sam was close enough to hail Mr Hobson, the
referee blew for kick off, and the match began.

Sam flung himself, gasping, onto the substitutes' bench.
During those first few seconds he saw that Mark Dawson
was on the pitch, after all. All hope suddenly died within
him.

Then he caught sight of Brandon Bullock, and it was all

he could do not to go on the pitch and attack him.

'Whath haffened to you?' asked Beaky incoherently. Sam had been so engrossed in his own troubles that he had not even noticed him sitting there, clutching a large, bloodied handkerchief to his nose, while Jimmy Clarke strutted around in the goal mouth.

'My dog escaped. What happened to *you*?'

'My noeth,' said Beaky sadly. 'I bangthed it on the pothst.'

Sam nodded sympathetically. And Beaky filled him in on the game so far – they were losing 2–1: Jake having scored for Rovers, while Danny Myers and a tall ginger-haired lad had both scored for Titmarsh Wanderers.

'Mark's playing well,' said Sam casually. 'I thought he was away this weekend.'

'Yeah, but he got here for half-time and Old Hobson put him on this half.'

Sam could hardly believe it. If only he had been there, he could have played all first half. As it was, Mr Hobson was hardly likely to take Mark off and substitute Sam if Mark had only just gone on. And Mark was playing really well too. Sam watched Mark kick the ball off the line, preventing what looked like an almost certain goal. Brandon Bullock thundered in, on target again, and once more Mark kicked it away – but conceding a corner to Titmarsh.

'Go Rovers!' and 'Go Wanderers!' yelled the crowd, 'Knock 'em dead!' (It was surprising, Sam thought, how worked up a crowd made up mainly of people's mums, dads and little sisters managed to get.)

Danny Myers was going up to take the corner. Brandon was standing at the near post, and was not above giving the Rovers players a shove when the referee's back was turned. Sam suddenly noticed that Brandon's right hand was bandaged. He eyed it suspiciously, wondering if it was the result of Biter's teethmarks (it seemed unlikely that anybody would be able to lock Biter up in a caravan, even with a bone, without having something to show for it). But now the ball was curving in, from a good strong kick by Danny; Brandon was jumping up to meet it, his left arm was rising . . .

'Hand ball!' howled Sam and Beaky together, as the ball plummeted from Brandon's fist and into the back of the net. Brandon was running around the pitch, punching the air, and the referee – the referee could not have noticed, for he was letting the goal stand! Titmarsh led 3–1.

'But he practically punched it in!' Sam protested to Beaky. 'The cheating toerag!'

The whole Bellstone Rovers team was incensed, as was their half of the crowd – the language flying around was quite scarifying. Even Mrs Harris, who had now arrived, was hissing, as was Elfrida, while Spider was trying to stop a snarling Biter flinging himself onto the pitch. 'Thath's Gregth's granny,' said Beaky shocked, and pointed at a little old lady who was trying to spit at Brandon. (She missed, unfortunately.) But Sam was too intent on the match to care.

As were the players on the field. Rovers, enraged by Brandon's blatant cheating, were attacking hard. Jake and Sunil took the ball forward at every opportunity, and their opponents were forced to get back and defend their goal. The Titmarsh players could no longer get the ball to their forwards, and Brandon Bullock, wanting to be where the action was, decided to forsake his place by the enemy goal in favour of getting back and tackling hard. As he barged in, following the ball around the pitch, he was annoying his own team-mates as much as the Rovers players. They shouted at him to get away, and there were various scuffles and skirmishes and near collisions.

Over the next ten minutes, Brandon must have come close to being sent off several times. Twice, it seemed to Sam, he did not even pretend to be aiming for the ball when he went in to tackle. Both times a Rovers player went flying; but although the referee frowned, and shook his head, he did not raise a yellow card, and Brandon was still on the pitch.

But now Jimmy Clarke, Rovers' substitute goalie, had the ball and was rolling it out to Mark; he passed it to Jake, who dribbled it up the right wing. Greg was in the penalty box, shouting for the ball, but most of the opposing players seemed to be in the box too, determined not to let them get it. Jake looked as if he were going to cross, then changed his mind and ran straight at goal. Three of their players abandoned Greg and converged on him, whereupon, niftily, he back-heeled the ball to Greg.

Crunch!

Brandon had intended his tackle for Jake, but Jake was already past him, and Brandon went sliding on across the sodden ground, his studs raised, straight into Greg. The ball went skittering off through the mud, and Greg was on the ground, yelling and clutching his ankle. A small concerned group – the referee, Mr Hobson, the nearest Bellstone Rovers players – gathered around him.

Sam held his breath. To his great relief, he saw Greg get back on his feet. But he was not running back to his place on the field. Instead, supported by Mr Hobson, he was limping back towards the bench. The referee turned to Brandon and solemnly produced the yellow card. 'One more of those son, and you'll be off.'

Meanwhile, Mr Hobson cast an eye at his substitutes' bench: Beaky, bleeding profusely in his excitement, and Sam, alert, eager, and hardly believing what had happened.

'Sam,' said Mr Hobson. 'Are you ready to go on?'

'You mean – to play up front?'

'Yes.'

It was strange, Sam discovered. He had dreamt of this moment a hundred times – but now it had arrived, he would have given anything to be somewhere else. He had always imagined himself running confidently onto the pitch. Instead, his feet felt numb, he was distinctly shaky round the knees, and there were butterflies in his stomach he advanced across the grass. He did not hear the raging words that Mr Hobson sent after him, nor

Beaky's 'Good luck'; and he did not see Jake grinning or hear Elfrida and Mrs Harris cheering. But he did notice Brandon. He was smirking – but with an edge of menace behind the smirk.

Rovers had a free kick from the edge of the box, and Jake had just one thing on his mind. With just a short run-up, he clipped the ball over the wall and sent it sailing into the top corner of the net. The crowd went wild, as did Jake's astonished team-mates. Elfrida hugged a startled Mrs Harris round the waist. 'Imagine him being able to kick it so far!' said Mrs Harris, impressed despite herself.

'Oh that's nothing to Jake,' said Elfrida grandly.

On the pitch Mark yelled to Jake, 'You've been watching that Beckham video again,' as they all made their way back to the half-way line.

As the game restarted, Sam tried to get himself involved. The ground was slippery with mud after so many days of rain. Sam found himself flailing around, struggling to get accustomed to his new position, and to stop himself drifting back down the field towards his usual spot. When Jake passed to him from the wing, Sam was surprised, and lost his feet; he went over and missed the ball altogether. As he scrambled up, red-faced, he was aware of Brandon laughing at him.

There could only be fifteen minutes left. But now, when Rovers desperately needed to score, it seemed their opponents were growing more confident. They were pressing into Rovers' half, determined to get another goal themselves, and forcing the Rovers players back to defend. It was Jake, sprinting across the field, who went in to nick the ball away from their forward. He tackled, and the ball bounced off the side of his foot and rebounded towards the halfway line. Only Sam was anywhere close.

Without even thinking about it, Sam ran towards the ball and trapped it with his foot. Then – the first rule of football, Mr Hobson always said – he looked up. There was nobody to pass to: everybody else was back, defending. And the goal looked an awfully long way away. Much closer was Brandon Bullock, who was coming towards him with a very evil look on his face.

'Run, Sam!' bawled Elfrida from the crowd.

'Run, Sam!' howled Mrs Harris, jumping up and down.

'Yeah, go on Fatty, run!' mocked Brandon.

And Sam ran. He ran as he had never run in his life before. The pitch stretched away interminably, the mud was sucking him down like quicksand, and he could hear the breaths tearing out of his chest, as if he would collapse at any moment. But still he ran. He pulled away from Brandon Bullock who looked, if only Sam had been able to turn and see his face, more surprised than he had ever looked in his life. At the last moment Brandon flung himself into a desperate tackle, but he was too far behind, and his feet went flying out from under him, sending him sprawling into the mud. Sam had forgotten Brandon. Now there was only the goalie left to beat. He was coming out of the goal, tall and determined-looking, with his gloves outstretched.

Sam did not consciously decide when to shoot for goal. He was not aware of choosing a time or an angle. Instead, it was with a strange sense of unreality, almost as if he were looking over his own shoulder, that he suddenly saw the ball leave his right foot. It was not, in all honesty, the driving strike he had often imagined; but the angle was perfect. It went right past the desperate goalie's legs and from there, to Sam's astonishment, it rolled into the back of the net.

Sam was so astonished he almost sat down in the mud.

Loud cheering rose up all around the pitch and Sam could hear Biter barking wildly. The rest of the Rovers players were mobbing him, yelling and shouting, but it was only when Jake clobbered him triumphantly on the back, so hard he almost fell over, that the full reality sunk in. As he steadied himself he could not help a huge, foolish grin from appearing on his face. He had scored!

Five minutes later the final whistle went and the score was three all. The referee announced a penalty shoot-out. A mini-conference took place on the halfway line to decide the five penalty takers for Rovers. Jake, Sunil and Mark volunteered, but nobody else seemed very keen. 'How about you Sam?' said Mr Hobson, and the rest of his team-mates made agreeing noises. Still in a state of shock, Sam found it had been decided: he would take the fourth penalty.

'Just blast it,' said Jake encouragingly, and walked out to take the first one. He scored of course, swerving his into the top corner, as did Mark and Sunil, with well-placed shots that sent the keeper the wrong way. Titmarsh had missed two, and with the score 3-1 to Rovers, the ball was rolled to Sam. If he scored this, then Rovers were through to the semi-finals of the Cup!

He did not even manage a good connection. In the run up, weak as a baby, he slipped on the mud, and saw the ball go slithering harmlessly off to one side, miles from goal. It didn't really matter. Although the next Wanderers player took his penalty well, and Rovers' Jimmy Clarke had his saved by the Wanderers goalie, Brandon, going last, sent the ball sailing through the air, right in the centre of the posts – but some ten feet above the crossbar. The crowd erupted and the Rovers players ran joyously back towards their goalie (past a scowling Brandon on his knees). Bellstone Rovers were through to the next stage of the Cup. And Sam was the hero of the hour.

* * *

'Wow – that was fantastic – Hobson'll always have to let you play up front now.'

'Brandon looked sick as a parrot when you ran past him.'

'You know, football's more exciting than I thought.'

'I'm so glad you won, dear, although really, playing in these conditions, it can't be safe.'

Sam was hardly listening. He was in such a good mood, the only way he could express his feelings was by seizing a piece of stick and fighting Biter for it. Meanwhile, Jake, Elfrida and Mrs Harris continued their dissection of the match while Spider listened and nodded.

'Just like Brazil we were!' Jake triumphed. 'We out-played them! It serves that Brandon right!'

'I think Sam was faster than he expected,' Mrs Harris said. Sam had certainly been a great deal faster than *she* had expected.

'Yeah, and if he hadn't yelled at Sam like that then he might have had some breath to run after him,' Jake continued. 'But the goal was class – sheer class –'

'It was more interesting than I expected,' Elfrida said. 'I think I like football after all. I don't see why girls shouldn't play. I think I might get a team together at school – you can be coach if you like –'

'You must be joking!' said her brother.

'Well, then, Sam can be coach. I reckon he's a better player than you are anyway –'

Before Jake could respond to this, Spider signalled to them to hush. In the silence that followed they suddenly became aware of Mrs Bullock, standing a short distance away, talking to Mr Hobson. Hoping they were not being too obvious, they all edged a little closer.

'But that – that's impossible. Outrageous! I simply don't believe it –' Mrs Bullock was clearly very upset. Mr Hobson was smiling politely, but as if his patience might be wearing rather thin.

'Mrs Bullock, you came to me for a professional estimate. I visited your residence, as you recall, and inspected what was left of the object in question, and I told you my view of the matter then. You asked me to consult further with colleagues, and to take certain pieces for closer examination. I have done so, and what I have found confirms my original opinion. Had the urn in question been genuine, there is no doubt that it would have been worth a significant amount – although not, I think, one thousand pounds. But it is merely a very poor quality replica. It is worth no more than fifty.'

'Fifty pounds! But I spent close to a thousand!'

'Then you were very foolish to do so, without taking professional advice. I am sorry, Mrs Bullock. But as you know, I have been in this business for many years, and I have no doubt. Were you to seek compensation from your insurers or from those who destroyed the object you could not ask for more than fifty pounds.'

'But – but – but –'

Fortunately, Mrs Bullock was too preoccupied to notice what was going on only a small distance from her. It would have made her feel no better – indeed it would have made her feel a lot worse – to see 'those revolting Griswald hooligans' rolling around in the mud, laughing fit to burst their sides.

Chapter Seventeen
Water, Water Everywhere

It rained again the following day. This time it poured and poured. Bellstone River rose, and soon Bellstone Meadows had a new lake. Several of the main roads flooded, then the school basement flooded, and school was cancelled. Water ran down the middle of Thistle Lane, and ducks could be seen paddling there. Gardens became quagmires of mud and water.

Sam and the Griswalds enjoyed themselves, at least some of the time. During breaks in the rain they chased ducks, and constructed rafts, and held raft races, then raft rescues and raft shipwrecks. Mrs Harris was not so happy.

She kept phoning the police to find out if the water was likely to get any higher, and she made Sam go with her to the big supermarket in Greater Titmarsh to stock up with supplies 'just in case'. Mrs Griswald was not happy either. Most of the plants she had put in her garden looked as if they would drown. And Mrs Bullock was positively furious. The eddies of water carried mud and all sorts of rubbish, and Bellstone was looking less tidy than it ever had before.

The Griswalds had not forgotten the treasure which they believed lay at the bottom of the Bullocks' garden. They even borrowed Sam's copy of *Archaeology is Fun*, and perused it for information as to what kind of burial site the Bullocks' garden might be. They were, of course, hoping that it was the kind which held lots of gold, as well as bodies. Jake and Elfrida were all for digging up the garden as soon as possible, by torchlight if necessary, but Sam pointed out that they could hardly do so while the place was knee-deep in mud. And besides, he added, it was very important that they first developed the correct techniques for excavation, otherwise they might destroy valuable evidence as they uncovered it. The Griswalds had bought this for the moment, but Sam suspected they would soon grow impatient. He himself still had horrible visions of the Bullocks creeping up on them as they attempted to excavate their back garden – and what might result. The Griswalds might have given up their theory of the-Bullocks-as-murderers, but Sam, for all he tried, could not.

He wanted to put off the moment of truth as long as possible.

Jake was sufficiently fired with enthusiasm for all things archaeological that he started surfing the Internet for information on burial sites, and he even paid a visit to Bellstone Public Library. On his way home he stopped by to see Sam.

'Look what I've found,' said Jake, waving a piece of paper at him.

'What's that?' Sam tried to look interested, although as he was secretly almost one hundred per cent convinced that the Bullocks' garden was *not* an archaeological site of any kind, it was not easy.

'It was in a pamphlet Mr Hobson wrote, called *Bellstone Through the Ages*.' Jake read aloud from the piece of paper. '*Although the Bellebriggan tribe undoubtedly resided in the vicinity of Bellstone, and opposed the Roman invaders, the existence of their legendary Warrior Queen, Elfriga, is still open to question. However, a Roman centurion of the period does refer to her in letters home as reportedly being "a woman of irascible temper and monstrous size, whose cruelty of nature is well renowned"*. Huh!' Jake sounded disgusted. 'Sounds more like a Bullock than a Griswald!'

Sam grinned and agreed. 'Better not tell Elfrida, though,' he suggested. 'You know how fond she is of Elfriga.'

'And it doesn't say anything at all about treasure!'

As Sam had never believed in Queen Elfriga's treasure

anyway he was not especially disappointed by this. But he thought it better not to say so. 'Still,' he pointed out, 'it doesn't matter whose burial site it is really, does it? As long as it's there?'

'Huh!' Jake was disgruntled. 'I'm beginning to wonder. I just hope you know what you're talking about, with all this archaeology stuff.' Sam said nothing. 'Anyway, have you seen Spider? He's been gone all day.'

Sam shook his head. 'I expect he'll turn up,' he said.

* * *

When Sam went to bed that night the rain was worse than ever. He lay there listening to the wind rising and howling through the trees. There was a rumble of distant thunder. Biter was under the bed, whimpering, and he wouldn't come out.

Sam turned over uneasily. Downstairs, he could hear the rise and fall of his mother's voice as she called the police to ask about the rising water for the umpteenth time. Then he sat up. It seemed to him that he could hear something else, over the storm.

The hairs rose on his neck. Someone, or something, was tapping on his window.

* * *

In the Bullocks' garden, all was dark and cold. The moon was covered with cloud, and the shadows were deep. So much rain had fallen that almost half the garden was under water, and the garden shed and the bird table stuck up like strange islands in a lake.

There was a rustling by the fence. Shadows moved
within shadows. Suddenly there was the sound of a door
quietly opening, then closing. A small, bobbing light
appeared, and was almost immediately shaded. Two dark
figures slipped down the steps and round the side of the
house. They crept down the path to the gate, and out into
Thistle Lane.

As they moved along the wet lane it could be seen that
one of them was carrying an unwieldy object on their back.
They paused at the gate to the Harris house. Then they
passed through but did not go to the door. They made
their way to the side of the house and crept into the back
garden.

They did not go silently, however. Their footsteps

splashed and squelched on the wet ground. And they were arguing.

'My feet are soaking! And I think the torch is about to give out,' complained a shrill female voice.

'Shuddup! You'll wake them.'

'No I won't. Anyway, I don't think this is such a good idea. I reckon we should just leave her there.'

'Oh, put a sock in it. What if she drowns?'

'She won't drown. She's too high up.'

'Well, we still need to feed her, don't we?' A pause. 'Of course, if we didn't, and she died, I suppose we *could* blame it all on them –'

'Don't be disgusting!'

They were drawing close to the beech tree which supported Sam's tree house.

'Right. We'll see if being locked up has improved her mood –'

Then they stopped short. The ground dipped around the roots of the beech tree, and the hollow had filled with water. It was impossible to approach the trunk without wading through it.

'I'm not going in there! She'll be all right – you'll see.'

'But we haven't fed her in two days!'

'Keep your voice down!'

With much muffled bickering, they began wading towards the tree trunk, still struggling with the large object, which they were now trying to extract from its covering of old sacking.

'We'll have to put the torch on –'

'We'll be seen –'

'No, we won't –'

A dim yellow light appeared, revealing the cross and irritable faces of Brandon and Christabel Bullock. They were up to their knees in mud, and Brandon was struggling with the extendable ladder on his back. Christabel was holding a small tin of cat food.

'Honestly!' she squeaked, trying to hold her raincoat above the water, her small, prissy face pursed up with dislike. 'I don't know why we decided to do this. I mean it's exactly the kind of thing *they* do. Sneaking around in the middle of the night –' She broke off, and let out a muffled scream.

A dark shape had appeared in the leaves above her. Looming, faceless, catlike, yet human, it leapt out of the branches and over her head. It landed on the ground beyond the water, at the same time as two almost identical shapes sprung down beside it. Brandon and Christabel, knee deep in mud, were surrounded.

A powerful flashlight snapped on above them, bathing them in yellow light. Brandon and Christabel, dazzled by the brightness, looked exactly like a pair of startled goldfish.

One of the figures on the ground whipped off its balaclava.

'Ahah!' declared Jake Griswald with relish. 'Caught red-handed. Yes, this is the kind of thing *we* do – and you should have remembered that we do it better!'

Brandon and Christabel blinked as their eyes adjusted to the light. What they saw did not reassure them. In a semi-circle around them, with extremely unfriendly expressions on their faces, stood Sam, Jake and Spider. They were all clad in black (Spider and Sam still wearing balaclavas) and looking extremely mean. Glancing back over their shoulders the Bullocks could make out that the figure still in the tree, and directing the flashlight, was Elfrida. They could also now see the ropes hanging from the branches.

'But – you got down without a ladder,' bleated Christabel.

'Do you think we care about ladders,' said Jake scornfully. 'Come on, admit it. We've caught you red-handed!'

'I don't know what you're talking about,' said Brandon snootily. The snootiness would have been more convincing had he not been wrestling with a ladder in the middle of a pool of murky water. At that moment, he lost the battle with the ladder and it fell over with a splash. Spider jumped neatly to miss the end of it.

Brandon glanced round and his eyes fell on Sam. 'Sam! You've got some sense. You're not mad like them. Why don't we all go back to bed? After all think how much trouble you'll be in – think what your mum will say –'

Sam's voice was quite steady as he replied, 'Actually, Brandon, my mum thinks you're a creep.'

Brandon just goggled at him.

Christabel said, 'But you can't keep us here! We haven't done anything wrong! And you've climbed into our garden loads of times.' Nevertheless she did not move forward. There was something menacing about those three figures: Spider, silent and faceless; Sam, sturdily prepared to defend his territory exactly as he did on the football field; and Jake, half crouching, his hands already forming rigid knife-hands as he readied himself for a kung-fu attack.

'Now you know how it feels,' Elfrida told her triumphantly, 'to be surrounded. This is how Morris felt, when your mother fed him to your horrible cat.'

'Yes, well,' Brandon was blustering now. 'She's going to be absolutely furious when she finds out you've been threatening us.'

'Oh come off it,' Jake scoffed. 'Quit pretending. We all know the truth! We all know what you're up to with that ladder and that cat food! You've come to feed your cat!'

'We've come to rescue her!' said Christabel quickly. 'From you!' But she was too late.

'How did you find out?' Brandon demanded at the same moment.

'D'you really think we wouldn't notice what was going on in the tree house?' said Jake scornfully.

'But Mrs Harris said nobody could go in!' Christabel howled. 'And Sammy always does what his mum says!'

'But we don't,' said Jake.

'And she took the ladder away, and locked it up!'

'D'you think that makes any difference to us? Anything

you can get up, we can too, only ten times as quickly.'

'And I don't always do what my mum says,' Sam intervened. He was feeling very angry. He had more-or-less grown used to the Griswalds treating his tree house as their own – but it was a bit much when the Bullocks did too. Especially when they were trying to frame him. 'What about that crash outside the town hall?'

'That was a fluke –'

'No, it wasn't. We've corrupted Sam, you see,' explained Elfrida helpfully from the branches.

'Yes,' said Jake. 'He's almost as bad as us now. Almost another Griswald.'

'And,' Sam added forcefully, 'I'm not stupid. I can work out what it means when Biter spends all his time sitting under the tree house. Of course there's a cat up there!' In fact, he was only annoyed with himself that it had taken him so long.

'Right,' said Jake firmly. 'And now you two are going to get up that tree and let her out.'

There were a lot of protests, and a lot of flailing around in the mud, before this was achieved. Although Sam, Spider and Jake could easily make their way up to the tree house unaided, Brandon and Christabel, it seemed, could not. The ladder had to be retrieved, and propped up against the trunk, and held steady for them while they were shoved and cajoled up into the branches above. As Jake said, it was a wonder they had ever got up there in the first place – especially carrying Delilah.

'She was muzzled,' said Christabel.

'That's cruel!' Elfrida shot out of the leaves so unexpectedly, and spoke so ferociously, that Christabel nearly fell off the ladder.

'Impressive, though, you have to admit,' Jake said. 'I wouldn't like to put a muzzle on that cat.'

'I did it,' said Christabel with dignity. 'Brandon kept dropping her every time she bit him.'

At last, they were all on the platform at the front of the tree house. Mrs Harris's rather puny attempt at a padlock had been cast aside, and replaced with an altogether more impressive version, which presumably belonged to the Bullocks. After various threats, they were persuaded to remove it. The door creaked open.

The torch and the flashlight swept from side to side. Then Christabel Bullock cried out, in a scared voice: 'She's not here!'

For several moments, there was total silence, as everybody took in the sight of the cat's travelling basket in the middle of the floor. It was empty, except for a blanket and a small piece of red cloth. Then Brandon turned on the Griswalds. 'All right then,' he said, in his usual bullying tones. 'What have you done with her?'

'We haven't touched her!' said Elfrida, contemptuously. Sam and Spider, their faces in shadow, said nothing. Jake, for once, was speechless, plainly aghast. Brandon and Christabel stared at them, cross at first, then uncertain, then horrified. They turned round and began searching desperately. Christabel upended the cat basket, and Brandon peered into all the corners. But there was nowhere she could have gone.

Elfrida picked up the piece of red cloth and waved it at them. 'The muzzle, of course. You pigs! I 'spect we could report you for cruelty.'

Brandon and Christabel did not even try to deny it.

'They couldn't – surely – could they?' Christabel muttered to her brother.

'But where is she – I mean – I don't understand!'

'It's them – those Griswalds – they must have taken her –'

'But they can't – not through the padlock – and we locked the travel case too –'

'D'you think someone's really taken her?' said Jake to the others in a low voice. 'But how could they?' Then he caught sight of his brother's face. 'You! You did it! But how could you? Not with one arm still in plaster – and one hand bandaged up –'

'You might have told us!' squeaked Elfrida.

'Somebody must have helped you,' Jake accused.

'Hush,' said Sam. 'They'll hear you.' He was grinning.

Jake's jaw dropped. '*You* helped him!'

Sam grinned even more broadly. He liked and admired Jake – thought he was the best footballer he had ever met, a good friend, and a great criminal mind. But it was good to take the wind out of his sails for once. 'Yeah,' he said. 'We did it this afternoon. While you were at the library.'

'But how?' muttered Jake, careful not to let the Bullocks hear.

Spider and Sam said nothing, but their eyes flicked to a small hole in the roof of the tree house.

'Wow! You got through there!' He looked at Christabel and Brandon, but they were now desperately searching the travel case – as if a cat Delilah's size could be hidden under a blanket. All the same, they moved out onto the tree house platform.

'So where is she?'

'Actually, we let her go.'

'You let her go!' Jake was outraged. 'But she's the evidence!'

'Yeah, well,' said Sam. 'It's cruel to keep animals locked up.' He exchanged a glance with Spider, who winked. In fact, although Sam had no intention of telling Jake this, they had not had much choice but to let her go. Taking her muzzle off had been a mistake. A big mistake. Climbing out of a tiny space, into a beech tree, with a cat biting your ear, was no fun at all.

'Well, you might have told us,' said Elfrida, disgruntled.

But nobody replied. For at that moment there was a flash of lightning overhead. Christabel shrieked her head off, and everybody else (except for Spider) yelled. But above the racket, they all heard the same bloodcurdling noise. Sam, feeling someone nudge him, turned to look where Spider was pointing. There, on the other side of the fence, high up in the Bullocks' poplar tree, all her fur standing on end, yowling her head off, and horribly lit up by the lightning – was Delilah.

For a few seconds the noise was truly terrible. The thunder rumbled, Delilah yowled, while in the distance was the sound of Elfrida's cats and Biter joining in. On top of which the rain was now deluging down. And then, above all this, they heard a new sound.

'Help! Help!'

Everyone recognised the voice, although nobody had ever heard it asking for help before. It was Mrs Bullock.

In a moment, Spider was out of the tree house and down into the garden. He covered the distance to the fence in a few easy steps and leapt to the top. A coat now covered the barbed wire – left there from earlier in the evening when Spider had been keeping a close watch on the Bullock residence – and so his hands came to no harm as he disappeared over to the other side.

Everybody else went round by the road, Christabel and Brandon coming last, both whingeing and complaining.

Mrs Bullock was standing on the doorstep, the flood waters eddying around her feet. Sam and the Griswalds took a few moments to recognise her. She had her curlers in and was wearing a frilly nightie.

'Help!' she screamed. 'Help! Water's coming into the house! And the storm has taken out the telephone!'

Christabel and Brandon both went completely white. Sam, for probably the first time in his life, felt sorry for them. It must have been truly terrible, to see their mother in such a state and not know how to help.

For a moment, there was a stunned silence. Then: 'My *Super-Matrix*!' howled Brandon, racing towards the house. 'My stereo!'

'My new TV!' howled Christabel, stumbling after him. 'My mobile phone!'

They both ran straight past their mother, and disappeared.

Mrs Bullock looked dismayed. And for the first time in his life, Sam felt sorry for *her*. Still, if there was one thing about the Griswalds, they were good in a crisis. Within seconds, Spider had sent Elfrida back to Sam's house to fetch help. Jake had already run into the house, and Sam made haste to follow. They were both horrified to find water cascading down the front steps, like a miniature waterfall. Worse than that, Mrs Bullock seemed to be having hysterics.

'My lovely house,' she moaned. 'Not a thing out of place. You couldn't find a tidier house in England –'

'It's only the kitchen,' pronounced Jake, making a rapid inspection. 'If we get working we can easily shift everything.'

But Mrs Bullock did not seem to hear him. She had collapsed onto a chair, and they were not sure if she was laughing or crying. Jake looked at her, then at Sam. 'I reckon she's hysterical,' he said thoughtfully. 'And what do you do when people are hysterical? You slap them on the face.' A huge grin slowly appeared on his face.

But before he could put this into action, Mr Bullock came in, and Mrs Bullock recovered of her own accord (thus depriving Jake, as he said later, of 'probably the best moment of my life so far'). They all set to work, moving things out of the kitchen. Every now and then they could hear Christabel and Brandon in the distance, removing their own most favoured possessions to the highest part of the house. Brandon even tried to rescue a pizza from out of the fridge which Sam and Jake were carrying into the hall, until they yelled at him and threatened to drop the fridge on his foot.

Soon after this, Elfrida turned up with Mr and Mrs Griswald, Luke, and Mrs Harris in tow. To Sam's relief, Mrs Harris was quite calm. She had brought Biter with her on a lead.

'Elfrida explained that Biter had raised the alarm,' she told Sam, 'and that you had all gone next door to investigate. The poor Bullocks! You'll be pleased to hear that *our* house is completely dry. *Their* house is much nearer to the river, of course. I expect they wish they had a dog like Biter to raise the alarm. You know, I feel so much safer now, knowing that nothing can happen without Biter waking us.'

Sam was extremely pleased to hear this. He knew that if Biter made Mrs Harris feel safe, then she was never likely to send him to the Dogs' Home, no matter how many people he bit. So he did not reveal that Elfrida had been less than truthful in her account. For Biter had been hiding

301

under the bed when Spider turned up at Sam's window; and he had not even emerged when Sam climbed out of the window and into the night.

Mr Griswald was carrying waterproofs, wellington boots and whisky; Mrs Griswald was carrying a hot thermos flask of tea and yet more spades and shovels to build banks against the water. Luke had brought his camera, and annoyed everyone by taking photos of them as they cleared up. (He was, he announced, planning to sell the pictures later to the *Bellstone Gazette*.) Mrs Bullock, after her third or fourth swig of whisky, surprised everyone by becoming quite cheerful, and bursting into the *Tidy Bellstone* song.

In all the confusion it took a while for Sam to notice that Spider was missing. Then he realised that he had not seen Spider since they'd come into the house. And he remembered that, outside, the waters were still rising . . . and that even Spider was not invincible.

Quickly, Sam took his torch and went back out into the garden.

It was surprisingly bright. The storm clouds had passed over, and a huge autumn moon hung low in the sky. The water had stopped rising, and stretched out calm and unmoving in the moonlight, like a beautiful, silver lake. As Sam watched, a pair of moorhens appeared, and floated serenely across what had been the Bullocks' lawn. But there was no sign of Spider.

Then there was a noise from the poplar tree. Sam had forgotten about Delilah, but now he moved closer and pointed his torch upwards. Immediately, he caught sight of Spider. He was balanced on a branch, with the struggling Delilah wedged beneath his one good arm.

'Are you all right?' called Sam. He could hardly believe that Spider Griswald might actually be stuck up a tree. Then again, with one arm broken, and one hand bandaged, it was expecting a lot, even of Spider, that he should be able to climb a tree and bring down a reluctant and complaining cat. Sam saw that several of the branches below Spider's had come away from the trunk: perhaps they had been struck by the lightning earlier. And at that very moment, the branch Spider was holding on to began to come away as well.

With a twist of his body, Spider managed to lever himself and Delilah onto the branch above. But now he was definitely stuck.

Sam thought hard. 'Wait a minute,' he yelled. Then, as fast as he could, he ran for his own garden. To his relief, the ladder was still propped up against the beech tree, a sack lying beside it. But it took several long and desperate minutes before he had manoeuvred it all next door.

It was something of a struggle to get the ladder to the tree, but he managed it. He propped it up as securely as he could and hoped that the soft soil would hold it firm. He tried not to remember that he much preferred to go up ladders when somebody was holding the bottom – if at all. After all, it couldn't be so much worse than climbing up to the tree house roof with Spider. Although, somehow, with Spider leading the way, that had not seemed so bad.

He tried not to look down as he reached the branch below Spider's. With Spider's feet still looking a long way above him, Sam wedged himself carefully and opened up the sack.

'Right,' he yelled. 'Drop her!'

Almost instantly, a yowling, hissing, snarling ball of teeth and fur came plummeting down towards him. Sam felt her claws whip through the air only millimetres away from his face. Then she disappeared into the sack and he quickly closed it. From inside came a horrible yowling and mewing, and Sam thought the seams might burst. But they did not.

Spider slid down beside him. There was a pause as he and Sam looked at each other.

'Thanks,' said Spider.

Sam came the closest he had so far to falling out of the tree. He was still struggling to regain his balance – and to tell Spider not to mention it – when a camera flash went off. He looked down, and found Luke Griswald peering up at them through a long lens.

'The *Gazette*'s going to love this,' said Luke with a grin.

Sam gaped at him. Regardless of whether the *Bellstone Gazette* published the picture, Sam reckoned that Luke had just recorded a truly historic moment.

Chapter Eighteen
After the Deluge

The *Bellstone Gazette* did publish the picture, a few days later, and there was a report to go with it.

CHILDREN ARE HEROES
Brave Newcomers Rescue
Distinguished Citizen and Cat
Valuable Historical Remains Uncovered in
Flood Drama

A distinguished local citizen and her family would have been victims of the floods, had it not been for the plucky kids next door.

Mrs Bullock, leader of Bellstone's Tidiest Town in England Campaign, and her family were asleep when the Bellstone river burst its banks and swept through their house. Luckily, neighbouring kids Richard Griswald (13), Jake Griswald (11),

Sam Harris (11) and Elfrida Griswald (9) were immediately on the scene.

'Sam's dog Biter raised the alarm,' Elfrida Griswald explained. 'He's a wonderful dog – he deserves a medal for what he did.'

The children alerted the emergency services, then helped to get the Bullocks and their possessions to safety.

During the commotion, Richard Griswald, more usually known as Spider, spotted the Bullocks' cat up a tree. With the help of Sam Harris, he braved the rising floodwater to bring her down. Local fireman Bert Biggerstaffe commented, 'It was an amazing rescue. There will be a job with us waiting for him when he leaves school.'

Elfrida said on her brother's behalf, 'We love all animals. We're glad we were able to reunite the Bullocks with their cat. And this will be a lesson to all kids to keep their pets inside during storms.'

The cat, Delilah, had been missing for several days, and the Bullocks had offered two hundred pounds for her return. Police say Spider and Sam will receive the reward shortly.

But the floods did more than ruin the Bullocks' carpets and Mrs Bullock's expensively landscaped garden. For it also uncovered valuable archaeological remains.

Mr Hobson, a local history expert, explained, 'The Bullocks' garden appears to be on the site of a medieval midden, or rubbish tip. It is a fascinating remnant of Bellstone's past and contains animal bones in large numbers. Experts also expect to find quantities of preserved dung. It was all rubbish to their owners, but it will tell us many things about how our ancestors lived.'

He suggested that these remains had probably been hidden for centuries. 'When the Bullocks had the garden bulldozed recently it probably removed an entire layer of soil, and now the floods have washed away another.'

The Griswald children were among the first to notice strange debris in the Bullocks' garden. Elfrida Griswald said, 'We saw bones floating in the flood water.' But the Griswalds' most important find has already been identified as an old chamber pot, which they have generously presented to Bellstone Museum.

Strangely enough, the Bullocks' garden would not have been affected by the floods had it not been for Mrs Bullock's own Tidy Bellstone Campaign. The campaign removed rubbish from the upper Bellstone river a few weeks ago, allowing the water to flow more freely. Richard, Jake and Sam, enthusiastic members of the Campaign, were responsible for the undamming.

Jake Griswald commented, 'We spent hours and hours hauling rubbish out of the river, and we got soaked and covered in mud. Mrs Bullock gave us the job specially, and I hope she's pleased with the result. We certainly are. We will really enjoy watching the archaeologists digging up the Bullocks' garden, perhaps for years and years to come.'

The Mayor of Bellstone said, 'Thanks to these children, a fascinating part of Bellstone's past has been uncovered. We owe them a debt of gratitude. This kind of public spirit is what makes Bellstone what it is.'

The Bullocks were still recovering from their ordeal yesterday, and did not comment.

'Absolutely astounding,' said Mrs Harris to Sam in an awed voice, having read the article for the third time.

'Astounding,' agreed Sam. He meant it, too, although he suspected that his mother and he were astounded by rather different things. Sam was mainly astounded by the whopping lies the Griswalds  had told – and that they had got away with them.

Mrs Harris turned back to the article. 'I do think they say rather a lot about the Griswalds, though,' she said at last. 'I mean, why didn't you say something, Sam? Then you could have been quoted too.'

'Oh well,' said Sam. 'The Griswalds are better at that kind of thing than me.' It was true enough. Whatever Jake and Elfrida might say about having corrupted him, when it came to barefaced cheek and outrageous invention, the Griswalds were still his masters. Sam would never have been able to keep a straight face; in fact, it had been difficult enough just listening, when Elfrida told the reporter how much she loved Delilah, and Jake explained how much *he* loved the Tidy Bellstone Campaign. Jake had tried to get Sam to explain all about archaeology, but Sam had thought it best to leave that to Mr Hobson.

'Still, at least you have your photo in the paper.

Although you do look a bit gormless, Sam. I mean really. You look as if –'

'As if I'd just been slapped round the head with a wet fish,' said Sam. 'Well – I was surprised, you know.' And so would you be, he thought to himself, if Spider Griswald had just spoken to you – for the first time, ever. 'By the way, Mum,' he added. 'You were right. Archaeology has turned out to be quite interesting.'

Sam left his mother still gazing, enraptured, at his photograph, and went into the garden. Biter was scrabbling around under the tree house. He had finally come to realise that there were no more cats in residence, and was just looking for sticks. Sam whistled to him, and they went out into Thistle Lane.

Shutting the garden gate behind him, Sam smiled as he remembered the final events of the Bullock flood. How Elfrida had spotted yet another bone floating about on the flood water, and throwing caution to the wind, had brandished it at Mrs Bullock. How Mrs Bullock had denied all knowledge. How the police had said it must all be investigated. How Sam, the next morning, had had the brilliant idea of taking the pot he and Elfrida had found, together with all the bits of bone, round to Mr Hobson, to ask if he thought they could have anything to do with Queen Elfriga . . . and how, although Mr Hobson had said it could have nothing to do with the Bellebriggans, he had immediately become very excited, had got straight on the phone to some eminent archaeologist friends, and taken them straight round to look at the Bullocks' garden. And how it had turned out to be a fascinating archaeological site after all.

Sam and Biter had just reached the Griswalds' gate, when a policeman came out. Sam regarded him rather nervously – policemen, visiting the Griswalds, usually boded no good at all. But then he remembered what the article had said, about himself and Spider getting a reward. And besides, he looked a friendly kind of man.

'Hello,' he said. 'Are you here with the reward?'

'What's that?' The policeman looked at him closely. 'Wait a minute – you're the lad who was in the paper. The one that helped young Richard Griswald rescue that cat.'

Sam nodded.

'Well, I wasn't calling about the reward – although according to my Chief, it's in the post. Or it will be when the Bullocks hand it over. No, it was that little business of the bus shelter, and the mayor's Jaguar. The fact is, in view of recent events – well, nobody, including the mayor himself, sees any need to take further action.'

'That's great!'

'Well, accidents do happen, don't they? And there is such a thing as benefit of the doubt. Especially in view of recent events. Very impressed we were, with you young folks and the quick way you acted. I wish more young people were as community-spirited.'

'Err – right,' said Sam, wondering if the Griswalds had ever been described as community-spirited before.

'Especially surprising, given their background,' the policeman went on, jerking his head in the direction of the house behind him.

'How d'you mean?'

'Their dad, that's what – Fingers Griswald, they called him. His turf was in London, you know – that's where I used to work, once upon a time. I remember my boss talking about him. Oh, he led them a merry dance!'

'What! You mean he *is* a master criminal!'

The policeman pursed his lips, in the manner of one who could say a lot more, should he be so minded – but who would have to be persuaded first.

'Fingers!' Sam thought rapidly. 'You mean like Sticky Fingers or Fingers in the Till – you mean he was a thief?'

'Oh no. That wasn't it at all. They called him Fingers on account of how fast his fingers moved when he was working, drawing and that.'

'Oh.' Sam was undeniably disappointed. 'Yeah, I know he's an artist.'

'Was he just! The best Van Goghs he did.'

'Right.' Then Sam realised what he had said. 'Van Goghs! You mean he was a forger!'

'Well – the paintings were only a sideline. It was the bank notes – that's what really got him into trouble.'

'Wow!' Sam was stunned. 'And I thought they were making it up.'

'He's been going straight for a long time. Or at least, they haven't caught him!' The policeman laughed. 'I expect his wife keeps him in check. She used to be a copper, you know.'

With a cheerful whistle and a wave, the policeman departed, leaving a flabbergasted Sam staring after him.

* * *

He found the Griswalds in the caravan. On his way he passed Mr Griswald, who was sitting in a deckchair, wrapped in a winter coat, sketching Elfrida's cats, which were cuddled up together on the steps. There was a gentle, dreamy expression on his face, and he didn't seem to notice Sam as he passed.

The Griswalds were sitting around a camping stove (which Sam regarded with great suspicion) upon which they were heating a saucepan of some strange-smelling, sizzling liquid. Jake was holding a copy of the *Bellstone Gazette*.

'Come and have some mulled wine,' Elfrida greeted him. 'It doesn't have any wine in it, but it tastes lovely! We just invented it.' She gave him some, and Sam looked at it doubtfully, wondering if it was safe to drink.

'I just wish I could see the look on the Bullocks' faces when they read this,' Jake gloated.

'They'll be sick as parrots,' agreed Sam. 'Mr Hobson said Mrs Bullock almost cried when all those archaeologists trampled over her garden. *He* thought she was crying for joy, because of all those fascinating historical remains –'

'But actually, she's mad as a wasp in a jar,' said Jake, 'because they're going to be digging it up for ever.' They grinned at each other. They still could not believe it.

'That's why she was burning the evidence, of course. Mr Hobson had been going on at her about all the fascinating old remains in Bellstone, and she was afraid of something like this.'

'I wish it had been Elfriga's treasure though,' said Elfrida. She sighed. None of the others really cared, but Elfrida still yearned after Queen Elfriga. And it only made matters worse that Queen Elfriga's bowl had turned out to be what Mr Hobson called 'an eighteenth-century piss pot'. Elfrida had been fond of that bowl. Still, at least Bellstone Museum had been delighted to receive it. They had even put a small card in the case, naming the Griswalds as the benefactors.

'No – it's much better, having an ancient rubbish dump on her doorstep,' said Jake. 'Hah! It's just what those Bullocks deserve.'

Sam scrutinised his friend closely as he spoke. He was very aware that he, Sam, had spent a lot of time persuading the Griswalds that all kinds of valuable treasure was hidden in the Bullock garden. A medieval midden was not quite

314

the same thing. He couldn't help wondering if any of them was going to reproach him with this.

He need not have worried.

'It was you, Sam, who got us on to this whole archaeology business,' continued Jake approvingly. 'I must admit there were times I doubted you. The whole thing sounded like – well, like a pile of old rubbish, if you don't mind me saying so.' He grinned. 'Sometimes, you know, I wasn't sure you believed it yourself. But you had insight. You knew your stuff. Next time you come out with something like that, I won't need convincing. What idiots the rest of us were – thinking Old Big Nose was a murderer!' He laughed, and Sam joined in quickly. 'As if she would have the guts for something like that!'

'Of course, I didn't realise it was a *midden*,' Sam said. 'Bits of old food, and animal dung, and scraps, and broken jars, and old tealeaves, probably – if they had tealeaves then . . . Still, if you listen to Mr Hobson, you'd think it *was* treasure. He thinks it's brilliant.'

'The main thing,' said Jake, 'is that they'll be digging up Old Bullock's garden until the end of time. They'll make a right mess. Hah! It looks a right mess now, what with all that mud, and rocks, and *bits* everywhere.'

'Yes, and we're heroes,' said Elfrida smugly. 'We sounded the alarm. We discovered the historical remains. We told Mr Hobson. We rescued Delilah. Although,' she could not help adding, 'I can't think why you wanted to, Spider. I wouldn't have. I'd have left her up there.'

'You've forgotten the two hundred pounds,' Jake reminded her.

'And she might have drowned,' Sam pointed out. 'She was surrounded by water. And I don't think cats can swim.'

'Well . . .' Elfrida was divided between her love for animals in general, and her animosity towards this animal in particular. 'I expect she *can* swim. She's not really a cat. She's a – a – fiend in cat shape.'

'Well, I think it was a brave thing to do,' said Sam. He glanced sideways at Spider, who smiled at him. Since Spider had summoned him that night, to make him his accomplice in his climb to release Delilah, and since their adventure in the Bullocks' poplar tree, Sam had felt they had a special understanding. True, Spider had not said anything to him since, but Sam did not mind. After hearing Jake and Elfrida give their press interview, he thought he understood why Spider chose to remain silent. Jake and Elfrida did more than enough talking for three. They probably did enough for a hundred.

'Yeah, you might have told us you'd found Delilah, though, Spider,' said Jake.

Spider shrugged. His shrug seemed to imply that he had not thought it of much importance. Not something worth worrying them about, anyway.

Sam grinned and put his arm round Biter. At that moment, he felt life was perfect, that nothing could ever be any better than it was now. But then again: 'You know,' he said, 'if they spend too long digging up Mrs Bullock's garden, she might not be able to take it. I mean, she really does hate mess. And it's bound to be messy, isn't it – looking for all those historical remains. Perhaps – perhaps she'll move away.'

He felt happiness ballooning up inside him at the thought. But to his amazement, he saw the other three frowning at him.

'That would be no fun,' said Jake.

'What d'you mean?'

'Well, how would we be able to remind them all the time that we'd won?'

'And who would we fight and fall out with?' asked Elfrida.

Sam, who thought it might make a nice change not to fight and fall out with anyone, turned, desperately, to look at Spider. But Spider was nodding in agreement with his siblings.

Sam shook his head. At that moment he knew he would never truly understand the Griswalds. They were definitely insane. The truth was the Griswalds did not enjoy a quiet life. They liked action and excitement – even if that also meant trouble and turmoil.

'I'll tell you one thing,' said Jake, 'we're definitely staying in Bellstone. Mum loves that bit in the paper. And everyone's being nice to her.'

'We might even get a medal,' suggested Elfrida hopefully. 'After all, we are heroes.'

Jake said, 'Maybe they'll present it at the town hall.'

This, Sam thought, was typical of the Griswalds. They never knew when to be grateful for a good thing; they were always looking for more. And while they might be the heroes of the moment, he had a feeling it was only a matter of time before they would be plunging into disaster again. When they did so, he had no doubt they would be taking him with them. That was what being friends with the Griswalds was all about.

And yet, strangely, the prospect did not daunt him. Perhaps Elfrida was right – they *had* corrupted him. He was almost looking forward to what they would get up to next.

'What we should do,' Elfrida was saying, 'is dig up Bellstone Park. Maybe if we joined the Tidy Bellstone Campaign that would give us an excuse. After all, Queen Elfriga must be buried somewhere.'

'What I think we should do –' Jake began, but Sam interrupted.

'Never mind all that!' He waved his hands expansively, as Biter began barking with excitement. 'Don't you realise? Two more matches – and Bellstone Rovers might even win the Cup!'

Afterword
Did Queen Elfriga Exist?

The truth is, you will not find Elfriga or the Bellebriggan tribe in any history book. (Not unless you can find Mr Hobson's pamphlet on the subject, but sadly it is out of print.) But there were warlike women among the British tribal leaders at the time of the Roman invasion in the first century. One of these was Queen Cartimandua of the Brigantes. But the most famous was Boudicca, today more commonly known as Boadicea, who was the Queen of the Iceni, and who led her tribe in an uprising against the Romans. She destroyed Colchester, London and part of the Ninth Legion before she was finally defeated.

Not much is known even about such an important historical figure as Boudicca. And very little is known about the Dumnonii tribe, who lived in the southwest of Britain during the same period. This tribe, historians believe, may well have been divided into warring factions. Perhaps one of these could have been the Bellebriggans, and perhaps their queen, Elfriga, could have led them in a smaller and less successful (and hence unrecorded) uprising against the Romans . . . And perhaps she could have had a great-great-great-great-great- (and so on) granddaughter called Elfrida.